Na Bolom

House of the Jaguar

NA BOLOM

HOUSE OF THE JAGUAR

FORREST HAYES

Hidden Jungle Press

PRESCOTT ◉ ARIZONA

Hidden Jungle Press
PRESCOTT ⊙ ARIZONA
FIRST EDITION

Cover Design: Kelly Shorten – KMD Web Designs
Interior Design: Coreen Montagna, Kate Robinson – Starstone Editorial
Editorial: Matt Teel, Kate Robinson – Starstone Editorial

ISBN-13: 978-0692758632
ISBN-10: 0692758631

Printed in the USA by Kindle Direct Publishing

We have two minds. One thinks, the other knows. The mind that knows goes back many lifetimes. This is the mind of the one heart, of all things: the trees, the plants, the clouds, the rivers, the mountains. The more time you spend with this mind, the more you will see Spirit around you.

CHAPTER 1

The Denver Museum of Natural History

Peter Campbell stared with vacant eyes at the giant fossil skull, not seeing its oblique lines or cavernous openings. Instead, he searched within for the answers he could not find outside himself. Setting down the tungsten-tipped air scribe used to clear away the hard mineral deposits, he leaned against the large oak table and refocused on the skull—a newly discovered predator from the Jurassic age.

As he studied the fossil, his mind wandered back to the jungles of Chiapas, and to Jazmin. He had heard nothing from her in four weeks. Shutting out the sounds of the other paleontologists and archaeologists working throughout the large basement lab, he wondered why. Something was wrong; he could feel it deep in the pit of his stomach. Had she been hurt? Was she sweating through a malaria-induced delirium? Had she been abducted by some South American slave trader? After all, she was a beautiful young woman living deep in a remote jungle. Anything could happen.

Worse yet, the uprising in Chiapas last year still hadn't played itself out, and the Clinton administration had done nothing to intervene. What if she was lying dead on the jungle floor? How would he know?

His thoughts sickened him. They had agreed he would wait a month to hear from her before taking action, and today was the day. But what exactly should he do? They hadn't developed a plan. He could call the U.S. Embassy in México. But relying on the government for help meant more waiting. He cringed at the thought.

Snail mail in the backcountry of México lived up to its name, so he'd kept himself absorbed in his work while waiting to hear from Jazmin. The first few weeks had been bad enough. Now he needed sleeping pills at night, and an excess of black coffee during the day.

He knew that getting a letter out from a remote area could be difficult, even though the village was only a few hours' drive from the nearest post office. "The men and women of the village go into town to trade in the square," she had said. "Do not worry, *mi amor*. I am sure the sweet villagers will deliver my letters to San Cristóbal for me."

Apparently, that wasn't the case.

Peter grabbed a couple of antacid tablets from a countertop as he walked the few steps to his desk, wiping dusty hands on his even dustier pants. He sat in his swivel chair, absentmindedly stroking the edge of a mahogany picture frame, studying a photo of the two of them. His gaze followed the silky, reddish- brown hair that fell lavishly over her slender shoulders, and tried to remember its scent. Instead, he heard her last words before boarding the plane: "My heart is with the jungle, and with you. You will come to be with me there, no? Then my heart will not be torn."

He had stood in the terminal not knowing what to say when she turned and ran to board the plane. Her words hung in the air like a darkened cloud. Something had changed. They always spoke of making Colorado their home. She seemed happy to start a new life in Colorado ...

"Wow. Now there's a beauty."

Peter jolted as someone snatched the photo out of his hand. Standing beside him was Nate Greenburg, in his mid-twenties and already pot-bellied, eyes glued on Jazmin. "Nice legs."

Peter responded with a deep, impatient sigh. "Yeah."

"Not yours. Hers."

"I caught that, Nate." He grabbed the photo back. "What are you doing down here?"

"I'm driving your staff to the Dinosaur National Monument to look at the new sauropod discovery everyone's talking about." Nate nudged him with the tip of his toe. "You're the head of the department. I assumed you scheduled the trip."

Peter shook his head. "Yeah, maybe."

Nate continued to study the photo over Peter's shoulder. "She's quite a catch. What's her name?"

Peter leaned back in his chair in resignation. "Jazmin . . . Jazmin Rivera."

"A Latin beauty, huh? I haven't seen her around."

"I haven't seen much of her either."

"You make a nice-looking couple."

Peter looked around the room, hoping for an escape, and caught sight of Shelly heading toward him. She pulled long locks of her tightly curled red hair away from her eyes, and bent down in front of him, blocking Nate's view.

"Are you coming along with us? The field trip's going to be fun."

Peter fumbled with the photo, then placed it back on his desk. "Thanks, Shell, but I really have to finish this skull. You know if it's not mounted and standing in the main entrance of this museum scaring the hell out of women and children by this time next week, John will have *my* head!"

Shelly cast her all-knowing look. "Peter, just mount the damn thing. It looks fine. No one will know the difference. Since Jazmin left, all you've done is work on this project. You're obsessing."

"It's not just the project. Jazmin—"

"Listen, Jazmin grew up in the jungle. She can take care of herself."

Shelly punched his arm. "The skull's fine and Jazmin's fine. Take a break, big guy. It'll be good for you to get out and breathe a little fresh air. You need to exercise that rugged body of yours. If I'm not mistaken, I'm seeing a bulge where your belly button used to be.

Shelly was right. It would be good to get out. He felt like hell, hadn't exercised in weeks. He guessed Shelly was looking forward to sitting next to him on the bus. But he was obsessed with thoughts of Jazmin, and now something had to be done. He hadn't told anyone they had agreed to take action today. Not Shelly, not John, no one. He'd hoped it wouldn't come to this.

Shelly looked over her shoulder and pointed at the skull. "Besides, being around that ugly thing all day would depress anyone."

Peter smirked, grateful for her concern. "You'd know ugly after staring at dino dung all week. But how, exactly, do you figure following Nate's big butt around all day will improve my mood?"

Nate wheeled around from where he stood studying the giant skull. "I heard that. Okay, everyone," he said, turning to face the large open space of the lab, "grab your things. The magical mystery tour is about to begin."

Peter looked up at Shelly. "Thanks for the pep talk, Shell, but I've got to stick around in case Jazmin calls. She's supposed to call today."

"Really?" She shrugged, a disappointed look clouding her face as she squeezed his hand. "Okay."

He stood and kissed her cheek to soften the rejection.

"All right, you lizard-lovin' cave dwellers!" Nate hollered. "Time to make your way upstairs and out to the bus." He gave Peter a mischievous smile. "Good day, Dr. Campbell."

Peter rolled his eyes and waved as the staff filed through the double doors of the lab. The room went quiet. Microscopes and magnifying lenses mounted on giant swing-arms stood motionless atop overcrowded desks. Countless fossils sat in hollow silence, as if awaiting their caretaker's return. Now only the screensaver images of dinosaurs leaping and flying across the desktop monitors brought any life into the large space. Peter felt lonely and uncomfortable in the silence. Strange, since he normally felt right at home in a room full of fossils. But not today. Not now. His gaze returned to the photo on his desk.

He sat and rubbed his temples in an attempt to clear his mind. He needed to focus on work. Besides, why should he worry? As Shelly said, Jazmin's a capable woman. She can take care of herself.

He reluctantly turned from the picture of Jazmin's smiling face and looked across to the other side of his office at the skull, his constant companion these days. It belonged to a powerful bipedal predator, a newly discovered species of tyrannosaurid, in the same family as the giant *Tyrannosaurus rex*. Although small for a tyrannosaurid, the skull was massive, nearly three feet long.

Peter stood up, grabbed his coffee and walked the ten steps over to the skull. Leaning against the table, he placed his hand on the rough fossil, trying to regain some enthusiasm for the project. He studied the massive jaw, the window-like openings behind each eye, the extensive line of serrated teeth. (What was it Jazmin had called them? *Stilettos in a vise.*)

The rest of the body stood nearby. Twice the size of a grizzly, this predator could have shredded the backside of an elephant. But there were no elephants when this creature roamed the earth.

"Lucky elephants," he mused.

Yes, those teeth were the things of nightmares. He brushed a hand over the fine, serrated edges and winced as a small bead of blood formed on the tip of his finger. They were still sharp after tens of millions of years in the ground. He felt a familiar fear run through his body as he licked his finger.

It had the legs of a giant: eight feet high at the hip, with the tibias measuring twenty percent longer than the femurs—a sure sign of a sprinter. This one combined the ferocity of a carnivore with the speed of a thoroughbred. Dino could run . . . and kill.

As a scientist, he couldn't help but admire the way Mother Nature had equipped this monster. It was an evolutionary *tour de force*, a marvel of Darwinian eat-or-be-eaten engineering. But there was something else about it, something less . . . objective. Less scientific. Something he hadn't spoken aloud, not to his peers, not even to Jazmin.

The thing gave him the creeps.

It made him uneasy. He wasn't sure why, but it had started shortly after the skull arrived at the museum and it persisted. Every time he worked with the skull, a cold fluttering started deep in the pit his stomach, making it difficult to think. His mind often drifted. Then he began to hear things. Animal calls. Footsteps. Once he thought he smelled the pungent aroma of the jungle.

More disturbing still, he felt watched. Or stalked. Like some hidden predator was hunting him.

He never mentioned it to anyone because he knew how it would sound. Hell, it sounded weird to *him*. Once he heard a deep sonorous growl and jerked to a standstill only to find Shelly standing nearby looking frightened.

Shaking off the interruption, he tried to relax into his work. Checking some of his measurements, he picked up the air scribe and ground away the last of the hard mineral deposits surrounding the teeth.

Finished, he leaned down and looked at it man-to-beast. "Okay, Slasher," he murmured, "what else can you tell me?"

He looked through the empty sockets of the huge skull and could see the wall beyond. What might the creature's eyes have looked like? The eyes always intrigued him. What type of vision did it possess? Did it see color? Did it see in two dimensions or three? Did it see through the darkness? No one knew. No eyes had survived the test of time. "I'll bet those big eyes of yours were cold and unsympathetic," he said. What color were the eyes? Were they green or brown? Jet black? And what might the pupils look like? Horizontal like a gator? Vertical like a cat? Round like a human?

No, he thought. Not human-like.

Then something flickered inside the darkened cavity, a movement, a flash of color.

He half-jerked his hand away. *What was that?* The hair on the back of his neck raised like an animal's hackles when his scientific instincts flooded in. He didn't know whether to move away from it or look at it closer. He waited a second before he leaned in.

There was nothing in the socket. It looked dark again. But he'd seen something, he knew it.

It happened again.

This time, Peter kept his heart in his chest, took two deep breathes, and leaned in as close as he dared.

I'm a scientist. And this is a scientific phenomenon. Something has crawled into the skull and that's all. Keep your head on, Peter.

Something *was* there. An image. Had Nate pasted a picture to the inside back of the skull? He'd kill him for that.

He shifted his weight and raised himself to peer into the eye socket on the opposite side of the skull. Another image, blurred and reddish, changed into distinct colors and patterns. It felt as if he were looking through a camera and trying to bring the lens into focus.

"What has that idiot done?"

But even as he said it, the image started to solidify, the shapes and colors became more defined, and he realized this wasn't a trick. He couldn't see through the skull anymore.

Peter instinctively pulled back. What was this?

And then he was looking into huge reptilian eyes the size of his fists, staring out from the skull. A fierce reddish color, with black vertical slits running through the middle, like lightning bolts in black. Peter slid off the table and steadied himself.

The eyes remained like giant marbles reflecting the lab's artificial light, and then, with the alert ease of a predator, they began to shift from side to side. He felt the blood drain from his head.

"What the hell's going on?"

The eyes shifted back and forth, silently scanning the room from the depths of time. The lab suddenly felt cold and unfamiliar. He tried to distance himself from the skull by stepping back, but it felt as if he was pressed against a wall and he stopped short. Catching his movement, the giant eyes turned in his direction.

Peter froze, but his mind raced through all possible explanations: the drugs he'd taken in the eighties; the homeopathic remedy he recently started; the full-spectrum lights they just installed; the black coffee.

There has to be an explanation.

Unable to pull his eyes from the predator, he felt an ancient terror grip his heart, override his logic, pull him relentlessly into its timeless void. Visions of frightened creatures flooded his mind, familiar visions. Running . . . panting . . . high-pitched desperate cries, a stampede . . .

Suddenly, a voice that seemed to issue from the heavens blurred the scene—a human voice. Distant at first, then recognizable as the intercom's crackle.

"Dr. Campbell? Are you there?"

Jean, the department secretary. Peter willed himself to take a deep breath.

"Dr. Campbell? You have a call."

He kept the skull within the edge of his vision.

"Dr. Campbell?"

He reached for the phone and pushed the blinking light. "Yes…Jean, thank you."

"Thank you? Thank you for what?"

"Nothing . . . sorry."

"You sound like you just finished running a four-minute mile. Those dinosaurs chasing you around down there?"

He took a deep breath and shook his head. "Something like that."

"There's a gentleman on line one. He's apparently asking for you."

"Apparently?"

"Well, I think he's speaking Spanish, but Spanish is all Greek to me.

The only thing I understood him say was your name."

"Okay. Thanks." He punched the blinking line, avoiding eye contact with the skull. "Paleontology."

"¿*Señor* Campbell?"

"¿*Sí* ?"

"*Mensaje . . . de . . . Yasmin.*" The timid voice spoke in broken Spanish.

Peter shot out of his seat and lunged for the handset of the phone, spilling his coffee across his desk. "Damn," he said in English, then switched to Spanish. "¿*Un mensaje de Jazmin Rivera?*"

He glanced again at her face in the photo, keeping the savage eyes of the dinosaur skull pushed from his mind for the moment.

"Where is she? Is she okay?"

"*La señorita dice de venir pronto.*"

"Come quickly? Where? . . . ¿*Adonde?*"

"*Villa Lacandón. Pronto.*'

"Quickly? Why? What's wrong? Is she all right?"

There was a pause. The man breathed heavily and seemed on the verge of saying something. Had the man heard him? Had he understood?

"¡*Hola!* . . . Are you still there?"

"*Ven pronto,*" the man said again.

Peter searched for the right words. "*Sí, comprendo.*"

More silence.

Peter shouted, "Wait! Who is this? Have you seen her? Is she——"

A click. Then dead silence.

"Damn it!" Peter slammed the phone handset down. With a defeated sigh, he picked it back up and dialed the operator, daring a glance at the giant skull.

Its hollow recesses revealed only shadows.

CHAPTER 2

eter hated large cities, especially this one. México City was dark and cool when the plane landed, the air thick with the stench of diesel fumes. Grateful to see that his backpack had arrived with him, he hauled it over to the next staging area and waited for the flight to Tuxtla Gutierrez.

He hated waiting too. Patience wasn't one of his virtues.

He dropped into a chair and picked up a copy of *El Sol de Acapulco*. The front page of the business section featured an unpleasant photo of Mexican President José Aguilar. Jazmin had mentioned him once or twice. His face was all falling lines—sagging cheeks, drooping moustache, lowered brow with piercing black eyes. Peter immediately disliked him. The man was no environmentalist, that much he knew.

When asked about the North American Free Trade Agreement opening México to the U.S. timber giants, Aguilar said he had given the go-ahead for logging in the Costa Grande area between the luxury Pacific coast resorts of Zihuatanejo and Acapulco. *El Presidente* praised the agreement, which he claimed would bring in much-needed industry and hundreds of jobs for the local populations. But when asked about environmental impact, he dodged the question, suggesting that his administration would look into it further.

Peter shook his head. Quite the soul of discretion—the Mexican government was already granting permission to log the area without any proper environmental impact studies.

The flight to Tuxtla Gutierrez took only an hour, and the plane arrived as a brilliant yellow sun began to rise over the horizon. Peter grabbed his carry-on and headed for the exit door almost as soon as the landing gear touched the pavement. The tropical air was already warm and moist; walking down the ramp was like wading into a swimming pool.

The small airport offered few amenities, none of which were open yet, and he killed two hours sitting in front of a dark vacant booth waiting for a rental car. The Jeep he finally secured was slightly rusty and certainly less comfortable than he was used to, but he knew he'd be glad to have four-wheel drive on the back roads.

At seven thousand feet, evergreens and oaks replaced the broad-leaf forests of the lower elevations and the air felt cool on his arms and cheeks. Rain began to pelt the windshield and he pulled over to put the ragtop up. It should have felt good to be there. But not now. Not like this.

Within an hour, the rain cleared and the outskirts of San Cristóbal de las Casas came into view—a sleepy town of single-story pastel buildings, wrought-iron barred windows and red tiled roofs. Peter's legs ached from hours of sitting, and he needed supplies. He pulled into the square and parked in front of a small adobe store.

Free of the vehicle and stretching his arms over his head, he took in his surroundings: brightly dressed natives carrying handmade rugs and straw baskets filled with food, traders in wooden stalls hawking their wares, a boombox blaring salsa music from the front of a retail store. Children played in the side streets, kicking a ball and chasing one another through the narrow corridors. Farther down the square stood the requisite military Jeep and men in uniform.

Stifling a yawn, he grabbed his red backpack and walked into the store where a weathered-looking man stood behind a long wooden counter. They exchanged smiles and nods. Peter filled a basket with mangoes, guava, and ripe *platanos*—bananas—then spotted *machetes* hanging on a far wall. He could use one in the jungle...and it might come in handy if he needed something to trade. Same with the carton of chocolate bars next to the cash register.

The storekeeper rifled through the basket to ring up Peter's order. At first glance, he was just another tired old man with little hair and few teeth. Up close, Peter could see he was really quite young, another reminder that life in México could be hard.

Behind the counter, in a back room, three barefoot children stared blankly at a black-and-white television, sucking on raw sugar cane. *They'll be toothless soon as well,* he thought.

The storekeeper flashed a gap-toothed smile. "*¿A donde vas, amigo?* . . . Where are you going, friend?"

"The Lacandón village, south of the city," he replied in slow Spanish.

"No, no, *Señor*," the man said, shaking his head resolutely. "You must not go there. It is very dangerous to go into the jungle alone."

"I must go," Peter answered, surprised at the man's concern. "A friend needs me there and I must go to her."

"A woman?"

"*Sí*. Jazmin Rivera. Do you know her?"

The man leaned across the counter and whispered. "This is not good. There is danger in the air, and it follows the woman."

"So, you've heard of her?"

"*¡Sí !* She has written things in the paper. This woman wants to save the Lacandón land. She is a good woman, very brave, but there are powers here that do not want her around. *Señor*, going into the jungle alone is a very bad idea. There are bandits, and snakes," he said, getting louder, "and jaguars!"

"I understand it may be dangerous, *Señor*. But I must go."

The storekeeper stared at him, then leaned across the counter again and whispered, "You should have more than a *machete*. You should have *una pistola*."

Peter weighed the suggestion. He had no permit, and it would be risky to carry a gun illegally. But the man was right. Going alone into the jungle without a gun was also risky.

He lowered his voice to match the shopkeeper's. "Well, do you know where I—where a man like me—could buy a gun?"

Glancing suspiciously around the empty store as if someone might be eavesdropping behind a sack of potatoes or a pound of sugar, the shopkeeper turned and entered a curtained doorway into a back room. He returned holding an automatic handgun, complete with shoulder holster. Placing it on the counter, he looked anxiously about the room and slid it toward Peter.

Peter released the snap on the leather holster and pulled the gun out, surprised to see an Italian-made 9mm Beretta. It felt solid and balanced in his hand. He knew enough about handguns from his tour of duty in the National Guard to check it for wear. It was a fine piece. He wondered how a poor storekeeper came across such a weapon.

Unable to hide his approval, Peter smiled as he ejected the magazine and set it on the counter, then slid the action back and forth to inspect the firing pin. Slipping the empty magazine back into the butt of the handle, he placed the gun back on the counter. The tips of his fingers left faint prints in the thin sheen of oil coating the gun. The gun looked well maintained.

The storekeeper eyed the store entrance. Glancing back at Peter, he asked, "You want it?"

"Does it shoot straight?"

"*Sí, sí*, it works very good. I never use it. But I must clean it once a month or it will rust in the humid air. I am a slave to this gun."

The gun was spotless. In fact, it looked brand new. Peter looked it over once again, contemplating the risk. It might come in handy.

"¿*Cuanto cuesta?* . . . How much?"

"*Dos mil pesos,*" the storekeeper said.

About two hundred dollars—a fortune by the storekeeper's standards, but a bargain for a gun of this quality. Peter wondered again how the storekeeper had acquired it, but he couldn't linger to ask. Besides, it was illegal to own or to sell a handgun to a foreigner. The storekeeper was taking a sizable risk.

Slipping a wad of bills from his pocket, Peter counted out two thousand pesos. The man smiled as he picked up the money, then reached under the counter for a small wooden box. From it he produced a cleaning rod, a small can of oil, and a full box of bullets. "Here," he said, "take these. The gun will do you no good without bullets."

Peter thumbed through the bills again and placed another two hundred pesos on the counter. The toothless storekeeper pushed it back toward him. "I overcharge you for the *pistola,*" he said, grinning again. Peter knew otherwise. Glancing over the man's shoulder, he gestured toward the children staring at the television and stuffed the two bills into the storekeeper's shirt pocket. Then he thanked the man, packed his newly acquired supplies into his red backpack, and headed to the Jeep.

He drove out of San Cristóbal and into the jungle, winding through the dense forest of pine, mahogany, and ceiba with greenish-yellow moss hanging like wet flags from the branches. The strong musty smell suggested a greenhouse long out of control, an explosion of unchecked growth and diversification. In spite of himself, he relished the heady rush of pungent air, thick with the scent of sticky flowering buds. Raindrops and noonday sunshine washed over the unsettled country and mingled on his windshield.

An hour passed before Peter noticed vehicles stopped ahead in the road.

An alarm went off in his head. People were walking from car to car, searching the vehicles—men carrying automatic weapons. A holdup? No. The men wore military uniforms—a military checkpoint.

He slammed his hand on the steering wheel. "Of all the damn rotten luck!"

If the soldiers found the Beretta, he'd sweat out the next six months in some filthy Mexican jail, eating cockroaches and paying off crooked lawyers. But there was no turning around. They had already seen him, and now traffic blocked him in from behind. He crept toward the checkpoint, his heart pounding with every inch. Finally, the soldiers finished with the car ahead and waved him forward.

The unfamiliar uniforms included black berets and shirts bearing red arm patches with a black panther. Not the usual Federal troops. He glanced again at the weapons slung from their shoulders—Colt M40 carbines, maybe, he wasn't sure. He gripped the wheel tight, expecting the worst.

Two men approached. "*Buenas tardes, Señor.* Your passport, please."

A bead of sweat ran down Peter's forehead. He dug into his shirt pocket and handed his passport to the soldier.

"What brings you to Chiapas?"

Peter's mouth went dry. "I'm a paleontologist with the Denver Museum of Natural History, in México on business. I'm headed to . . . Palenque."

The soldier on the far side of the Jeep opened the passenger door and began rummaging through his knapsack, pulling out clothes and toiletries. Then he grabbed for the red backpack, fumbling with the zipper until he caught sight of the *machete* hidden under the passenger seat. He dropped the backpack and pulled out the long knife.

"*Capitán,*" he said.

A thick, formidable man with deeply bronzed skin and a bushy, Pancho Villa mustache strode forward. More Indian than *mestizo*, he carried himself with the aura of a well-heeled man, someone used to fine things. He wouldn't look out of place on an expensive stallion, a proud *caballero* or *vaquero*. Dressed like the clean-shaven soldiers but with bars on his shoulders, he was the only one without the sleek carbine. Instead, he wore a handsome hand-tooled leather hip holster. Snapped inside, some sort of revolver peeked out, its polished steel gleaming like silver against the light tan handle grips, fashioned from staghorn. Clearly, this gun and its proud owner had a history together.

A soldier interrupted Peter's thoughts, muttering something as he poked around underneath the Jeep looking for contraband.

El Capitán glanced dismissively at the long knife but said nothing. *Machetes* were common in the jungle.

"I need it in the field," Peter said. "When I'm doing my work."

The *capitán* didn't nod, didn't shrug. He stared again at the passport, started to say something, and then noticed the carton of chocolates on the seat.

Peter put his hand over the carton and smiled. "Chocolate for the hard-working soldiers?"

The *capitán*'s eyes narrowed.

Peter held a bar up. "*¿Chocolate?*"

One of the soldiers hovered near the passenger door, waiting for permission to grab the candy. But the *capitán* frowned. Maybe he smelled the bribe for what it was. On the other hand, didn't most Mexican soldiers and law enforcement officers levy *la mordida?*

Maybe his small stash of dollars and *pesos* would buy his release if they found the Beretta . . .

The *capitán* shot a furtive glance at the other soldier, handed the passport back to Peter, then nodded brusquely. Peter offered him the carton. The *capitán* tossed a soft chocolate bar to the far side of the jeep and kept several for himself. He gobbled down one of the bars in two big bites and opened another.

The backpack was lying exposed on the backseat. Sweat dripped down Peter's forehead and armpits. "What exactly are you looking for, *Capitán?*"

"*Banditos,*" he grunted. "Zapatista rebels."

Peter smiled. "Do I look like a Zapatista rebel?"

The *capitán* sneered, then turned again to look at the growing line of vehicles. He licked the chocolate from his fingers, stroked his mustache back into place, and said, "Go."

Peter needed no more encouragement. He shifted into first, hit the accelerator and sped through the roadblock. When he glanced in the rearview mirror, the soldiers were already searching the next vehicle, a Mexican family in a big American station wagon. But the captain was still standing in the same spot, watching the Jeep with an intensity that made him shiver.

A half hour later, Peter turned off the main road and his progress slowed to a crawl. Mud holes, branches hitting the sides of the Jeep— he was thankful for the four-wheel drive. He reached back, pulled out the Beretta, and placed it under the seat. There would be no checkpoints in the backcountry.

He drove until he reached a fork in the road, then chose the most traveled route. At the end of the road, he could see a cluster of thatched huts tucked into a mountain clearing. Peter's spirits rose. This was the X on the map Jazmin had copied for him—the Lacandón village. It looked inviting, typical of villages in the backcountry.

And yet something felt wrong. No dogs barked as he drove closer. No smoke drifted from the fire pits. All was quiet. The village looked deserted.

He parked a couple hundred feet up the road and slipped the gun into his pocket.

On foot and walking cautiously, his mind raced. Hut after hut looked undisturbed, but all personal belongings were gone. And no sign of Jazmin.

Had they been forcibly removed? There was no indication of a struggle. The villagers seemed to have simply packed up and left.

Searching the perimeter, he came across an obscure trail. He followed it and soon found fresh tracks, tire–tread sandals, and good clear impressions from a pair of boots—all heading into the jungle. The boot impressions were small, with four diamond shapes on the heel and three at the toe. He removed a leaf from the middle of one of the prints, revealing the faint impression of the letter *N*.

Nikes!

His heart beat faster. The prints were Jazmin's. They had to be; they bought those field boots in Denver and he knew their tread design by heart.

He ran his fingers over the impression and smiled. She'd gone with the tribe.

Peter checked the time—1:01 p.m. At this latitude he still had plenty of light left, and might be able to catch up with the villagers before dark. Perhaps he would sleep in Jazmin's arms tonight...

Holding that thought, he ran back to the Jeep and quickly sorted through his equipment and supplies, loading only the gun and the most essential gear into his backpack. Soon he was on his way.

The air was heavy with humidity, and his clothes quickly dampened with perspiration as he moved through the thick underbrush and along the trail. Flies and mosquitoes buzzed around his face as he crossed the rugged foothills and forded creeks. But after hours of hiking at a fast pace, the sun began to set and the sky turned pink, and he still hadn't caught up with Jazmin.

He stopped to check his compass and study the tracks again. If he kept going with the flashlight, he might find Jazmin before daybreak. He was tempted to continue; she might be over the next hill. But tracking in the dark was difficult and dangerous. He might lose the trail. And moving through the jungle at night would increase his chances of encountering predators.

Of course, camping was risky too. The jungle was no place to be alone. Monkeys and parrots screeched in the surrounding hills. A large black bird cackled loudly from a nearby tree, scolding him.

Peter decided to set up camp, though a lingering uncertainty gnawed at him as he crawled into his sleeping bag. Something didn't feel right. He second-guessed his decision not to light a fire.

He fell asleep quickly, but lurid images of the tyrannosaurid skull jarred him awake. He lay thinking about the mysterious phone call that offered more questions than answers, the close call at the roadblock with the soldiers in unfamiliar black uniforms, and the disappearance of the tribe.

Everything felt connected, but he didn't know how.

CHAPTER 3

Peter tossed and turned on the mat, weaving in and out of slumber. Dreams of Jazmin mingled in the back of his mind with the chatter of spider monkeys high up in the forest canopy, the steady beat of rain on the nylon tent, and the whistles and hoots of birds greeting the sunrise. *I need to get up*, he thought, but he sank back into an uneasy sleep.

The noise grew louder and he bobbed back into semi-consciousness. The jungle always greeted the day with raucous enthusiasm, he reasoned. But as he forced his eyes open, he was startled to find that it wasn't morning. The world around him was still pitch black.

And what sounded like a serenade, wasn't one at all: it was an alarm. The sounds weren't getting louder—they were getting closer.

Predator!

His heart leapt. He had to keep himself from springing up and drawing attention.

He eased his hand through the backpack, silently searching for the Beretta. He cursed himself for not keeping it out where he could easily find it in the dark when he felt the smooth leather of the holster.

The monkeys screeched directly overhead and then something snapped just outside the tent.

A twig.

The creature was only a few feet away.

He sat up slowly, held his breath, and raised the gun, listening, knowing the animal on the other side of the nylon wall was listening too.

Without warning, an ear-splitting scream directly in front of him sent shockwaves through his body as a section of the tent tore away violently.

Peter fell back against the rear of the tent and squeezed the trigger. Nothing happened.

God, the safety! Now nothing stood between him and the creature except damp jungle air.

He flipped the gun's safety off.

His heart pounded. He waited in the blackness. Had the creature fled? At first, he heard only the gentle sound of rain dripping through the trees above—then something else. A fast rhythmic sound, barely audible.

What was that?

And then he saw the faint glow of yellow eyes and knew. The sound was the creature's breathing.

It sprang the instant their eyes locked, striking him in the chest like a sledge hammer.

Claws sank into his flesh with brutal force. He screamed as he desperately tried to hold the powerful beast back. Flashing white fangs and the smell of damp fur overwhelmed his senses.

Frantic to keep it away from his neck, he tried to free the hand that clung to the Beretta, but the animal was too strong, too fast. He shoved back and kicked with all his strength, firing his weapon at the same time.

The beast jumped back, but in the dark, Peter wasn't sure if it had been hit or merely scared off. He shot again, then again, and again, pulling the trigger until the gun emptied. Gulping down air, he sat still and listened, but his ears rang from the loud blasts.

He heard nothing but his racing heart and ragged breath.

Since his ears were no help, he groped for the flashlight and flicked it on. Only veils of white mist and deep shadows crept between the trees. He frantically searched through what was left of the tent for the heavy, compact box of bullets tucked deep into his backpack. As fast as his bleeding hands could move, he reloaded the clip and shoved it back into the handle. He was almost disappointed when no red eyes glowed back. He wanted to kill the son-of-a-bitch.

A big cat—of all the stinking luck.

He lowered the gun and turned the flashlight on the tent. It sagged in tatters and his clothes lay several yards away.

He steeled himself to look down at his wounds. The sight sickened him. His shirt hung in shreds, revealing long lacerations running down his arms, chest and abdomen, exposing raw pink flesh oozing with blood. Sweat ran down his chest, mingling with blood and settling in a growing pool of red beneath him. For a moment, he could only watch in silent disbelief as his life drained onto the jungle floor.

His stomach fired a queasy, sickening alarm, and his mind raced in a panic.

Damn! Why did I come here alone?

Why did Jazmin lure me here and disappear?

Where the hell did she—

He stopped himself. Anger and fear would only steal precious energy. He learned years ago that accepting circumstances was the first rule of survival. Anger, denial, and self-pity wouldn't keep him alive. He'd have to think positive to survive the night.

Every movement was painful as he held his shredded abdomen and struggled to drape the torn rain-fly back over the tent. He went through the first aid kit: iodine, quinine, hydrogen peroxide, two rolls of elastic bandages, pain relievers, sterile gauze pads...

A threaded needle. "Thank God," he whispered. His hands shook so uncontrollably that he couldn't have threaded the eye to save his life— which is what this had come down to.

He swallowed a handful of aspirin, used some water to clean his wounds, and assessed the damage. The gaping wounds on his left side and arm were the worst. Holding one end of his scarf in his teeth, he wrapped it around with his free hand, fashioning a tourniquet for his arm. The bleeding slowed, which would buy him time.

His chest and stomach wounds were another matter. He could only apply pressure, using the elastic bandages from his first aid kit. He opened the bottle of hydrogen peroxide, clenched his teeth and poured it over the deep lacerations. He screamed through clenched teeth as the angry bubbles sizzled into raw flesh, then turned to fire. The pain shot to his head in a bright flash. Everything went black.

When he came to moments later, he was lying on his back. He struggled to sit up and then picked up the bottle of peroxide again. This time he would move slowly, careful not to push beyond what he could endure. He couldn't afford to pass out again. The big cat would be back if none of his shots had hit their mark.

He finished cleaning his wounds and reached for the threaded needle. He clenched his teeth around a torn piece of cloth from his tattered shirt, held his breath, and then pushed the needle into his limp arm. His world blackened again.

"Can't," he said, struggling to stay conscious. "I can't do it." Fighting fear and nausea, he clumsily wrapped his body with the elastic bandages and fell back against his blood-soaked mat. He knew wounded people often died from general trauma and dehydration rather than the direct effects of their wounds. He couldn't expect anyone to come looking for him before daylight even if someone had heard the gunshots. The indigenous people were afraid to venture into the jungle at night.

"Stay awake," he said over and over.

Calm down. Drink lots of water. Survive the night.

He knew he'd never stay conscious lying down. He waited for the strength to sit up again, but it didn't come. Carefully rolling onto one side, he tried pushing against the ground with his elbow, when blackness washed over him like a tidal wave.

He awoke with a terrible thirst.

How long had he been lying there? Not long; it was still dark.

He attempted to move his hand toward the canteen but it didn't respond. It didn't even twitch. He wondered if he'd be found lying dead from dehydration next to a container of water.

The flashlight still illuminated the tent, but as he attempted to sit up again, everything spun out of control. Sweat ran off his brow and into his eyes. He tried to clear his head by breathing deeply. He needed to gather his strength and prepare for another attack should it come, but the tent kept moving and swaying while his heart beat inside his head. After several failed attempts, he closed his eyes and tried to push the nightmare away from his thoughts.

Jazmin's smiling face appeared in his mind's eye, illuminated as if she sat in front of a fire. She was talking to him, but he couldn't hear her words. She tried to reassure him and he felt comforted by her. "I hope you will be okay without me," he whispered, wondering if she would forgive him for dying without saying goodbye.

His body throbbed with merciless pain, and the image of Jazmin vanished.

His mind shifted back to the big cat.

Please, God. Don't let it come back.

Time drifted. The cacophony of the jungle kept him conscious, but uneasy. So many familiar creatures, howling, cawing, screeching, fighting for his attention. He stirred feverishly on the blood-soaked floor of the tent.

They're trying to tell me something.

He recognized the screeching of nocturnal monkeys and the deep croaking of bullfrogs in the distance when another sound caught his attention. He knew that cry. But his mind was turning off, no longer able to take in new information.

What is that sound?

The creature's name slammed into his mind as he slipped back into the darkness. Gathering all his will, Peter's lips weakly formed the last word to race through his mind as he fell from consciousness.

"Jaguar!"

CHAPTER 4

The ocean stretched out before him in an endless horizon. Peaceful. Alluring. Unfathomable power lay just below its glassy surface, a power with no recognizable limits, a power Peter could not begin to grasp. Despite his longing to become one with it, the deep and gentle currents beckoned then receded, beckoned then receded.

He opened his eyes to an unfamiliar world of sound and texture, out of focus, then clearer. Strange shapes danced over him. Deep shadows. He turned his head and recognized smoke drifting up to a thatched ceiling of palm leaves. Sunlight streaked through walls of stripped saplings and vine.

And then pain—pure unadulterated pain. He wanted to get up, run from the pain, but couldn't. He gritted his teeth and tried to lift himself onto one elbow, but a painful restriction stopped him short.

Is this my body?

Gazing down, he saw bandages circling his upper body, his arms. Claws, teeth, terror . . . He took a deep breath and his head spun . . . *Someone saved me.*

He was lying on a straw cot, elevated on wooden poles fashioned from saplings. Bundles of herbs hung from the ceiling, ghost-like in the smoke-filtered sunlight. The smell of wood fire and sage washed over him . . . Bracing himself, he finally managed to ease slowly up onto one elbow.

"It is about time you woke up," a voice behind him said in Spanish.

Peter jolted forward, lost his balance, and tumbled off the cot. Stinging pain shot through his torso like hot irons as he hit the ground. He turned his head as far as possible and looked into the shadows for the source of the voice. He saw the faint outline of a man sitting cross-legged on the earthen floor.

"Who . . . who the hell are you?"

The man remained motionless, and Peter remembered he had spoken Spanish.

He tried again. *¿Quién . . . eres tú?*

"*Soy Chan.*"

Peter struggled to translate his questions. "Where am I, Chan?"

"Safe in the womb of our mother," he replied in Spanish.

"Womb of our mother" meant little to Peter, though he was glad to hear of his safety. "What tribe?"

"Lacandón."

Peter breathed a ragged sigh of relief.

"You followed us when *bolom* attacked you. My people watched and listened. We heard your gun in the night. The spirit of darkness came back for you."

"Spirit of darkness? The jaguar?"

"*Sí. Bolom*, Spirit of Darkness."

Peter shifted until he could lift one of the crude bandages from his arm and inspect the laceration. The wound was purple and swollen, but clean, well-stitched, and free of blood.

"How did you do this?" he asked. "Wounds like these take weeks to heal."

The man stood and removed the draping from the doorway. Bright sunlight flooded the hut and Peter had to close his eyes for a second and turn away. "I heal you," Chan said. The bright sunlight set his white cotton tunic aglow like a paper lantern. He looked heaven-sent.

"I am good healer, no?"

He walked to the space beside Peter and peered down, his high cheekbones and sunken cheeks accenting a wide nose and generous mouth. Long raven-black hair touched with silver outlined his deeply lined face. His eyes, nearly obsidian-black, radiated wisdom.

With the grace and confidence of a younger man, he reached down and helped Peter up onto the cot. Peter tried to suppress his moans, but the pain of this simple movement overwhelmed him. The room blackened, then came back into focus again.

"Thank you."

The old man stayed silent.

"You're a native," Peter said in Spanish. "How do you know Spanish?"

"Missionaries," the old man replied. "They came to our village many years ago, when I was a boy. We were told many disturbing things about Spirit and ourselves." He shook his head. "They stayed many years."

"They're gone?"

"*Sí.* They depress everyone in the village. We tell them to leave."

Peter started to laugh, then clenched his teeth and took a few deep breaths to overcome the pain. A new anxiety overcame him. *Jazmin.*

"Is a woman here?"

"There are many women here. Busy women. They have no time to lie around like you."

Peter smiled weakly, enjoying the old man's humor. "How long have I been here?"

"*Dos semanas.*"

"Two weeks?" Peter gasped. "It's no wonder my wounds are so well-healed."

Chan gazed thoughtfully into his eyes. "It takes time to bring someone back from the dead."

The old man's penetrating stare drew Peter in. He looked steadily into Chan's eyes, then quickly looked away, uncomfortable with his sudden seriousness.

When he looked back, Chan's eyes had softened again. "Maybe I am not such a good healer," he said. At first just his eyes smiled, then he started shaking with laughter.

Medicine men were usually over the top, and couldn't be trusted as far as Peter was concerned. Was he delirious?

Peter began to fade again, and then he suddenly felt Chan's hands moving over his chest and abdomen. He opened his eyes slightly to see that Chan was not actually touching him. It wasn't body heat that he felt, but some sort of subtle, tingling energy. The sensation was soothing. He closed his eyes again and found he didn't give a damn if it made sense or not. It felt good. That was all that mattered.

"What's that strange smell on me?" he asked.

"Manure," said Chan. "Keeps the rot away."

Gangrene. He'd heard of using manure to keep gangrene from forming in open wounds, but he had never seen the practice.

The shaman continued as if in prayer, speaking in a language Peter could not place. His calm, hypnotic presence was mesmerizing. Peter's world began to fade, but many questions nipped at his mind, keeping him awake.

He searched for the right Spanish words. "Why did the village move?" There was no response. Peter waited, wondering if Chan would answer before he passed out again. He had worked with native people in the tropics before. Their pace was slower, hampered by heat and humidity, and tempered by a culture that felt no need for change. He had to slow down, be patient. Several minutes went by before Chan spoke again.

"The jungle spirits told me it was not safe in our village. The standing-people warned of danger. Cloud spirits were dark and worried. Rest now. We have much to do . . . little time."

"Little time?" Peter searched Chan's eyes for an explanation. "Why?" He didn't think these people even had a concept of time beyond the natural cycles of daylight and darkness and the change of seasons, and suddenly time was an issue.

Chan looked down at him with his piercing yet comforting deep-set eyes. "Sleep. Let Spirit heal you. They will come soon, and you must be strong enough to run for your life."

CHAPTER 5

Peter awakened to a different jungle from the one in which he had fallen asleep. The trees and plants appeared to be smaller, yet more pungent, more alive. There was no village, no villagers, nor any sense of human presence. Unmoored, with no thoughts beyond the present, he sniffed the air, then began pacing through the dense foliage.

No longer a primate, he moved through the heavily wooded forest without memory of a human consciousness, an alert bundle of animal nerves. A sudden sound emanated from a thicket of palms. The rustling trees behind him demanded his full attention. Frightened, he quickened his pace, holding a clear mental image in his awareness: a creature, a predator, staggering in its power and ferocity. This image of a two-legged killer flashed repeatedly in his mind, but he had not identified the animal through visual contact. He had smelled it.

Tall trees swayed behind him; some simply brushed aside, some snapping like twigs. He began to sprint, but something was wrong. He was limping, his right leg injured. The pain slowed him as he ran through the forest and out onto a vast savanna.

The savanna teemed with exotic birds and great herds of animals. The mucky smell of the large herds seemed inviting. Great herds of animals normally suggested safety, but his instincts told him otherwise. There were no creatures of his kind in sight. He searched for their signature in the air, but he picked up no scent. He shuffled his feet desperately. There was nowhere to hide; no canyons nor woodlands to disappear in, no lakes nor swamps to swim into, just earth and sky stretching into an endless, drying wetland. Worst of all, the creatures of the savanna would not prevent the predator from pursuing him.

A high-pitched, strident bugling emanated from his throat, echoing over the treeless flatlands as he raced across its vast expanse, but no one returned his calls. Now he could only run. A quick look back at the edge of the jungle revealed nothing threatening, and he slowed down for a moment, anxious for the opportunity to rest. A second glance gave no visual hint of a predator, but he knew it was still there, watching. Stopping at a shallow channel of water to drink and rest his wounded leg, he scanned the area again, and then bent down to drink.

His clear reflection shone in the rippling water, a large bipedal dinosaur with a duckbill and a semicircular plate-like crest standing atop the head. The crest rose steeply from wide-set eyes to a height of about one foot, then curved down toward the back of the head. He was a mature *Corythosaurus*, a four-ton plant eater of the late Cretaceous period.

Sensing danger again, he raised his head high and sniffed the air for a chemical signature, studying the edge of the savanna. He shifted uneasily, not liking what he smelled. Or heard. A huge predator was crashing through the trees and onto the savanna. One ton of hungry *Tyrannosaur*, twenty-five feet long, with a nimble, ten-foot stride. The fact that the predator was smaller than a full-grown *Corythosaurus* was insignificant— the *Tyrannosaur* was to him what a mountain lion is to a bison.

He ran on, the wind rushing by with a steady drone. Mud sprayed out fifty feet in every direction, punctuating each lunging step. After running for miles at a steady gait across the tepid wetlands, he began to tire. His wounded leg shot painful signals to his brain and he slowed his pace. He looked back at the huge predator, steadily gaining ground. The *Tyrannosaur* focused straight ahead, showing little interest in the large herds of ceratopsids whose horns stabbed defiantly at the sky. These great beasts were a good source of food for the *Tyrannosaur*, but the herds were too large. Alert to the predator's presence, they had quickly formed protective circles—too dangerous for an attack.

The *Tyrannosaur*'s muscular body gleamed bronze in the midday sun. The closer it drew, the more terrifying it became. It sprinted up close behind, then beside him. Nothing more than hapless prey now, he flinched, taunted by the terrifying red eyes with black, dagger-like pupils.

Peter awakened, screaming from his gut. Sweat rolled from his face and body. As he lay panting on his cot, he struggled to an upright position and surveyed his surroundings. He was still in the Lacandón village, back in the safety of the hut. His lungs ached and his chest wounds shot daggers of pain from his hard breathing.

"What the hell was that?" he asked aloud.

"Your lesson for the day," Chan's now-familiar voice responded behind him.

Startled, Peter turned to see Chan sitting on the earthen floor, patiently watching over him. Between breaths, he blurted out in Spanish, "I'm really beginning to hate waking up around here."

Chan sat motionless, apparently unable to appreciate the humor.

"I had a dream." Peter's eyes lit with excitement. "It was incredible. There were dinosaurs . . . huge beasts everywhere . . . it was so real. But the most remarkable thing . . . *I* was a dinosaur. I smelled the air. Ran with the wind rushing by. My God, what happened to me?"

"Not a dream," Chan said with a barely perceptible shake of his head. "Experience."

Peter lay back down, exhausted from the episode. He slowly registered Chan's words.

"Experience?"

"*Sí*. You were a dinosaur. You liked being a dinosaur. Now you experience manhood. Now you think you are a man."

He contemplated the old shaman's words. "You're saying I actually was a dinosaur?" His body still trembled from the memory.

"You experience dinosaur," Chan said. He stood and moved to Peter's side, then placed his hands over Peter's chest as he had done before.

Peter automatically took in a slow breath and began to relax. "So, I really wasn't a dinosaur then. I just imagined it . . . right?"

Chan did not answer right away, measuring Peter's words. "No, not dinosaur." Chan spoke in a slow, reassuring tone.

Peter raised his head. "So, I just had the experience of being a dinosaur, like in a dream?"

"You could say this." Chan nodded. "*Sí,* like a dream."

Comfortable with this perspective, Peter lay his head back down on the cot while Chan continued his healing.

"*Sí,*" Chan said again. "Just a dream . . . just like this one."

Wincing, Peter struggled up onto one elbow. "What do you mean, 'like this one?' This is real. I'm not dreaming now. I'm a man." Unexpected anger and fear arose inside of him. "My name is Peter and I'm lying in this bug-infested swamp of a jungle. This is as real as it gets. And while I appreciate all you've done for me, there's been enough confusion in my life lately. I really don't need any more."

Exhausted by his effort, he lay back down.

"Dinosaur real, too," Chan said, apparently unaffected by Peter's outburst.

"There is no way that could have been real," Peter added.

"How do you know what is real, old friend?"

"I know because I experience life with all my senses and with full consciousness."

Chan sat down on a tree stump next to the cot. "Like dinosaur."

It was a simple statement, almost innocent, but it struck Peter like a blow to the stomach.

"Yeah," he responded automatically, before realizing the implication. He shifted uncomfortably on the cot. "I guess so. Well, it seemed real to me at the time."

"Like now."

"Yeah . . . like now."

"When you experience all of self, you will know what is real," Chan said. "Before you think you are a dinosaur. Today you believe you are a man. The jungle, the spirits called you here to remember."

Peter fought to absorb Chan's words.

The jungle called me here?

What the hell did the jungle want him to remember? Peter wanted to know more, but he was starting to fade, to lose his concentration. He needed comforting, and concern for Jazmin surfaced in his mind.

But before he could ask about her again, his mind spun into the timeless void of an uneasy sleep.

It seemed only moments later when his eye opened again, this time to total darkness.

Something behind him had moved.

He panicked. *What is it?*

He took a deep breath, struggling to calm himself. Something large and stealthy crept behind him.

Jaguar!

His dreams had tried to warn him. It had paced back and forth in front of him in his dreams, and now it was back to finish him off.

Peter strained to see but his eyes couldn't penetrate the darkness. Frustration welled up inside him. He reached for his gun, but had no idea where it was. He tensed at every sound, trying to account for them, holding his breath in wait for the sudden attack. He stared out into the darkness, wondering if the moment were real or just another one of his dreams or visions—whatever they were. He had been fooled more than once already.

He didn't dare move, not even to determine if he were in a human body or some other form.

He began to put the pieces together: he thought like a human, like Peter. *I must be Peter* . . .

He froze as moist, warmth breath suddenly teased the back of his neck. He braced for the attack.

A sudden movement from behind sent him catapulting off the cot and onto the earthen floor. He cried out in pain as he hit the ground, but another scream rang out at the same time.

"Peter!" a familiar voice cried out. "*¿Que pasa?* . . . What is the matter? Where are you?"

Peter lifted his head and responded in English. "Jazmin? Is that you?"

"*Sí, sí,* it is me."

"My God, I . . . I thought you were the jaguar."

He listened to her climb out of the cot in the darkness to kneel at his side, then felt her damp cheek against his.

"Jazmin, is it really you?"

She began shaking with sobs. "I was so worried, Peter. I didn't think you would ever wake up. You were so badly mauled by that cat. I am so sorry."

He fought back his own emotions as he wiped tears from her face. She had suffered with him during these nightmarish days. Somehow knowing that made it easier for him to accept his situation.

Soft chattering at the hut's doorway alerted him to the crowd of villagers, curious to see what the screaming was about. Their commotion filled the night air with a queer language made stranger in the dark.

"It was just a nightmare," Jazmin tried to explain to them. "Peter woke up frightened. That's all it was."

Jazmin spoke a few words in the Lacandón language, Yucatec Maya, then he recognized Chan's voice. The shaman had pressed his way through the crowded doorway to lean over Peter.

"*Bolom* is part of you now. Do not fear it. The spirit of *bolom* is your ally. It protects you in the darkness." His voice softened. "Know your allies and your enemies, old friend. This is your key to survival."

The villagers continued to talk among themselves as invisible hands helped him up onto his cot. Once he settled in, the villagers dispersed, leaving him and Jazmin alone again. She rejoined him on the cot, holding him close, but her face evaded him in the darkness.

He stroked her hair, grateful that he finally held her in his arms.

"I haven't seen you for six weeks."

"Almost seven," she replied.

"Why doesn't someone light a fire? I can't see a damn thing. And that's not a good thing because . . . because everything around here wants to eat me."

"I am sorry, *mi amor,* but a fire would give our location away. Chan says we are in danger."

"So I heard. Who are we hiding from?"

"The people who want to take the land away from the tribe and log the forest."

"Do you really think someone would come into these people's forest and run them out? Or kill them?"

"Chan thinks so. That's why he moved the village. He began getting messages that we were in danger."

"You never contacted me. I was worried sick."

"I tried. I missed you so much. I wrote you every day, but I had no way of getting a letter out of the village after they set up roadblocks. I wanted so badly to contact you, but Chan would not let anyone go into town. Weeks went by before he sent K'in to call you. The tension was building all this time."

K'in. He thought about the phone call and wondered if he would get a chance to wring the guy's neck.

"I ran into one of the roadblocks on my way here," he said.

"How did you get past them?"

"They weren't looking for me."

"Ah! *Si.* Of course. Thank God," she said. "After Chan realized the danger, he waited until the last moment before he moved the people deeper into the jungle. We packed our belongings and left as soon as K'in returned from San Cristóbal."

"Next time, send someone who likes to talk."

"I know," she said. "When K'in arrived back at the village I asked him to repeat what he had said to you. When he told me, I cried. I did not think you would come. I knew before we sent K'in that he would talk little, but he is the only one here besides Chan who speaks any Spanish. It was the best we could do. I hope you can forgive me, Peter."

"Of course." It felt odd to hear her say his name. Somehow, she sounded more distant. She had begun calling him *mi amor* before she'd departed. "You did what you could. I'm just glad you didn't try to get past those roadblocks. Those soldiers looked brutal in their black uniforms. No telling what would have happened to you."

"Thank you, *mi amor.*" She stroked his cheek. "After all you've been through, I thought maybe you wouldn't understand."

Mi amor—that's better, he thought.

"I'm not sure I understand anything anymore. Since I arrived here, I've been attacked by a jaguar with a very bad disposition, a *Tyrannosaur* that showed absolutely no respect . . ."

"Dinosaur? What are you talking about?"

"Chan didn't mention it to you? I had an incredible dream, only Chan said it was much more than a dream. It was so real I'd have to agree with him. I really felt I went back in time."

"When did this happen?"

"Hell, I don't know. I'll take a wild guess and say it was sometime between the last time I saw daylight and a hundred million years ago."

"Very funny," Jazmin said. "Are you sure you're feeling all right?"

"Like I said, I'm not sure of anything right now. Chan knew I was dreaming about the jaguar. How does he know these things?"

"He just does. Chan hears the voices of the forest." She took a deep breath, and exhaled slowly. "Spirit speaks to him . . . many strange things happen."

"Like what?"

She paused to think. "Some odd things happened in those first few days after the village men brought you in. Whenever I came into the shelter, I became faint. A strange energy filled the room. I never experienced anything like it before. Sometimes there were several villagers around you, other times just Chan, but that strange energy was always there. I always felt weak, and I could never stay long."

"Yeah. I felt it too. I've been unconscious so long. Maybe that's why. I didn't have the strength to stay conscious through the healing process. Chan has some kind of power in his hands, too."

They reflected for a moment. "Another thing," Jazmin said. "Butterflies kept flying 'round your shelter. They were nowhere else; just here . . . beautiful little blue butterflies· Sometimes I sat and watched them, but I could not see a logical reason for them hovering around your hut."

"How about an illogical explanation?" he asked, his eyelids drooping with fatigue.

"I asked Chan." She gently stroked his hair. "He said the butterfly was a sign of transformation."

"Transformation," he muttered. "Oh, yeah. Been doing lots of that lately."

They held each other, listening to a rare breeze playing through the trees, and the deep sonorous roar of a howler monkey. Then all settled into a still hush, except for the gentle rhythmic chirp of crickets.

Wanting to hang onto the moment, Peter fought the urge to fall asleep, pushing himself toward the surface of consciousness. "Jazmin?"

"¿Sí?"

"Don't let me fall out of this damn cot again."

"Okay, *mi amor*," she said, kissing his damp forehead. "I won't let you fall."

CHAPTER 6

Streaks of light rifled horizontally through the walls of the hut, waking Peter. Enchanted by the light, he paused to reflect on the gentle probes that sought out and erased the shadows. In his few short weeks in the jungle, he'd already slowed down and had begun to measure time in natural cycles rather than by his watch. It was something he had to accept. He wasn't going anywhere; not for a while, anyway.

People stirred outside the hut, disrupting his contemplative moment. He eased his head up to peer between the hut's loosely woven bamboo slats and out into the surrounding village. Women and children were preparing the morning meal, yet the camp was quiet, the only sound an occasional murmur. He wondered if the Lacandón were simply a quiet people by nature, or if they had grown cautious, like hunted animals.

Jazmin lay at his side. He smiled, then put his nose in her hair and inhaled the familiar scent. Easing onto his side, he leaned on his good elbow and studied her face. As always, her beauty drew him in. She spent little time on her appearance, and wore no makeup. But her face was darker than he remembered, tanned by the warm Chiapan sun and moistened by the humid tropical air. He stroked her velvety hair, gently separating a lock from the flow of colors that fell across her shoulders, then studied her features: a proud, patrician nose, high cheek bones, and full lips. The gentle arc of her upper lip dipped in the center to meet the full lower lip in a feminine, seductive way.

Always, it was her eyes that melted his heart. He longed to see them again as he focused on her motionless, wide-set eyelids, willing them open. He urged their shining light to pierce his soul again.

Stirring, Jazmin murmured some vague sentiments in Spanish, straightened her legs, and as if on command, opened her eyes. Her mouth turned up into an easy smile and she rose from the waist, pressing her lips firmly into his. Peter began to melt into her, but stopped short. He wanted more of her, but his lips were the only part of him that didn't hurt. As she held him closer, a deep pain arced across his chest and he eased back.

"*Buenos días*," she said. "I've been waiting a long time to say that to you, *querido*."

"Yes," he said, through his labored breathing. "This is a huge improvement to my mornings, too."

She squeezed him impulsively. Peter grimaced. "*Ai!* Careful, I'm still pretty delicate."

"Oh, of course. I am so sorry, *amorcito*. Does it hurt terribly?"

"Only when I inhale. Or exhale. Or move."

Jazmin's mouth turned down and her eyes grew wide with concern. "I am just grateful Spirit gave you back to me. I have missed you beyond understanding. There is so much I want to share with you." She held him for a moment, carefully avoiding his most tender areas. "Other than the pain, how are you feeling?"

"Good, for a cripple suffering from hallucinations."

Jazmin stroked his face and kissed him. "Be gentle with yourself, *mi amor*. You've been through so much."

"Hopefully I won't have any more nighttime surprises."

"Do not worry. You are safe here. The spirits of the jungle protect you."

"That's encouraging," he said, skeptically. "The good news is I'm healing quickly. I'm just a little sore now."

"Just a little sore, huh?"

Peter lay back down, not wanting to test his stitches anymore. Jazmin kissed his lips tenderly and eased herself from the cot, her body lean and firm under the same thin cotton tunic the tribe wore. Only the twine she pulled around her waist guaranteed that her sleek figure was not lost in its folds. She combed her thick, silky hair from her shoulders and gathered it into a ponytail, securing it with another piece of twine. Watching Jazmin was a luxury, and for the moment, Peter ignored the pain of his wounds.

"I must change your bandages." Jazmin pulled away the sheet they had slept under. Working methodically, she unwrapped the cotton strips binding his torso until he lay exposed except for his boxer shorts.

"I'll boil the wrappings and reuse them when they dry."

He glanced down, sucked in his breath, and quickly looked away. "Jesus." Crude against the angry red scars, black stitches covered his body from chest to thighs.

"Do not fear your scars, *mi amor*. They are healing well, and you will be like new soon."

She stroked his face, then began to wash each row of stitches with a cloth, occasionally rinsing it in a bowl of water sitting next to the cot. She moved from one area to the next, carefully dabbing along the suture lines.

"Do they hurt?" she asked with a sympathetic look.

"Not when you touch them," he lied, stroking her thigh. "Chan said he would be removing your stitches soon."

"Good. They itch."

Building up his nerve, he lifted his head again to study the long, tortured lines of black stitching that ran down his body. How had he survived the attack?

"You know, I've endured one lousy plane ride, wrestled an angry cat, and survived a mysterious shaman's lessons to see your beautiful eyes again."

Jazmin turned her crystal gaze on him and smiled broadly. "Yes, you did. You are my hero, coming here after a phone call from a stranger. I could not believe you came alone."

"I didn't think to ask anyone along. Didn't exactly have time to plan this…vacation." Her hand passed over a particularly tender wound on his chest and he caught his breath. "Anyway, you would have done the same for me."

She shook her head and smiled. "I don't know. Wrestling mean jaguars may be asking too much of me."

"A bit much for me as well."

He groaned as she lifted his arm above his head. "Maybe I'll feel stronger in a few days and we can hike out of here. They'll be worried about me at the office. I said I'd only be a few days. Besides, we don't want to stick around if bullets start flying. That pea-shooter of mine won't do us much good."

Jazmin stopped and looked straight at him. "Pea-shooter?"

"My handgun."

"*Ai, Pedro!* Where did you get a gun?"

"San Cristóbal …in a country store. A toothless storekeeper told me I'd need it. I guess he saved my life. Besides," he added, "if we stay much longer, that old shaman will turn me into a mushroom or a dinosaur or something."

"That old shaman saved your life!" she snapped.

Peter recoiled at her sudden rebuff, the first time he sensed her anger. "I know he saved my life. And I'm very grateful for that. But there's something strange about Chan."

"You will like him once you get to know him. He is like a father to me."

Peter sighed. "Jazmin, I just don't think we should get involved in their fight. It's too dangerous and the bad guys have the guns."

"We are already involved." Her face suddenly flushed. "It is not just *their* fight, Peter. It is *our* fight too."

They went silent. Frustration welled up inside of Peter. How much more would she ask of him?

"How did you get so good at this?" Peter asked, referring to her nursing skills.

Her eyes sparkled in the dim light. "Chan has me doing this every day since he sewed you up. We have kept you clean, especially your wounds." She helped him turn over to face her once again. "I enjoy bathing you now that I can look at your cuts, bruises, and those horrible stitches without feeling sick."

"When did that change?" he asked.

She hesitated, and her face became serious. "When I realized you would live." Tears welled up in her eyes. "*Lo siento*. I am sorry I yelled at you."

Peter took a deep breath. "You've been through a lot too." He brought her down to him and held her close, gently kissing her. "We'll talk more about it when I'm rested, okay?"

"Okay." She rubbed her nose against his and kissed him again. "I missed you so much."

"I know. I couldn't think about anything but you."

She caressed his face. "I'm so grateful you came, and at the same time, I'm so sorry."

"Me too." He winked at her.

Jazmin's smile returned. "Peter, when we talked last night about the roadblock, you said the soldiers wore black. Are you sure? The *Federales* wear green uniforms."

"I'm sure." She helped him roll onto his other side. "And they had black berets with black panther insignias. I didn't recognize the uniforms."

"That is strange," she said, looking confused. "Those are Mexican Special Forces uniforms."

"Special Forces?"

"One of our scouts said soldiers had set up roadblocks, but I didn't know they were Special Forces. That was just a few days after I sent an article in to the local paper in San Cristóbal." She brushed a fly from his damp face, and unrolled a clean bandage.

Peter thought about the roadblock again. "Strange they would bring in Special Forces just to man a roadblock."

"They set up the roadblocks after the paper printed my story about Chan's remedies. I told them how he treated everything from deadly snake bites to cancer."

She carefully applied the white gauze around his badly scarred hand. "I was a little . . . how do you say? Early?"

"Premature?"

"*Sí, sí*. Premature, but I encouraged the people to write the government to save the land for further research. I know I was right in doing so."

"They obviously wanted to isolate the Lacandón village. And no doubt wanted to keep you from going back to town."

"I think you are right. I was stirring up trouble. And I doubt they were going to allow anyone to return to the village either."

"No. Probably not. I think they were trying to isolate the tribe."

"K'in avoided the roadblocks, and went through the jungle on foot."

Peter raised his head, clutching at the cot for leverage. "Did you say you've found a cure for cancer?"

"Chan has the cure. I must document his work and prove that it works. Maybe I am premature, but I think he cures every case that comes to him." Jazmin stopped working and looked at him. "Some cases were diagnosed years ago as terminal, but Chan has somehow made them healthy again. Look what he did for you. When the men brought you in, I couldn't find your pulse. You were covered in blood . . ." Her voice caught in her throat and she blinked to hold back her tears. "Oh, Peter, I don't know how he did it, especially without blood transfusions, but I know in my heart he brought you back from the dead."

He felt a jolt of fear run through his veins. Jazmin turned away shaking with sobs, and crossed herself. Like so many of México's natives, she still clung to her Catholic rituals.

"I'm sorry you had to go through that," he said.

Their thoughts softened, and they stayed silent for some time. Then Peter's anxiety returned. Lying helpless on a cot was not something he was used to; furthermore, he was determined not to get used to it. He wanted to move his body, get off the hard cot, and flex his muscles, but movement meant pain. He tried to shift his weight but his left arm was not responding, and the simple act of lifting his head invited undesirable sensations.

"I feel like an invalid," he complained.

"You are an invalid, for now. So get used to it, and stop complaining." She gave him a kiss.

"Hell, I was just getting started." He smiled weakly. "So anyway, Chan treats all kinds of disease?"

"Yes. I have seen him treat poisonous snakebites, malaria, fungal infections, heart problems, diseases introduced by Europeans, tumors—lots of things. Yet, some of the plants he uses are thought to be chemically inert."

"Inert?"

"Yes. These plants had no significant effects in the lab, so researchers thought they had no chemical value. But Chan uses them to treat all kinds of disease. This jungle is a pharmaceutical gold mine. I am just afraid they will destroy it before we can learn its secrets." She looked down. "I shouldn't be preaching to you. You know how it is here."

"I understand. It's easy to get emotional when you're in the middle of a disaster. But if Chan is such a miracle worker, why would anyone want to run him off?"

She shrugged. "Money. Isn't it always about money?"

"Money and power," he agreed. "I read where President Aguilar just signed away another fifty square miles of forest on the west coast for the logging companies to carve up. But the article didn't mention the Lacandón's land. Besides, I thought it was protected by law."

"Yes and no. They have the right to sell the natural resources on their land to the logging companies, and the other Lacandón tribes have already said they would."

"Why? These people seem to be quite capable of living comfortably off this land."

"Chan's people, yes, but the other Lacandón tribes have become dependent on Western society. They were relocated to areas where they can no longer maintain their *milpas.*"

"*¿Milpas?*"

"Their farming plots."

Peter thought back to the man's picture in the newspaper. "So instead of moving onto some God-forsaken reservation, Chan moved his people deeper into the forest. And now he's got some people upset."

"I think so. The logging companies want this land. If the government only understood the value of this jungle, they would never allow anyone to destroy it. Chan has shown me trees that are thousands of years old. The plants he uses in his remedies grow only under the ancient trees. These plants need shade and the nutrients that drop down from those trees. They don't grow anywhere else. If the trees go, the plants and their remedies go with them."

Peter sighed deeply. "So, you start talking about a cure for cancer and

the logging interests get nervous."

Jazmin's eyes looked inward for the right words. "I am afraid we are in a corner."

"Yes." Peter grinned. "You've boxed yourselves into a corner, all right. But why did Chan move the village? You said he had heard some things. Did someone come into the village and threaten you?"

"No. But he did receive messages warning him of danger."

Peter turned over slowly and looked at Jazmin. "Really? What sort of messages?"

She hesitated. "I was afraid you were going to ask. It . . . it is hard to explain. You see, Chan——" she cleared her throat, "*speaks* to the jungle."

"Speaks?"

"Yes. He talks to and listens to plants, animals, and..." Jazmin threw her hands into the air. "Many things."

Peter shook his head. "So, you're telling me the village moved, and I risked my life chasing you into this bug-infested jungle just because Chan talked to a monkey, or a blade of grass?"

Jazmin's face flushed.

"No," she said, drawing out the word in hesitation. "It was a cloud."

"Oh, yes . . . that's just great."

Jazmin's eyes fired with passion. She leaned closer and looked into his eyes. "I don't expect you to understand right now, but things are different here. And it's not just Chan. I have communicated with plants and trees myself. It was always with Chan's help, but I do know it is possible now."

"You've communicated with plants?" He tried to keep the skeptical tone out of his voice.

"Yes!" She looked hurt that he would question her.

"Okay. I'd like to know more about that later. But for now, I'd just like to know who's chasing the tribe."

Again, she paused. "So far, no one."

"No one?"

"No."

"I see," he said.

"Peter, I've seen Chan do miraculous things, and he says it is always with the aid of the spirits here in the forest. I trust him. If the plants and trees can communicate to Chan to help heal the sick, then why could they not have communicated to him that the tribe was in danger?"

"Okay. I wouldn't stake my life on it, but at least I understand where you're coming from." He paused and grinned. "Well, I guess I *am* staking my life on it."

"And doing very well, I wish to say."

"Okay. I'm sorry. But why am I here? You obviously didn't plan on my taking you out of here, so why did you send for me?"

Jazmin took a deep breath as if preparing for a long debate. "Well, I am not sure."

He swallowed hard at the anger that welled up inside him. "You're not *sure?*"

"It was Chan who sent for you."

"Chan! What the hell…" he stuttered. "He doesn't understand my background or training. I'm a paleontologist, not a botanist. And I'm certainly no politician. What part could I possibly play in this ongoing drama?"

Jazmin took his face gently into her hands and searched his eyes.

"You've suffered coming here, Peter, and I don't expect you to understand this right now, but Chan knew you had to help us. I don't know how he knows these things, but I trust him with my life."

"Yes, and mine!"

"*Sí*, and yours too," she said. "I am sorry. I cried for days after they brought you into camp. It was awful. If I had known this would happen to you, I would never have allowed Chan to send for you."

"Okay," he said, regretting his anger once again. "Inform the university about your findings. I'm sure they could work up enough interest to send some more people out to help you observe and gather data."

"It is too early. They want empirical data, and there is not time to gather it. All I have of my field equipment are the few things we were able to carry with us. Besides, this forest is in grave danger *now*. And I don't think they would be interested in my findings, anyway."

"Why on earth not?"

"Because I am not convinced the pharmaceutical companies could bottle and sell Chan's medicine, and that is where the money comes from." She finished bandaging his wounds and sat down on the stump by the cot.

"Oh? Why?"

"After two months of watching Chan do his healing work, I realize that every healing he does involves ritual. He always asks the plant spirits for help during his ceremonies."

"So?"

"Don't you see? It's not just the chemicals in the plants that heal, but the *spirit* of the plant. Chan has to communicate to the plant about what it is he needs, and then he asks permission to use it. As I said, several specimens he uses in his healing work involve plants known to be chemically inert in the lab. But they work here for Chan."

"I see. If the pharmaceutical companies can't easily bottle and sell the cure, they won't be interested in saving the forest?"

"Exactly."

"But they sell all kinds of drugs without ceremony now, without the permission of the gods. And, hell, half of them don't work. I think you're being a little pessimistic."

Jazmin offered a weak smile and squeezed his hand. "See, you are helping already."

"Good," he said softly. "But right now, I need your help. My back is killing me." Peter shifted to one side, groaning. "I need to get up and stretch."

"Are you sure that is a good idea?"

"I'll be fine."

With Jazmin's help, Peter eased himself up. Wincing with the pain, he lifted his feet over the edge of the cot. His legs shook as he placed one foot, then the other down onto the cool, earthen floor. Light-headed, he gripped the side of the cot and inhaled deeply. It felt good to be upright again. The effort encouraged him, but the scars on his chest and abdomen were taut, hindering him from standing fully erect.

He smiled, proud of his achievement, until he looked down at his emaciated body. Suddenly dizzy, he began to black out. Jazmin shrieked as he began to teeter. She tried to hold him up by his shoulders, grunting with the effort. She began to lose the battle when powerful hands grabbed Peter from behind.

"You are taller than I thought," Chan said as he helped Peter back onto his cot. "I thought you were a little, short person."

Jazmin propped Peter up with makeshift pillows of old shirts she had filled with grass. All Peter could do was shut his eyes against a spinning world.

Chan selected leaves from bundles of herbs hanging from the ceiling and placed them in a small gourd. He left the hut and returned holding the gourd filled with a steaming, hot liquid, and handed it to Peter. Chan had allowed a breakfast fire, but it was small, and a young woman kept constant watch to prevent it from smoking.

Peter sniffed the foul-smelling mixture and gave Jazmin a quizzical look. "I'm going to take a wild guess and say this isn't coffee."

"Do not worry, *amor*. You won't miss your coffee after a while."

Chan's face grew serious as he gestured to Peter to drink from the gourd. Peter braced himself and sipped the strange concoction tentatively. He looked from Chan to Jazmin, then took another sip.

"Not bad," he said, cringing.

"Drink," said Chan, pointing his chin toward the brew.

Something about Chan always startled him, and now he realized what. Native people rarely spoke so directly. He often worked with tribal people in remote areas and found them too humble, secretive, or shy to offer advice. Peter played the game long enough to know he usually needed to gather information in layers, asking the same questions several times, talking in circles, playing dumb, and then asking again. Once he had gathered enough responses, he weighed each against the others until they began to acquire a semblance of accuracy and credibility. This was not the case with Chan.

Peter braced himself, and downed the entire cup of the strangest, foulest brew he had ever tasted. He fought to hold it down. Chan's eyes sparkled in amusement. Sometimes something inside Peter's body feared Chan. Now he trembled as if his body carried a memory separate and independent from his mind. These conflicting emotions were fascinating to his scientific mind, but not particularly enjoyable. He felt out of control.

"Your journey begins here," Chan said, taking the cup from Peter's hands. "Your journey will take you many lifetimes ahead. Or maybe you will lie down and die like other people, huh?"

"The only journey I want to take," said Peter, "is back to my home."

"Where is home, my friend?"

Peter pointed north.

Chan gave him a puzzled look. "Perhaps your journey will take you home." He paused for a while, then said, "Spirit's world nourished our ancestors. People spoke to the standing-people, to animals, to mountains, our cloud friends. They heard their voices. This is true knowledge. You have forgotten it. You separate yourself from Spirit."

"No, I don't talk to trees, but I've worked outside in the field for years."

"Do you hear the jungle's messengers? Did you listen for their voices when you entered this sacred land?"

"Well . . ." He looked at Jazmin, then back to Chan. "I avoided the poisonous plants I knew were indigenous to the area, and I stayed alert for signs of danger."

"*Sí, sí.*" Chan nodded. "But you did not hear the voice inside you. The jungle has eyes and ears. It listens and watches. It calls to you, but you have no ears to hear, no eyes to see. The jungle has many messengers." He gestured with a sweep of his hand. "But you have forgotten them."

"What do you mean I've forgotten? I've only been in this jungle a few weeks, and I was unconscious most of the time."

Chan leaned in close to him. "You have been here from the beginning of time."

An uncontrollable shudder surged through Peter's body, and he fought the urge to vomit.

"You knew the spirits," Chan continued. "You must reawaken to this knowledge. Hummingbird energy is here. Spirit moves like the wind."

"Hummingbird energy?" He didn't really give a damn about hummingbird energy right now.

"Hummingbird rules the heart—our fears, our sorrows. It will show you the way. Look at your fears. The jungle is dark and mysterious, but we must not destroy it. Fear the jungle, and you destroy yourself. To kill the jungle is to die."

"Yes," Peter said. "I know the world's ecosystems are in trouble. But it's probably already too late."

"You fear the jungle just as your brothers do. You do not hear the voice of Spirit. It speaks to you now."

"I know a lot about listening to the jungle."

"Then why camp where the jaguar did not want you?" Chan asked.

He looked to Jazmin for help. "I was tired, and it was getting dark. It was the first clearing I'd come to."

"Did a creature not talk to you in this clearing?"

Peter thought Chan's question over, then remembered seeing a bird sitting in a tree nearby as he set up his tent. "There was a black bird making a lot of noise."

Chan's eyes widened.

"It was getting dark, but I think it was a raven—a large black bird with a stout build and a long, heavy beak."

Chan looked thoughtful. "*Sí*, I know this bird."

"It squawked at me while I put up my tent. Are you saying it was talking to me?"

"What did your heart say at that moment?"

"I don't know. I wasn't thinking about the bird. I was worried. I hadn't found Jazmin or your tribe. I was afraid I might get lost. It was getting dark and——"

"Raven is a good messenger," Chan interrupted. "Raven tells you to listen to your heart. You were not sure of your way. You were only a short distance from where our scouts listened and watched. They would have brought you safely to camp."

"How could I have known this raven was a messenger?"

"Raven is a messenger. Something is wrong when raven scolds you."

"You said I can move lifetimes ahead," Peter said. "What did you mean?"

"Spirit speaks very fast now. We must vibrate with it. The Ancient Ones spoke to Spirit, and listened to the stars. They knew this day would come."

"So, what happens next?"

"Great change comes when our vibration is high. Fears run away when we face it. We can face the darkness," he said, "or ignore the Spirit's signs, and let the world tear us apart. It is your choice. It is time for you to make a choice, old friend."

With that, Chan turned and started out of the hut. "You have had enough."

Stopping at the doorway, he looked back at Peter with a mischievous smile. "Raven gave you one more clue something was wrong that day. Do you know what it was?"

Peter looked again to Jazmin for clues, but she stared back blankly. "I have no idea."

Chan stepped out of their small enclosure and into the courtyard. "There are no ravens in the jungle."

CHAPTER 7

As thick as his dreams, the sweet morning air filled Peter's nostrils. It would be a hot day. He opened his eyes, and instinctively turned his head to see Chan sitting at his side in silent meditation. If Jazmin was up and out, Chan was always at his side when he awoke, but somehow it always surprised him.

The first rays of light had yet to stab their way through the dense jungle canopy, but Jazmin was already gone. This too, was a pattern. He remembered her drowsily kissing his cheek when she arose, saying she was working in the *milpas*.

Chan's long, dark hair fell loosely over his shoulders, accented against his white tunic. He sat with eyes closed, motionless, his toes buried in the soft earthen floor. There was something indefinable about Chan's presence. Even with his eyes closed, his entire awareness seemed focused in the moment.

Chan inhaled deeply, opened his eyes, showing no surprise that Peter was watching him. "You are stronger today."

"I'm feeling much better, thanks to you."

They fell silent again, studying one another.

"I've been wondering about that dream," Peter said, "or vision, or whatever you call it."

Chan stared at him.

"You know, the one I had as a dinosaur. It's been nagging me. I was hoping you could tell me more about it."

Still receiving no response, Peter tried again. "Actually, it isn't the first time I've experienced something unusual with respect to dinosaurs. Just before I came here, I had a vision."

Chan raised his brow.

"I was at work. I study dinosaur fossils. That's my job."

Chan cocked his head, apparently baffled by Peter's words.

"Bones! I study bones," Peter explained. "Fossils—they're bone and mineral. The day I left for México, I was studying the skull of a giant predator—a big dinosaur that ate other dinosaurs. I'm in my office looking at it when suddenly, its eyes came to life. It scared the hell out of me."

"The jungle calls you."

This again? thought Peter.

"The past calls you. Today calls you. Tomorrow calls you. Now you are here to meet them."

"Right." Peter nodded, unsure of Chan's meaning. "But can you tell me about the dinosaurs I've been seeing?"

Chan looked at Peter as if measuring his ability to understand. "The world is made of our thoughts. Long ago, we wanted to experience the physical body. We created the dinosaur." Chan laughed and slapped his thigh. "Very exciting! We became big like the tallest trees, fast like the wind. *Sí*, very exciting."

"We created them? Interesting." He could see this conversation lasting all day. And while he knew the vision had seemed real, right now his body needed to get up and walk around.

Chan rose to help as Peter eased himself up and looked under the cot for his boots. "No, no," Chan said. "Feet should touch the earth mother."

Peter hesitated. He had a difficult time just standing barefoot on the uneven ground, much less walking. But Chan was adamant.

Standing required all his effort and he leaned heavily against the old shaman as he rose from the cot. Pain shot through his upper body. He stopped, collected himself, and then took a step. More pain. When a second step produced the same sensation, he went lightheaded.

Neither man gave up. They eased along, stepping outside the hut into the full sunlight. Peter squinted, and fumbled instinctively in his pocket for his sunglasses. Apparently, they hadn't survived the attack.

Lacandón children played along the edge of the encampment and stopped to stare at the two men. The horseshoe-shaped village was without walls, except for the sleeping quarters Peter shared with Jazmin. The open-air design of the village blended seamlessly with the surrounding forest, hiding them from prying eyes. As they made their way through the small compound, Peter was relieved to see it was invisible from above as well as from the ground. They would not be easily detected if someone were hunting for them by plane.

Several elders rocked in their hammocks in the corners of the camp. Women of various ages prepared food while the children turned away to play with a village dog. The women averted their dark brown eyes as the two men passed by. The villagers all wore the same white cotton tunic and casual hairstyle, or lack of it. Their thick, black hair flowed around their faces and fell halfway down their backs. No one spoke as the two men slowly made their way through the village entrance.

They passed into the deeply shaded forest. Although Peter found walking painful and awkward, he felt energized by contact with the soft, cool ground. Even in the high humidity, the fresh air invigorated his under-exercised lungs. He eagerly inhaled the fresh scent of flowering plants as they hobbled toward the sound of water.

"It's great to be outside again," Peter murmured.

The trail ended at a small creek that bubbled through the forest. Silver minnows darted about in the clear water as Peter sat and dipped in his feet. A welcome breeze soothed his face and teased his hair. His senses awakened, and for the first time since the jaguar's attack, he felt invigorated. It felt good to be alive again.

Perched several hundred feet above a vast valley floor, the village nestled into a thickly wooded mesa where two climate zones mingled. The higher elevations of pine and oak were interspersed with the tropical broadleaf forest of the valley below, two worlds colliding in an abundance of wildlife and vegetation.

Peter looked back over his shoulder toward the village. He was surprised that he could barely see it. Chan kept them well hidden.

Peter lay down and watched the great white clouds float overhead in a deep blue sky. The clouds' quiet spaciousness, and boundless freedom, offered him a renewed sense of joy and hope.

"What is it you meant when you said *we* created the dinosaur experience?" Peter asked, breaking their long silence. "Are you saying that I, Peter Campbell, created the dinosaur?"

Chan opened his eyes. "We created the dinosaur."

"Maybe *you* did, but I just dig them up."

"We created Peter."

"Me? We created me? So, who am I if I'm not Peter?"

"Who are you?" Chan looked at him. "Sí, who *are* you?"

Peter had no idea how to respond.

"As a dinosaur," Chan continued, "you could not find the answer to this question. As a man, you can . . . *¿Muy bien, no?*"

"I guess so." Peter laughed. The quest for enlightenment never seemed like an attainable goal. It was something people talked about, sometimes strove to achieve, but never actualized. "I never really thought about it before," he said. "You're saying we created those incredible dinosaur bodies that roamed the earth for millions of years?"

"You could say this."

"And then along comes a meteorite that destroys all of us."

Chan looked confused. "Meteo . . . "

"Meteorite," Peter repeated. "Big rocks that fall out of the sky. Scientists believe a big one fell out of the sky and hit the earth, destroying all the dinosaurs."

Chan looked as though he thought Peter was out of his mind. "Rocks do not fly."

Peter smiled and shrugged. "Well, some people think they do. Actually, a big meteorite wouldn't look like a rock because it would be on fire. It would look like a fireball falling out of the sky."

Chan shook his head as though wondering how anyone could be so gullible. "Rocks do not burn."

Peter laughed and shook his head, uncertain how to explain.

Chan said, "We destroy the dinosaurs."

"We destroyed them? Why?" Peter asked. "That doesn't make sense."

"Dinosaurs have claws, tough skin." Chan held up his hands as if they were claws and shook his head. "No good." Chan pointed to his body. "These bodies touch, taste, talk, smell the earth. Mind thinks. Hands are very good. They heal, bring pleasure to a woman. Very good, no?"

"Well, I can't argue with that."

"Dinosaurs not good." Chan shook his head with disgust. "Dinosaurs dumb. Dumb bodies, dumb minds. They cannot move to higher vibration. We destroyed dinosaurs."

Peter dipped his hand into the creek, sending silver minnows scurrying for shelter once again, then pointed at his chest. "So this body has a greater ability to attain a higher vibration than dinosaur bodies?"

"Dinosaur bodies are no good," Chan answered, still shaking his head.

"Are you saying the dinosaurs couldn't evolve to a higher vibration so we destroyed the dinosaur bodies and came up with this human form?"

Chan thought for a moment. "You could say this."

"So, the dinosaur gave way to a better design," Peter said. "What's wrong with these bodies then? The dinosaur was around for tens of millions of years . . . humans have roamed the Earth for only a few hundred thousand years, yet it looks like we're already spiraling toward extinction and taking thousands of species with us."

The two men sat still for some time. Squawking overhead, several green and yellow parrots flew into the tall canopy overhead and began feeding on fruit. They scolded one another loudly as they fed, occasionally tearing off leaves and small branches, and sending them to the ground.

"Our bodies are not the problem." Chan looked up at the birds. "It is the mind. We must stop the chatter."

"So, our minds are holding things up?"

Chan's face remained blank.

"You said we created the dinosaur and Peter Campbell. It sounds like you're saying we created this world; the forest, the trees, the wind, the jaguar that nearly killed me, meteorites, everything."

Chan's face lit up with a smile and his eyes sparkled. "Life is a great responsibility, no? Are you ready to move to a higher vibration, old friend?" He studied Peter with wise eyes that seemed to look through him.

Peter started to feel uneasy.

"You need a good soaking." Chan stood and helped Peter into the cold water. "Your color bad. Come. Sit with our water friends. Drink. Let them wash your spirit clean."

Peter looked at his reflection in the water. He looked gaunt and pale. Chan gently pushed him down into the icy mountain stream, causing him to panic, but the shaman was too strong for him to resist. Bathing in frigid water while trying to heal was contrary to everything he had been taught. He would catch a cold, or worse.

But Chan held him submerged up to his neck for several minutes. His skin contracted into goose bumps as he attempted to relax in the gentle currents. Why Chan wanted to bathe him in the frigid water, weak as he was, he didn't know, but soon the nausea disappeared, and his energy level rose.

"You face your death, no?" Chan patted the water as Peter crawled out. "Now you can face your day."

"Damn, that was cold. I did think I might die for a second."

Peter lay on his back next to Chan, and watched the clouds drift slowly by as a toucan croaked in the distance. The peace and warmth of the day seduced him into quiet melancholy.

He wondered about this strange shaman and the plight of his people while countless birds and butterflies darted about in the forest canopy. Peter marveled at the dinosaur in his vision and the jaguar that nearly killed him, both creatures arising from the paradise around him. His life had changed completely in the last few weeks, yet the jungle had changed so little throughout eons.

"*Bueno*," Chan said. "You're stronger. Your color better."

"What does my color look like?"

"Like a rainbow. A beautiful rainbow—spattered with monkey poop." Tickled with himself, Chan laughed and slapped the ground repeatedly.

Despite his best efforts, Peter could not contain himself. He held his sore ribs to endure the pain of laughing. The old man's antics were contagious.

Chan reached to Peter's side and inspected his soaked bandages. Without explanation, he began removing the damp rags, unwinding them until his black stitches and angry red scars lay fully exposed. Peter turned his eyes away.

Chan began cutting the stitches away with his teeth and pulling them out. Peter flinched at the sharp, grabbing sensations. "You resent the jaguar. Do not feel angry at your jaguar brother. We had to find you. You were lost. *Bolom* came to help you."

"Yeah, and to eat me. It would have killed me."

"You were lost. The rain washed away our tracks. You could not follow us. The Spirit of Darkness brought us to you. You owe your life to *bolom*."

"But if the jaguar is such a great friend," Peter said, "then why didn't it take me by the hand and lead me to you? Why did it have to attack me?"

"That is not its nature."

The two men sat quietly for a moment.

"Sometimes Spirit must dig its claws deeply into us to get our attention." Chan chuckled, bit another stitch, then pulled it out with a sharp yank. Peter grimaced. "It was not *bolom* that wished you dead. It was sent to you."

"What do you mean?"

"Someone else does not want you here."

"Who?"

"That, you must find out."

Peter went quiet, studying his scars. Someone wants me dead? Why? He didn't even know anyone in Chiapas. None of it made any sense.

"Do not concern your mind with this now," said Chan. "Look past your scars and see the lesson. Every lesson is a gift from Spirit, no? Learn the lesson well and you need not repeat it. This may be your last chance to move to higher vibration on earth."

Another chill ran through Peter's body, one not caused by cold water. His mind and body were having a difficult time assimilating the new information.

Chan pulled out another stitch and Peter sucked in a sharp breath. "I'm sorry, but today's lesson is going a bit fast for me."

"There is little time. Your body must be strong." Chan looked past Peter as if seeing something just beyond his physical body. "When mind accepts a higher vibration, the body must follow. You need another soaking."

Walking for the first time, then having his stitches pulled out after an ice-cold bath had taken its toll. Peter wanted to go back to his cot, but he groaned, rolled over on all fours and crawled back into the cold creek. He washed specks of blood from holes left by the stitches and again lay shivering in the gentle currents of the creek.

"How's my color now? How long do I need to stay in this

freezing water?"

Chan laughed. "You may as well spend the night."

Peter stretched out and watched the clouds, trying to take his mind off the icy water. Time passed slowly. When a sense of calm washed over him, and he couldn't take anymore, he crawled out of the stream to dry in the warm Chiapan sun once again. He felt revived, and his scars didn't look nearly as bad now. When he was dry, he struggled into a sitting position and cleared his throat to signal Chan that he wanted to speak.

"I've been thinking about something. As I said, scientists think a big rock struck the earth millions of years ago and destroyed the dinosaurs. A meteorite would have to travel millions and millions of miles over light years before reaching the earth. How could we have planned this?"

"Spirit plans everything. Spirit plans our extinction now." Chan studied him for a second.

"Man destroys the forest spirits that feed him. The death of the forest is our death. You and I saw this, many lives ago. Do you not remember?"

"No," said Peter. "I don't remember. What do you mean?"

"You were here before. You saw our future. You said you would come back."

"Are you saying I had an appointment?"

The old shaman stood and looked up at the sky. "We will soon know if we are to leave the human form behind and go the way of the dinosaur."

"Do you mean our fate will soon be determined?"

Chan said nothing.

"That's difficult to imagine."

"Then it will be difficult for you to hear that what you do here will decide the fate of this very forest and yourself, my old friend."

CHAPTER 8

A week had passed since Peter first awakened in the village. This time he awoke at mid-morning, and as usual, Jazmin was gone. Chan was nowhere in sight. He raised himself into a sitting position and noticed the villagers quietly going about their duties.

Peter placed his bare feet on the ground, and after a preparatory deep breath, eased himself up. A wave of exhilaration ran through him. Shorts and a clean T-shirt lay at the foot of the straw cot where Jazmin had placed them. He smiled, wondering if she had anticipated his newfound strength or was simply exercising her usual optimism. Managing to get his shorts and shirt on without much grunting and wincing, he decided to go without his boots as Chan had recommended.

Peter brushed aside the doorway draping, eager for sunshine and a glimpse of Jazmin. Brown faces turned to look as he hobbled from his shelter and into the center of the village. Women stopped their household chores and children ran to their mothers, still uncertain of the strange white man who had been attacked by a jaguar. He offered them a friendly smile, and moved as quickly as he could through the throng of villagers. That wasn't too fast.

Peter paused at the edge of the village, gazing on the jungle's brilliant tapestry. He quickly spotted Jazmin sitting under a tree with Chan, the large umbrella-like leaves shading them from the midday sun. Jazmin stood, waved, then started up the slight incline to meet him.

He drank Jazmin in, fascinated as she strode toward him, glowing like a new moon bursting through the clouds. Jazmin moved with a rhythmic grace regardless of the harsh realities of life around her, always remaining utterly feminine.

"*Buenos días, mi amor*." She smiled, then switched to English. "How are you?"

"*Muy bien, gracias*," he replied, embracing her. "A little chewed-up, but happy to be alive."

"You are recovering quickly. That is so wonderful. It is good to see you up and walking."

"And necessary, from what Chan says. The dip in the creek yesterday has done wonders for me."

"Come. Let us sit with him."

She helped Peter walk toward Chan, who looked as if he were in a trance. They sat quietly, listening to the *wheeta wheeta wheeta* of a warbler soaring over the treetops and down into the valley.

Chan yawned and looked up.

"The logging companies have started hiring locals in San Cristóbal," Jazmin began. "And they are offering high wages to laborers; high by their standards, anyway. K'in spoke with some of the locals when he went into town to call you. I fear they will start logging this forest soon."

"But they can't," Peter said. "They need government permits, tribal approval . . . hell, they need legislative approval."

"They don't need it. The government simply turns its head. They even censor the papers. When I arrived in San Cristóbal, many people did not want to talk to me. They were afraid."

"What are they afraid of?"

"I spoke to a few people who had organized against the logging companies in other areas of México. They said that those who resist often pay with their lives. The logging companies murdered people in Guerrero and here in Chiapas. Their fears are justified. And, of course, these small towns always need the jobs the logging companies offer, which divides the people on these issues."

"So the government just stands by, and lets the logging companies bully the locals and take over the land?"

"I'm afraid so."

Chan glanced in Peter's direction. "The men who would destroy our standing brothers fear the ancient ones."

"The ancient ones?"

"He means the trees," Jazmin said.

"Why would they fear the trees?"

"They fear knowledge," Chan replied. "Our standing brothers are the keepers of our mother's history."

"But why would these people fear the knowledge these trees might have?"

"They are not ready to look at their past. The jungle holds their past, their fears. They destroy the trees to destroy their fear."

Peter stared at the ground, watching an endless line of large black ants march through the undergrowth. He wasn't buying Chan's beliefs about the trees, but the dislodging of indigenous peoples was an old story, one told many times before. There was little help and few resources for these people. He hated the exploitation of indigenous people, and tried to relieve his anxiety by focusing on the silent procession of ants patiently carrying bits of leaves and dead insects to their underground home.

"What hope is there?" Peter finally asked. "You can't fight these people. And you can't hide forever. What chance do you have to change their minds?"

"One of them has come to us. This one has come face to face with the moonless night. He will shine light into the eyes of those who would destroy the ancient ones. He will free them of the darkness."

Confused, Peter glanced at Jazmin.

"Do you mean a prophet has come?" she asked.

66

"No, he is just an ordinary man." Chan looked at Peter. "Yet there are no ordinary men. This one must find his *self*."

"Oh no," Peter said. "I know where you're going with this. We had this conversation yesterday. I'm a paleontologist, not a prophet."

"Do not fear, Sitting Raven."

"I'm sorry, Chan, but I don't understand any of this. I don't know why I'm here, who's threatening your tribe, why I'm having some very strange nightmares, or why you just called me Sitting Raven." He hesitated. "Why *did* you call me Sitting Raven?"

"It is your name," Chan said. "You must remember the Raven. Raven is your messenger. You must remember it always."

Peter ran his fingers through his hair, unsure he'd received an answer. "So why did you say I was one of them?"

"You fear the jungle's darkness just as our brothers who come to destroy it. You must look at your own fears."

"I don't know. Wrestling jaguars was enough excitement for me. Besides, this isn't my fight."

"No?" Chan said. "Is the forest not your mother? Do you not walk on her, breathe her air, drink her water? Are you separate from the forest?"

Peter sighed. "I can't change those people," he said, pointing toward San Cristóbal. "They don't give a damn about the future. They can't see a month ahead, much less a millennium."

"You can do what Spirit has appointed you to do, Sitting Raven."

Appointed! Peter began to feel an all-too-familiar uneasiness. He filled his lungs with air, trying to relax and avoid another agonizing experience.

"Look at your fear," Chan said. "Fear will run away if you do not run away first."

Disturbing emotions scrambled through Peter, but rather than ignore them, he observed them as Chan had suggested. His body shuddered as he concentrated on each emotion—anger, helplessness, fear. He reached down and placed both hands on the earth in an attempt to stabilize himself. Jazmin wrapped her arms tightly around him. Nauseated, he covered his stomach with his arms, then lay on the ground breathing deeply, still focused on his fear. Suddenly, without apparent reason, the trembling stopped.

"*Bueno*," Chan said.

Impressed by the effectiveness of his actions, Peter wondered if he had done it all on his own or if Chan had somehow intervened. For the moment he was glad the ordeal was over. He stayed face down on the earth. After a moment, he rolled over and looked up at Chan.

"What's happening to me? Where did that come from?"

"Many lives ago," Chan said.

Jazmin helped Peter back into a sitting position, and reclaimed her place next to him. "Are you okay?"

"I'll be fine, as long as we can keep this conversation from getting personal. Weren't we talking about the trees?"

"Standing-people show us the past," Chan said. "They have long memories. Our ancestors walked among them, heard their messages. They tell many stories about those who came before. Man is not ready for the Ancient Ones."

"How can you say that?" Peter asked. "Jazmin's embraced your teachings."

Chan smiled. "*Sí*, my daughter is special. If man's vibration were as hers, he would not destroy the jungle. When man's vibration is high, the standing-people will tell many stories about the earth and stars."

Peter hesitated before speaking about what was obviously a sensitive subject. But all this talk about trees and clouds was wearing on him. "How can trees speak? They have no brain of any kind. Ants have more brain matter than trees."

Jazmin sighed. "I have heard their voices."

He wanted to believe her, wanted her to share her experiences with him. But it all seemed so absurd.

"All things have heart and wisdom," Chan said. "They are part of you. Thought cuts the jungle into pieces, separates us. Wisdom makes us whole. Do not *think* the jungle away, old friend. The jungle has the same heart as you and I."

"That's preposterous!" Peter said, louder than he should have. "Trees simply can't have the same complex emotions or intelligence we have!"

"Who are you?" Chan asked.

Peter felt himself slipping into another one of Chan's traps and chose to remain silent. He was tired of the question and even more tired of not having an answer for it.

"Do you know your *self*, old friend?" Chan continued. "Do you know the mind that plays with the clouds and dances with the wind? Do you hear the voice inside that guides us through life? Or is all that brain matter getting in the way?" Chan laughed at his comment and slapped the ground, breaking the heavy mood.

Unable to hide her amusement, Jazmin laughed too, playfully patting Peter on the leg. "I know it is difficult to understand these things, Peter, but please try. Chan is saying our thoughts separate us from the world. I think so as well, but there is an inner knowing inside of us that connects us to all things."

Suddenly all eyes looked skyward. The beating of wings filled the air above them. Thousands of red-winged blackbirds darkened the sky like a cloud, their wing feathers accented by a splash of brilliant red and yellow glistening in the sunlight. The gentle whir and flutter caressed their ears when the flock passed overhead, but as quickly as the flock appeared, it was gone.

The air quieted again, but the mood had shifted inexplicably. The jungle had intervened to whisper its ancient song.

Jazmin sighed and gazed in the direction of the birds. "There is so much life here it's impossible to take it all in."

Peter said, "So there's consciousness within the tree."

"Everything is awareness," Chan said. "All things simply expressions of that awareness."

"All living things?"

Chan picked up a stone and turned it in his hand. "Like our rock brothers."

"Surely you're not suggesting a rock has awareness?"

"Chan says everything is alive," said Jazmin. "It makes sense if you think about it. If everything is a product of a living awareness, then as long as awareness holds an object like this rock together, it could be considered alive."

Chan studied the stone carefully. "Rock brothers very smart."

Peter covered his face with his hands. "Rocks," he said, shaking his head. "Just as I was warming up to the idea of trees having intelligence you throw in this rock thing."

"Okay," Jazmin said. "Let's talk about trees, then. Chan says the ancient trees have wisdom that goes back thousands of years and that older trees pass on their knowledge to younger trees. I think these teachings can be traced back hundreds of thousands of years, maybe millions. But the logging industry takes the older trees along with the younger ones, leaving only a few saplings. It's a recipe for disaster. Cutting down all the older trees is like going into a tribal community and taking away all the elders...like Chan."

"The analogy is appropriate, but—

"Peter, once this knowledge is gone there is no getting it back. The shock and loss to the forest, and the tribe, is incalculable. If the older trees disappear from the face of the earth, their knowledge and vibration will not be passed on to the younger generations, or to people like Chan."

"How does their vibration play into the scheme of things?

"No one really knows. But I do know one thing: much of Earth's history and wisdom will vanish before we even realize what it is we have lost."

Peter's scientific sensibilities awakened. "The planet is already in the middle of its sixth mass extinction. Half of Earth's living organisms that were alive ten thousand years ago are gone now."

"So, if I am not mistaken," Jazmin said, "losing the trees means disaster for *all* the communities of the world, including man's."

The mood turned somber while they quietly enjoyed the last cool breezes of the late morning.

Finally, Chan stirred. "Our standing brothers are here with us now as we speak." His voice was reverent. "Their roots go far into the womb of our mother. They feel her vibration. Their branches reach far into the heavens and listen to the songs of the mountains and stars. To lose the Ancient Ones is to separate us from the womb of the earth and the stars in the sky. We will leave our mother without her eyes and ears, without a voice to whisper her secrets into the wind. We will be lost to the heavens."

Chan looked up in the direction the birds had gone. "Who will hear our cries then?"

CHAPTER 9

Morning brought with it a high overcast sky stretching out across the valley as far as the eye could see. Peter relaxed, knowing the village would be safe from any prying eyes. He cleaned his gun to pass the time, watched closely by several children.

Suddenly, a brilliant red and black butterfly fluttered through the canopy. Close yet tantalizingly out of reach, this rare jewel danced through the trees, then into the village, enticing the children to chase it. Excited laughter mingled with the rich cacophony of songbirds and parrots chirping and cawing. Everywhere the sounds of life echoed and danced through the forest, soaring over the treetops and into the expansive valley below.

Peter slid the clip back into the butt of the handle, careful to keep his fingers off the oiled parts. The extreme humidity of the rain forest made it necessary to maintain everything regularly before rust, mold, and mildew formed on the metal, leather, or canvas elements of their equipment.

The butterfly was gone when he looked up again, but the ever-present Lacandón children had reclaimed their places nearby to follow his every move. He returned the gun to its holster, stuffed it into one of the side pockets of his backpack, zipped it, and hung the pack safely out of the reach of curious hands.

Each day in the village blended into the next in an unending cycle of food production, meals, and rest. The things that marked the passing of time for the Lacandón were not birthdays or holidays or the ticking of clocks, but the summer monsoons, the cycles of the moon, and the growing seasons. Perhaps the best way to live, he thought, since it kept the contentious world at bay.

Still, in truth, the lifestyle held little interest for him. Time had slowed to a barely perceptible crawl and sometimes seemed not to exist at all. He was used to a little more excitement and mental stimulation. But studying their primitive ways appealed to his anthropological mind, and kept him occupied.

Peter also focused on the necessity of regaining his strength. He began to work out, often pushing himself beyond his self-imposed limitations. But when his energy gave out and he had to rest, the days offered him little beyond the ubiquitous moment. He didn't like the stillness. He couldn't be sure what weird thing would pop into his head next, and he wasn't confident he'd enjoy it when it did. He guarded against those stray thoughts, searching for solid things to occupy his mind. Jazmin offered insights on the multitude of plants when she was in camp, but for the most part, he lay in a hammock and watched the villagers.

Life was pragmatic for the Lacandón. Everyone had their duties and carried them out with little confusion or discourse. They planted and harvested their crops, hauled water from the nearby creek, cooked, scouted, and tended to the children with little discussion and few complaints.

Peter felt anxious and impatient one minute, languid and watchful the next. Part of him simply wanted his wounds to heal so he could leave. Another part of him wanted to explore the land with Jazmin, and help her in her research. But none of him wanted to get caught up in the tribes' conflict, or face the dark depths of jungle mysteries that Chan had led him to. Having found Jazmin, he had accomplished his objective. As far as he was concerned, his obligation was fulfilled. There was just one problem with that; Jazmin wasn't going anywhere, not without the tribe.

Then there was Chan and his jungle logic. He said the tribe needed him, that the jungle needed him. But why? For what purpose? How could he possibly be of help? He had no political connections, no army, no scientific data, and no ideas. All he could do was lay back and heal.

The village was simple, no more than a camp—thatched roofs of green palm leaves sheltered the villagers from the hot summer sun and from the drenching rains to come. The addition of walls to the area he and Jazmin occupied was an exception, and he was glad for the privacy. The temporary village blended completely into the forest due to its lack of walls, which served to keep it well ventilated. Consequently, it was more comfortable outside the confines of their room than within.

The crowded, makeshift village provided shelter for sixty-six people, but despite its density and the uncertainty of their future, the atmosphere was relaxed and tranquil. By midday, most of the men, women, and children lay in their hammocks, swaying lazily to the heat and beat of the jungle, waiting. They waited for cooler nights and for their *milpas* to produce their bountiful yields, and they waited for the monsoon, which would soon start its torrential downpour. But most of all, they waited for the alarm they were sure would come to send them fleeing deeper into their sacred land.

Though skeptical of his role in the Lacandón dilemma, Peter took some comfort in knowing the village was ready to move quickly if necessary. Food waited in straw baskets and colorful hammocks, while crude wooden frames for hauling heavy loads sat in sheltered corners. Chan posted lookouts daily several miles in every direction, sending them out at the break of day to watch for anyone approaching the village. They didn't return until after dark. So far, no one had been seen, and it seemed unlikely the tribe would be taken by surprise. But an uneasy emotion stirred deep within him, an emotion he could not shake. For some reason he didn't feel safe, and he was beginning to trust his instincts.

From behind, all the men and women of the village looked

indistinguishable from one another, their jet-black hair draping in shaggy disarray over their shoulders onto loose white tunics made from bark cloth. Those who tied their hair into a neat ponytail were the only variation. Body ornaments consisted of simple beaded necklaces and earrings they made from the shells, rocks, and feathers of the forest.

The women were small, standing no more than five feet in height. But their darkly tanned bodies were proportional and strong, suggesting an enduring people who made their living by dogged sweat and by the strength of their backs. Most spent the greater part of the day outside the village foraging for food and planting new crops, while others stayed in the village where small children played at their feet and babies suckled their swollen breasts. The women prepared food as their ancestors had for centuries, pounding out maize for tortillas on a *metate*, shaping dough on a banana leaf, and lighting cooking fires using sticks and friction.

A woman in her early teens washed and prepared a basket of yams and fruit freshly harvested in the forest that morning. She occasionally glanced at Peter, then quickly looked away. None of the women would look at him directly, and the old men who lay in their hammocks ignored him entirely. Perhaps they were simply a shy people with cultural differences he had yet to understand, but something felt wrong. Not wanting to push the issue, he avoided eye contact and stayed out of the way.

The children's curiosity, on the other hand, had quickly overcome any lingering apprehension, and several stood nearby watching him intently. A bold child finally overcame his shyness and began asking questions Peter did not understand. Soon all the children were talking. More children approached, and after some quick dialogue and gestures, Peter pointed to several objects, saying the English name for each in hopes of hearing the Yucatec Maya word for the object in return.

One of the children pointed to a large bowl of corn gruel and volunteered the word *atole*. Peter repeated the word, then picked up a stick from out of the fire and pointed to the flame. All the children uttered the word *ka'ak*.

The adult women nearby continued to glance and look away, but the children were having fun with their new game and soon a small number of Maya terms, with the characteristic popping sounds, became part of his vocabulary.

The morning was nearly gone when Jazmin entered camp carrying plant specimens wrapped in banana leaves in one hand, and leading a child with the other. Peter cast an admiring look at her. Today she wore her own clothes—khaki shorts, yellow T-shirt, and a red bandanna with matching socks peeking from her hiking boots.

As she approached, he wondered when he would be able to fully appreciate her beauty again. As attractive as she was, he hadn't felt sexual since the attack. He still had a long way to go before he fully recovered, but that wasn't the only reason. His emotions had changed. There was something dark and oppressive holding him captive, something he couldn't put his finger on.

Several village women smiled as Jazmin entered the compound, and she greeted them in Maya as she moved toward him.

"It's so nice to see you up and busy," she said, setting her specimens down to kneel and wrap her arms around him.

"Well, I'm feeling up to it, and there's too much to do to just sit around all day. Besides, I'm getting bedsores lying on that hard cot." Peter studied her attire for a moment. "You make a remarkably good-looking target with that yellow shirt and red bandanna."

"Oh, you are right. I guess I do not think like a guerrilla yet." She sat next to him on the large log that faced the fire and removed her bandanna. "It looks like you have made some friends," she said, indicating the children.

"Look who's talking. I haven't seen you coming or going without a horde of kids surrounding you."

She smiled. "No, I cannot go anywhere without two or three tagging along. But I enjoy them." She laughed and stroked one of the children affectionately on the head. "They are the sweetest children in the entire world. Besides, they teach me so much about the plants and trees."

Peter smiled as she hugged another child. "I think you're just in time for lunch," he said. "If my observations are correct, we're having corn tortillas with squash, vegetable soup, and *atole*."

"*Atole*? You are picking up some indigenous words, no?"

"A few. The children are teaching me."

"I told you they were good teachers."

"Say, I've been wondering. Where are all the domestic animals? You know, the pigs, the chickens, the goats? I haven't seen anything here but one mangy dog."

"The tribe is mostly vegetarian," she said.

"I've never heard of any vegetarian Native American tribes. And I was looking forward to some good ole monkey meat, or pig's eye stew."

Jazmin laughed. "You're teasing me . . . But seriously, some villagers eat fish if they are out scouting, but they don't need to. Documenting the tribe's success with their vegetarian diet is part of my research project. The average Lacandón farmer cultivates over fifty species of plants a year."

"Hmm. Not bad."

"Yes, and with Chan's help, this tribe produces over one hundred different crops. No other people have ever cultivated such a great variety before."

"That's remarkable."

"They know precisely when and where to plant their crops. And they farm without disturbing the natural balance of the land."

An older woman announced something that Peter interpreted as "come and get it" and Jazmin walked over to the fire pit to serve up their meals. She greeted one of the women, then returned with a large gourd of soup and a stack of hot tortillas.

Peter watched as the villagers lined up for their food, then wandered off to eat the hot meal in their hammocks or near the fire. He peered into the soup. "Any eyeballs?"

Jazmin slapped him playfully on the thigh and giggled. "The stout older woman kneading the flour is Nuk. She is a very good cook. The pretty young woman helping her is Jaurita. They are very sweet ladies."

After eating his fill, Peter returned to his hammock to rest. Even eating tired him. Jazmin sat next to him, joined by several children.

"The jungle here is beautiful," he said.

"*Sí,*" she said. "Did you know that there is more diversity of life here in just two acres than there is in all of North America? The States alone have almost four million square miles."

Peter shook his head. "I knew the ratio was high, but I really had no idea."

"It is true." She kissed one of the children that clung to her. "The scientific establishment knows this, and there's a frantic effort to study the biology of the rain forests, but it is disappearing too fast. If we lose this tribe, their knowledge will take hundreds of years to regain, and if we lose the forest, we'll never get it back."

They sat in silence, watching the interactions of the people and the children playing. "This is one of the last tribes on Earth to be discovered and exploited, but they seem at ease," Peter said.

"They are happy because they are still in their home."

"But I'm not so sure they're too excited about me being here."

"I think they are just shy of a strange white man. At least the children seem comfortable with you. Give them time. As you have seen, they take everything in stride. They took all this moving business as if it was just another day. The jungle is their home and they are still in control of their lives. They believe in Chan, and they are confident he will keep them safe."

"Chan's as good as anyone to believe in. But if I tracked you into this jungle, *anyone* can."

"I've thought of that too. But Chan says he will be forewarned by Spirit of any danger."

"Well, I don't like it. Besides, Chan didn't seem to foresee my inauspicious arrival here."

"Inauspicious?"

"Not good, unfortunate."

Jazmin patted his hand. "But he knew you were coming."

"Right. Just like he knows they, whoever 'they' might be, are coming. That information won't do us much good if we can't determine when. On the other hand, do you really think someone will come this deep into the forest and attack these people? It seems unlikely. We've been here for weeks now and no one has even been spotted in the vicinity."

"I believe Chan. If he thinks someone is coming after us, then I think so too."

"Then we should plan on getting out of here. The old village is only a couple of days from here at a slow pace, and we could take the jeep out and head away from San Cristóbal. Besides, I'm sure everyone back home is worried sick about us by now, and I've got a ton of work . . ."

"A couple of days?" Jazmin asked in astonishment. "Didn't Chan tell you?"

"Tell me what?"

"We are seven days hike from the old village."

"A week!"

"Yes, for a person in good shape."

"How can that be?"

"After Chan sewed you up, the villagers made a stretcher and carried you for days. We are at least fifty kilometers from their village."

"Fifty? My God, I don't have any memory of being carried in here on a stretcher."

"And we wouldn't get past those roadblocks anyway," she added.

"I'm sorry—I assumed Chan told you. You have to get a lot better before we can travel that far."

"Okay. When I'm stronger we need to find a way to get out of here."

"Peter, I don't think that would be a good idea. Chan doesn't think so either."

"Why? You don't really plan to stay here as long as there's trouble, do you? That could be forever. This is an age-old conflict."

"Chan feels you are here for a reason. He hasn't said very many things, but somehow, he knows your being here is very important. In my heart, I know I must stay. I can't leave these people, or the forest. Please try to understand. This is a very critical time in their lives, and for the forest. They both need us."

Peter took a deep breath, looked around at the women and children in the village, then back to Jazmin's probing eyes.

"How can you be so sure Chan's right about me? All I've managed to accomplish here so far is troubling these people to feed and shelter me, and doctor me back to health. What can I possibly do here?"

Jazmin looked into Peter's eyes and then away. "I don't know."

"Okay, I give up trying to reason with you." He glanced at the children again, who had edged closer and now stood a few feet away. "Sometimes I feel like a display item around here. There's absolutely no privacy."

"The Lacandón are a social people, and in their minds anyone who wants privacy is probably up to no good."

"So, if we took off into the bushes alone for a while, they would suspect some ill deed?"

"What did you have in mind, *mi amor?*" Jazmin teased, rubbing his thigh.

"Well, that's not what I meant. I'm afraid I couldn't . . ."

"Oh, Peter, do not worry about your lust for me. That will come back in time." She hugged him. "I am just happy to have you alive."

The children pointed to the scars peeking out from Peter's unbuttoned shirt. "*Bolom, bolom*," they said.

"They want you to tell them the story of the jaguar. The children love stories. The adults do too, for that matter."

"Maybe that's why I'm here—to learn to be a great storyteller."

Jazmin rolled her eyes and patted one of the children on the back. Peter finished his last bite of tortilla, then stood to act out the scene of the attack for them. Moving to a clear spot on the ground, he knelt and started to put up his make-believe tent. The children watched attentively as he lay down and pretended to sleep. One by one the children crept in closer until a dozen stood nearly on top of him. With unexpected speed, Peter rose up and roared fiercely, grabbing at the hysterical children. They ran away in a panic, screaming wildly. The village filled with laughter.

"I think you missed your calling, *amor*," Jazmin said. "You should have been an actor." She stood and hugged him. "See you later. I have work to do. I'll be in my lab if you need me."

Peter followed her with his eyes as she made her way out of the village to her tent lab.

Just as Jazmin was out of sight, Chan appeared with an armful of some tuberous vegetable Peter did not recognize. Their eyes met. "Your color good," he said.

"Thanks to you I'm feeling much stronger today."

Chan made a gracious gesture and began walking away.

"Excuse me, Chan, but I want to ask you something. Why do your people act so strange around me? They won't look at me or talk to me."

"They are afraid," Chan said. "Afraid of the unknown."

Chan set his burden down and sat on a stump facing Peter. "Jaguar is a mysterious creature. It lives in darkness, kills without being seen. It is powerful, magical. My people look on you and see your scars. You are more than a man. Spirit of Jaguar is in your eyes. A great honor. But power can be used for good or ill. Among our ancestors were those who used the power of jaguar to destroy. How will you use this power, my friend? My people do not know."

Peter hesitated. "I really haven't thought about having any such power. It never occurred to me I was connected to the jaguar. Are you afraid of me too, Chan?"

Chan laughed and slapped his thigh. "I am not afraid of you, old friend. I am not afraid because I know you are only a pussy cat. He shook with laughter and slapped his thigh several times until his eyes teared up.

Peter just shook his head, unwilling to join in Chan's mirth.

"But do not feel bad," Chan continued. "*Bolom* has given you a great gift. Jaguar tested your courage. You did not run from death. You faced death and beat it. You are stronger now, wiser. Be proud of your scars. Wear them well." He placed a hand on Peter's chest. "No longer are you simply a man. You faced the darkness. You have claimed the power of the jaguar."

CHAPTER 10

A shadow darkened the entry of the little shelter as Peter awoke from his midday rest. He pushed himself to his feet and crept to the door to find a handsome Lacandón man in his twenties. The bow and quiver of arrows hanging over his shoulder identified him as a scout.

"*Hola*," said the man. "*Soy K'in.*"

"You're the one who called me at my office," said Peter, taking his hand. "*Me llamaste.*"

They studied one another for several awkward seconds. Peter had mixed emotions about K'in, still annoyed that the young man had hung up on him without answering his questions. And yet, K'in had risked his life going into San Cristóbal to contact him.

"*Muchas gracias*," Peter said.

K'in smiled. "*De nada.* I go now."

He nodded and started to pat K'in on the shoulder as the young man walked away, then pulled his hand back, unsure how the gesture might be taken.

He looked around the village and spotted Chan lying in his hammock. He slipped on some shorts and carefully made his way toward Chan with tender bare feet.

"*Buenas tardes, amigo*," Chan said from his hammock. "Your color is good, but your feet are soft."

He sat down next to the shaman. "Yes, I'm feeling better, but my feet will take a while to toughen up."

They watched the scout stroll out of the village. "K'in is a fine young man . . . doesn't talk much, though." They watched two women weaving baskets nearby, and then he said, "I wanted to ask you about the missionaries you told me about. Where did the priests go?"

"Life is about experience," Chan said. "Priests knew little of experience. They say they know Spirit and can speak for it." Chan waved his hand. "Spirit is unimaginable—it can only be experienced." He held his hand up, bringing his thumb and forefinger together to his face as if trying to see light between them. "Priests had a tiny idea about Spirit. They did not learn to listen to the voices of the jungle. The longer the priests stayed, the more unhappy they became. They were stuck. The moment we think we know Spirit, we separate ourselves from it." He scrutinized Peter. "This is your lesson, too, old friend."

"What do you mean by that?"

"You're stuck. But you have Jazmin."

"What does Jazmin have to do with my lack of openness?"

"You want to be close to her? Be close in experience. Know her world, and you will find your own."

Peter couldn't understand how Jazmin left him to begin with. If he was honest, he knew he resented her leaving and then disappearing with the tribe. "What exactly do you mean when you say Jazmin's world?"

"Her heart is here. My daughter vibrates with the trees. The little bushes sing to her." A parrot squawked just outside the perimeter of the village, and Chan stopped to listen.

Peter tried to concentrate intently on the birdsong as Chan had taught him.

"We must unlearn what we *think* about the jungle before we come to experience it. Allow the jungle to be a mystery, old friend, and the mysterious will reveal itself to you. Listen to the wind. Listen when a bird calls your name." Chan raised his eyebrows conspiratorially. "Spirit wants to share its secrets with you. The jungle is different today. Every day is new in the jungle."

"Yes. But the missionaries must have felt that."

"They refused to eat the jungle food. They planted seeds that came from far away. They brought cow and pig. They do not use the Spirit medicine of the jungle. The priests became heavy, very sick." He shook his head.

Peter was aware indigenous fruits and vegetables strengthened the immune system against local infections and diseases. He understood that the spirit of the food, as Chan put it, was an important dietary consideration. He nodded in agreement.

"They do not hear the voices of the jungle," Chan added, then looked Peter squarely in the face. "You do not hear the voices of the jungle. But you are lucky. Jazmin will teach you."

Peter could only rub his face in irritation. Deep down he knew it was true.

"The missionaries did not ask plant spirits for help," Chan said. "We have to *ask* the plants for help. We must make friends with the spirits of the jungle, or they will not help us. We taught the priests, but they did not listen to Spirit."

"So, they couldn't stay healthy. Is that why they left?"

"They left because we told them to go. They feared the spirits of the jungle. If they stayed here, they would have died, and we did not want their spirits. They would bring bad Spirit medicine to my people. They would leave their sickness and fear. We did not want it." Chan laughed and slapped his thigh. "We have many good stories of the missionaries."

"I've never heard a Lacandón story," Peter said, taking the bait.

A green and yellow butterfly flapped past, hotly pursued by several small children. Chan closed his eyes and rubbed his head, considering. "I remember one such story. One day, I took Father Rodriguez out in the forest to collect special plants for healing work. The other Father was very sick. The plant I looked for let me find it, but before we touched it, I told the Father he must ask permission of the plant before picking, or it will not heal his *compadre*." Chan leaned forward and whispered, "One must always ask permission of the spirits of the plants before picking them."

"You mean they won't heal us if we don't ask permission first?"

"Sometimes they do not give permission. If they say, 'no, do not pick me,' then I go to another plant. If plant spirit says 'okay,' then I thank my little friend for feeding me, and I pick.

"Father Rodriguez said I was crazy to talk to plants. He says God planted food for man. He said he will not bow to any plant."

Chan sat up in his hammock with a stern face completely out of character. Peter, K'in, and those around camp who watched and listened began to laugh as Chan displayed his preposterous grimace.

"The Father would not ask permission before picking our plant friends. He said plants have no intelligence. The Father began to pick. I did not pick the plant because I did not ask permission, and I know this kind of plant is the fire ants' friend." Chan's eyes lit up. "Oh yes, one must be very careful to ask the plant and the fire ant before picking. Soon the Father is covered in stinging ants. I laughed because the Father danced funny with ants in his robe."

Chan jumped around like a madman, slapping at his clothes and yelling while Peter and the villagers laughed.

"The Father was very angry. He couldn't take the plants. I said Hail Marys all the way back to village. Between Hail Marys, I notice my cloud friends high above. They came to play, happy to see me. I greeted them with gentle words, and I waved to them. Father Rodriguez heard me talking to my cloud friends. He says I am insane to talk to my cloud friends. He says they have no emotion, no intelligence, and to never speak to them again. My cloud friends grow dark. I feel badly for them, but I say nothing.

"We walk back to the village. My cloud friends follow. They want to tell the Father something, but he does not listen." Chan shook his head. "The clouds became sad, and I did not want to feel their tears. I stay many paces behind the Father. My cloud friends rain hard on him all the way to the village. Everyone saw the Father was all wet and I was all dry. Everyone in village laughed all night. But I felt sorry for the Father and his sick *compadre*. Surely, they were the most miserable men I ever knew."

CHAPTER 11

As the sun dipped below the distant mountains and stars began to illuminate the village, the mood relaxed. Children chased one another around the circle, and adults conversed in low voices, watching the dancing flames that kept the darkness at bay. Peter looked up at the clear evening sky, wondering why Chan was willing to risk the luxury of a fire. Once everyone was seated, all faces turned to their shaman.

"The gods look over us tonight, and protect us from the eyes of darkness," Chan began, as if reading Peter's mind.

Peter looked at Jazmin, wondering how Chan could be so sure their enemies' eyes were not watching. She simply smiled, obviously confident in Chan's decision.

The fire flickered against the moonless night, highlighting the surrounding trees. Yellow and blue flames danced atop the fire's orange base and smoke drifted lazily to the heavens. Following the smoke as it drifted upward, Peter inhaled the musky perfume of the jungle, gazing with wonder at the countless stars filling the sky with light.

The eldest villagers sat in quiet respect for the ceremony as examples for the younger members. Only the youngest children continued to play as Chan pointed to the Milky Way, cleared his throat, and began to speak.

"The River of Flowers blesses the Lacandón with its beauty and light. The stars are happy to see us together and well. They smile at us, and travel with us on our journey. We listen to their wisdom, and let them show us the way. Spirit moves quickly. We must adapt or be swallowed up. The faster Spirit moves, the more we must slow our minds. The Ancient Ones knew of this time of great movement. They spoke with the stars, and watched their journeys. They said the earth would vibrate like the hummingbird, and knew that if our vibration became different from our mother, life would become unbearable."

More logs were added to the fire, casting light upon the faces of the men and women around it. "Many are now coming into the world who can speak to Spirit. People will need their guidance."

Peter felt his stomach stir uneasily. He had heard this talk before.

"You, Sitting Raven, must be ready sooner—much sooner."

A tremor ran through Peter. Jazmin held him around his waist to steady him. How had he come so easily under Chan's spell?

"He wants you to say something," Jazmin said.

Peter's mind spun with questions. "Why were the Maya so interested in the stars?"

"Stars teach," Chan replied. "The Ancient Ones listened to the stars because they came from the stars. The priests became powerful, built great temples. But later, some ruled by fear."

Peter began to feel dizzy and nauseated. Chan came around the fire, removed Peter's shirt, dipped a gourd in a large wooden bucket of water nearby, and poured it over Peter's head. He flinched under the cold water, but felt an immediate relief from his nausea.

"The trees and clouds laugh and play with my gentle daughter," Chan said, returning to his place across the fire. "She came to this sacred land to dance with Spirit, and to learn their songs. Her time here is restful. But you, old friend . . ." He looked at Peter. "You came to do war. You are here to confront old enemies. The mountains and rivers and trees called you here to sit with us, and remember their secrets.

We waited many years for your return, Sitting Raven."

Peter's stomach tightened another notch. "How do you know these things, Chan?"

"I remember."

Peter breathed in deeply, and wiped the water from his brow with the short sleeve of his shirt. "You remember me from another life?"

"Your enemies remember you as well. For you and me, it was a time of great wonder, but also of darkness. The priests sacrificed the blood of the people to the gods. They sought the favor of gods to protect the city. Later they do these things to control the people. The spirit of the jaguar held the people in darkness."

Chan's dark eyes sparkled at him from across the fire. "Yes, I remember," he continued. "You remember too. Your body remembers *Na-Bolom*."

His stomach knotted and he winced in pain. Flashing images began to strike his consciousness like lightning bolts. Fleeting at first, the images raced through his mind, vanishing only to appear again.

Peter saw himself on the top of a stepped pyramid. Burning torches illuminated painted faces and feathered headdresses. Hundreds of spectators gathered at the pyramid's base as the sun gleamed golden on the distant horizon, gilding the tall structure's western face. The beautiful sight frightened and sickened him.

A man wearing an ornate crown of coral and rare gems glowered over him. Somehow, Peter knew he was the high priest. The man's face was severe—the prominent hooked nose, wide mouth, and thin lips possessed the deepened lines of an older man, but his years had not softened him. Familiar and repulsive, his face and jet-black eyes told a tale of hatred and evil deeds.

Several men held him down on a smooth rock surface, facing skyward. He struggled under the high priest's surly glare, and something that glinted from the priest's powerful hand in the setting sun's last rays.

The priest raised his fist at the precise moment the sun began sinking below the horizon and the golden serpent began climbing the pyramid steps. The second the sun disappeared, and the shadow slithered up the landing, the priest's hand flashed through the air.

A terrifying thud burst inside Peter's head. He flailed his arms wildly, then there was only blackness. Once again, he found himself back in front of the fire, drenched in sweat and wrapped in Jazmin's arms.

He gulped air in deep breaths, struggling to calm his heart.

"Are you all right?" Jazmin whispered in his ear.

"I think so."

"Where were you?"

Peter panted, his chest heaving. "On a pyramid—a Maya pyramid. A man stood over me. A high priest. I recognized him. Something happened up there that jolted me back. I heard a loud sound and blacked out." He turned to Chan. "What happened on that pyramid?"

"Do not bother yourself with these things, Sitting Raven. Concern yourself with the man. He haunts you still."

"Who is he?"

"You must find this out for yourself."

Peter turned to Jazmin, then looked to Chan again. "What did those people do to me?" he asked, still trembling violently.

Chan hesitated. "What you heard was the sound of your heart being ripped from your body."

Peter spewed the contents of his stomach before everything went black.

CHAPTER 12

The next morning, Peter climbed out of bed and stood on surprisingly steady legs. A good thing, since Chan insisted he use his newfound strength to accompany him and Jazmin to collect samples of plants found only in an area sacred to the Lacandón. The overnight outing sounded strenuous, but he looked forward to the exercise, and to his first opportunity to explore the vast Lacandón jungle. He needed to focus on something other than his slow convalescence, and the frightening images of his visions.

Jazmin filled the backpacks with boiled water, fruit, yams, tortillas, and a few unidentified vegetables—basically, the same meal they'd had for dinner. Peter didn't mind. His appetite was strong, he didn't have a picky palate, and could eat almost anything. That was good, because the Lacandón made little distinction between foods served for breakfast, lunch, or dinner.

Peter slung the pack over his shoulder, grabbed his *machete* and Beretta, and headed toward Jazmin's tent lab. The green twelve-by-twelve canvas tent stood just beyond the village, nestled under the shade of a large tree. He stuck his head in. Plant samples wrapped neatly in newspaper and stacked in a corner filled the tent with a complex, pungent aroma. Makeshift tables supported a single microscope and a plethora of lab equipment on one side of the tent. Most of Jazmin's work to this point had consisted of collecting data, and recording Chan's work with plants.

Jazmin turned and smiled, offering a kiss as he entered. "You look so strong this morning. You are gaining weight, no?"

"I'm beginning to feel like my old self again. It will be good to get out."

"*Sí, sí.* I'm excited. I feel so honored that Chan is taking us to his most sacred forest. We will meet the truly ancient trees. But right now," she said, ushering him out of the tent, "I want to show you the *milpas.*"

She collected her pack of supplies from the tent's entrance, and they started toward where Chan awaited them outside the village. Women and older men worked along the narrow trail. The younger men were out scouting. Chan seemed to be speaking with several men and women as the villagers came into view, but as they approached, Peter realized Chan was talking to the plants. They stopped and watched from a few yards away. He found Chan's gentle words and gestures striking, and this caused him to pause. There was something utterly familiar about the moment.

Jazmin leaned over and whispered in his ear. "He is asking permission to pick some of the fruits and other plant foods. Chan says *you* once spoke to the plant spirits as well."

Peter looked confused. "Is this part of their *milpas?*"

"*Sí.* All around us."

The *milpas* blended so well with the jungle that Peter couldn't discern where they began and where they ended. "How could there be an orchard here already, with trees bearing fruit, no less? They just relocated to this area."

"Chan started the *milpas* last season. The spirits of the forest told him to clear the area for an orchard, so the tribe came here regularly to work the new garden. When we arrived a few weeks ago, the plants and trees had already started to bear fruit, and much of the village was already completed."

"I'll be damned." Peter took his cap off and wiped his forehead with the sleeve of his T-shirt.

Chan caught his movement, and beckoned them forward.

"Buenos días," Peter said. Jazmin embraced Chan with a hug and a kiss on the cheek.

Chan appraised Peter. "Your color good today."

"I don't know about my color, but I feel great."

Chan's eyes twinkled and he gestured for them to follow, leaving the others behind.

Jazmin pointed out several plants as they started down a freshly trampled trail through the *milpas*. "These are *jicamas*," she said, pointing to either side of the trail. "And over there are yams and squash, intermingled with onions, lemon grass, chilies, and maize. When the rains begin, they will plant corn, black beans, and many, many other things . . ." She looked up at him with a sober face. "If they are not running for their lives, that is."

Peter peered through the tangle of plants and trees and nodded. "I can hardly tell there's a garden here, it blends in so well with the jungle. I assumed Chan's people were hunting and gathering what they brought into camp."

"About half of it comes from here. The rest is gathered from the forest's natural bounty. They always grow their gardens where the breadfruit and ceiba trees grow." She pointed to one of the trees. "These trees flourish on richer soils, which tells the villagers where to plant. You'll almost always see them interspersed along the gardens' edges."

"Wherever that is."

They continued on, Jazmin pointing out the gardens as they walked. "Cutting and burning the area to be farmed creates a nutrient-rich ash, but with the forest cover gone, there is danger of quick erosion. So, they plant fast-growing root crops like taro and chayote trees to anchor the soil. A few weeks later, they plant their staple crop of maize, along with manioc, avocados, guavas, rice, and mint—things like that."

"Mint," Peter said. "Thank God for mint. It's the only thing that makes that hot brew of Chan's palatable."

Jazmin nodded. "After four or five years, the gardens need to regenerate, so they plant tree crops of hog plum and palm, and many others. They call their orchards *pak che kol*."

"Come," Chan said, picking up the pace. "The ancient ones await us."

They left the *milpas,* and entered an open, grassy meadow where the sun beat down mercilessly. Peter felt himself tiring, glad when they entered the cool shelter of the darkened forest again. Even then, he had to stop every five to ten minutes to rest, but after little more than an hour, their hike ended at the banks of a slow-moving river thickly lined and hidden by an endless variety of trees.

A twelve-foot-long dugout canoe carved from the trunk of a mahogany tree was docked on the bank, covered with brush. A welcome sight—Peter was ready for a rest. As they unveiled the long, slender craft, he admired its simple, graceful lines, and crudely efficient workmanship.

They shoved the heavy craft into the calm waters and climbed in. "These canoes must last a hundred years," he said.

Jazmin nodded. "I am not sure they *ever* wear out."

Chan stood in the rear of the canoe, guiding it without effort through the swollen waterway using a long wooden pole. The craft wound steadily through the vine-entangled jungle, following the slow, nearly imperceptible current. Like a giant serpent searching out its next meal, the river flowed silently, turning one way, then the other, finding the path of least resistance.

Branches and vines dangled over the water, forming a thick canopy that sheltered them from the mid-morning sun. They passed an endless variety of flowers of vibrant colors and pungent fragrances. Trees, herbs, stranglers, orchids, ferns, and climbers all competed for the life-giving water and the sunlight that rarely penetrated the darkened forest floor.

"Isn't it beautiful?" Jazmin whispered as she dipped her hand in the cool water to pick up a pink bougainvillea blossom floating by. She sniffed it, then placed it behind her ear.

Peter sighed with pleasure. The beauty and sweet aroma of the flowering plants soothed him after the hike to the canoe. With Jazmin's lap for a pillow, he watched the forest canopy glide overhead.

At this moment he fully realized Jazmin was right—things were different here; a different time, a different mood, an altogether different world. The jungle had absorbed him, and now held him firmly in its web of teeming life.

Hours passed by before they pulled back onto shore. The water delivered them to a valley surrounded by jagged mountains—from one dream-like scene into another. Chan hid the canoe in the thick undergrowth, and pointed out an obscure animal trail. They proceeded on foot through the virgin forest.

Peter started to pull his long knife from its sheath, but Chan placed a hand on his arm. "Since the beginning, man has not left his mark on this land."

Peter nodded, and sheathed his knife. Though moving through the jungle would be more difficult without it, he would not dishonor Chan's wishes. The air was thick with swarms of insects, but they were rarely bitten, and he wondered if the bugs were kept at bay by the potions Chan gave him throughout his recovery. Whatever it was, the flies, gnats, and mosquitoes stayed away.

Their trek through the forest brought them to a still blue lake with waterfowl and songbirds. Blackbirds called out from a thick stand of cattails that lined the shore. The pristine lake reflected the blue sky and white clouds like a giant mirror; dragonflies cavorted at its surface, snatching an easy meal of insects; a water snake slithered across the lake in search of larger prey. Hundreds of multicolored ducks kept to the middle of the small lake, while a statuesque great blue heron stood near the shore, patiently searching out its next meal. The large bird stalked the nooks and crannies where the gnarled roots of trees writhed in the brackish water, occasionally stabbing the shallow depths with its long, sharp beak.

The trio sat along the bank of the lake to eat and soak up its beauty. Peter leaned against Jazmin, thankful for the rest. Papayas, mangos, and figs were the fare for the afternoon, and they ate with enthusiasm, saving the tortillas and yams for later. After lunch, they hiked into the dense undergrowth beyond the lake.

Skirting along the creek that flowed from the lake, they descended into a shallow canyon and stopped under the mist and thunder of a hundred-foot waterfall at its nadir. An old-growth forest of trees with towering trunks surrounded them, silent sentinels holding up the sky. Thirty feet around their base, the giants rose more than two hundred feet into the air, blocking out the sun. Jazmin had alluded to these ancient standing-people, the very heart of the Lacandón's sacred rain forest. They stared in awe and admiration at the overwhelming size and grandeur of the forest, untouched by man since the beginning of time.

Like the tentacles of a giant squid, the trees' massive roots rose from the earth to a height several feet out of the ground, reaching out in every direction. Peter thrilled at the sight. He raised his eyes skyward and stretched out his arms, yearning to be lifted up into the magnificent branches several stories above.

The creek meandered through the trees, forming small pools of deep green water. Along its banks, butterflies of every color and description mingled to drink in the mineral deposits along the shore. Ahead, a large flock of snowy egrets sat high in the treetops, ruffling their feathers and cocking their heads as the intruders entered their domain. All at once they took to the air, and within a few brief moments, they filled the sky like a windblown cloud.

After they walked a short distance more, Chan knelt beside one of the largest trees and lowered his head in silent tribute. Peter looked for a suitable resting place and leaned against the fallen trunk of one of the giant trees. He watched Jazmin walk a little further along the creek before she stopped. Apparently, she wanted to be alone. It was a time for silence; and like the grandest of cathedrals, the ubiquitous, towering forest seemed to demand it.

Throughout the day, Peter's heart had filled with emotions he could neither comprehend nor ignore. His emotions had overtaken his logic the day he awakened in the jungle, but now they overwhelmed him. Familiar yet ancient memories refined and awakened his senses. He could feel their presence, not just through his senses or by studying them rationally. Tens of millions of years of silent contemplation surrounded him, enveloping his awareness.

"What do you feel, old friend?" Chan asked after a long period of silence. "What does our mother say to you?"

"This forest is stirring up memories in me; memories I've long forgotten."

Chan sat motionless for several minutes, then stood and walked a few paces to sit with his back to another tree. The huge tree dwarfed him, reminding Peter of the giant redwoods in California—another forest world. He was not sure Chan heard his statement, and started to repeat it when old shaman spoke.

"You have not forgotten, Sitting Raven, or you would not be feeling these things now."

"Why am I feeling these emotions here?"

"The last time you were here, this forest was the same as you see it now. Man has not touched it; not with his hands or with his mind. And now your body remembers its ancient vibration."

"If man has never set foot on this land before now, how could I have been here before?"

"When you were here before you were not a man . . . there were no men."

Part of Peter wanted to argue, to demand an explanation, but a deeper part of his being acknowledged the truth of Chan's words.

"There is a message for you here."

"What kind of message?"

"Your body knows. Why don't you ask it?"

Peter tried to relax, clear his mind in anticipation of a great insight. For some time he listened to the leaves and debris that fell from the trees, shaken out by the gentle breeze passing through the upper canopy. The hours passed as they sat in silence. He listened for some deep grandfatherly voice to whisper ancient wisdom into his ear, but he heard only the buzzing of insects and the occasional call of a monkey or a bird, all of the forest's usual sounds. Peter's tension built. Finally, his emotions reached their peak, and he could no longer be still.

"Why don't you just tell me what it is I'm supposed to learn here?" he blurted out in a loud whisper. "You said there isn't a lot of time left, that I need to learn quickly."

Chan opened his eyes wide, surprised by Peter's abruptness. "No, there is not a lot of time left for you."

Again, a chill registered through him. He felt a familiar queasiness in his stomach, and wished Chan would stop speaking so cryptically.

"You do not need ideas, old friend. You need experience. Experience is the teacher. Talk is nothing." Chan's eyes bored through Peter, serene and timeless. "What do you feel? Ask this question. Be still. Let this question float away on the wind."

Resigning himself to the silence once again, Peter shifted his weight, tucked his legs under him, and leaned back against the large fallen tree trunk. He looked around for several minutes before his eyes rested again on Chan, silent and motionless in front of him.

Even in his white tunic, the old shaman looked as though he belonged to the forest, a permanent fixture of the landscape for millennia. Like the roots of a tree, his veins twisted down his legs and seemed to go into the ground, planting him into the soil. Peter felt mesmerized by Chan's meditative concentration.

The forest was imbued with this sense of permanence, like nothing Peter had experienced before. He longed to embrace it completely. He went into this longing and soon felt the forest's timeless peace engulf him in silence, betraying the many sounds around him. This peaceful presence beckoned him, penetrating his innermost being. Unrelenting, it pressed in on him until there was only the silence, a timeless awareness without limit. The jungle pulled him into itself. No longer separate, its silence and its sounds became a part of him, resonating deep within his innermost being. Then, there was only awareness . . . He heard the heartbeat and breath of the forest, then became the heartbeat.

The distinct sensation that time no longer existed crashed into his awareness. In one extraordinary moment, his universe changed. His mind became absolutely still, alert to every detail around him. All conflicts within him vanished, and he found himself in a place without desires, cares, or fears. Within this space, colors, sounds and smells came alive, distinct and vivid, somehow inseparable from him.

Peter's focus no longer had any specific reference point. He began observing his world from an undetermined place rather than from his body. His mind was still yet somehow vigorous in observing every movement: the beat of a dragonfly's wings, the shimmer of a leaf, the sweet smell of the creek. No sight, sound, or smell went unnoticed, but he was not only the observer. He was the observed too, by the wind flirting with leaves high in the canopy and the sun filtering through their veins. He was the water tumbling over the rocks and the sweet scent of the flowers wafting over the land. The moment lingered eternal.

An unaccountable amount of time passed before Peter heard a strident voice that brought him out of his symbiotic state. Hollowed and convoluted, the voice echoed in slow motion as though coming through a long pipe. It pulled him back into the world of conventional time and space, into the strict confines of his personal consciousness.

Chan spoke again, and the words came across clearly. "What do you feel, Sitting Raven?"

Suddenly aware of his body again, Peter gasped for air. He tried to stand, and reached out for something to steady him, then stumbled back to the ground. Frightened and disoriented, he glanced around, his mind racing in panic. Afraid, he cried out, "Who am I?" He grasped the earth as he looked up at Chan.

Chan studied him. "*Sí*. Who are you?"

"Your voice . . . it pulled me out of another dimension or . . . I don't think I could have come back into my body if you hadn't called me back." Peter groveled on the ground, trembling, trying to pull himself together. "I'm sorry. I don't know what's happening to me." Tears of exhilaration and fear ran down his cheeks.

"Do not be sorry, old friend." Chan walked to Peter and sat down beside him. "This is your lesson for the day. You remembered something important. Your body must adjust to a new vibration. Your tears will lead you to joy and laughter. Do not hold them back. Let them water this sacred ground. This is the greatest gift you could give our standing brothers. They will not forget you."

Peter's voice wavered. "I . . . I didn't want to come back."

"*Sí*, old friend." Chan stroked Peter's back. "Someday you won't."

CHAPTER 13

Peter experienced the deepest sleep of his life under the giant trees, and awoke the next morning refreshed. His dreams of the forest were strange, but restful. The trees had talked to him, encouraged him in some way, but he couldn't remember specifics.

He crawled out of the tent to stretch. It didn't make sense to feel so strong and rested after the exhausting hike—not in his condition. Had the forest healed him? He smiled inwardly, breathing in the trees' scent. Even his badly mangled arm felt strong. He didn't fully understand, but what did it matter? It felt good to be alive.

Today he and Chan would attempt to "strengthen Peter's body and spirit," as Chan put it, while Jazmin stayed behind to catalog and study the plant samples she'd collected. Peter had resisted the idea of leaving Jazmin alone for the day, having made the decision never to let her out of his sight in the forest. But Chan insisted the forest would take good care of her, and left no room for Peter to question his decision.

Peter noticed Chan sitting under the trees in the distance, and wondered where he had spent the night since he hadn't brought bedding. Crawling back into the tent, Peter sat quietly and studied Jazmin's face. She was more beautiful than ever. He nudged her cheek with his nose, then caressed her neck until she opened her eyes. She took him in her arms, pulling him next to her.

"Chan wants to take you into the mountains," Jazmin said.

"Yes. What about you? Do you still want to stay here?"

"*Sí*. I will stay here to collect plant samples and listen to the trees. They are so beautiful. I feel so rested."

"Me too. But do you think it's a good idea to stay here alone?"

"I will not be alone. The trees will keep me company. Do not worry, *mi amor,* I will be safe here with them."

"How long will Chan and I be gone?"

"I told him I would have dinner ready, and he nodded."

Peter prepared his pack and sought out Chan. Spears of light darted through the forest canopy as they hiked out of camp into the dense undergrowth. A faint light cast a warm greenish glow through the leaves, like stained glass, lighting their way. The chirping, screeching calls of birds and monkeys mingled with the gentle rustle of shrubs and the fleeting sounds of unseen animals as they breathed in the warm, musty air. A deer jumped into a thicket, and a giant anaconda slithered off into the underbrush. Everywhere, the jungle rustled with wildlife.

Chan moved quickly as if oblivious to the cacophony. Even with his renewed strength, Peter still struggled to keep up. But just a few weeks had passed since he'd awakened from his coma in the village.

Chan had insisted Peter exercise his body by hiking, saying he wanted to get away from the "noisy village." Peter had laughed at the irony; the quiet serenity of their makeshift village had nearly driven him crazy. It was anything but a strident environment, yet he had come to accept that more voices reached Chan's ears then reached his own.

Making their way through the thick brush, they crossed several pristine creeks. Sweat poured off Peter's body as they continued through the dense jungle, making it necessary to stop frequently to replenish his body fluids. European adaptation to colder climates was not serving him well, as his perspiration-soaked T-shirt attested. But sweating was not an issue for Chan, who looked fresh and drank little water as they moved across the vast terrain.

Passing through heavy foliage, Chan placed one foot directly ahead of the other, producing a narrow path. Barefoot, and without a *machete* to cut through the endless hanging vines and thick brush, he disturbed few insects and seemed unaffected by them. Peter had kept his *machete* at the campsite, and made a point of studying Chan's stride. Hiking was more difficult without his large blade to clear the way, but the more he mimicked Chan's smooth, easy movements, the less he noticed insects around him.

Even though he hadn't fully recovered from his wounds, he was a seasoned hiker with an athletic build, and felt he should easily keep pace with a barefoot man more than twice his age. But even as he strove to keep up, Chan stopped often to wait for him.

They crossed a valley of shallow streams, soon to be swollen with monsoon rains, then began to climb the rugged mountains. Large billowy clouds hung low in the sky, and hugged the steeply sloping range. Peter's lungs ached as their ascent became vertical and they worked their way up from the valley floor.

Ribbons of water cascaded off towering rock palisades, plummeting hundreds of feet into a thick green canopy below. Peter and Chan paused from time to time to enjoy white orchids hanging in clusters off rocky ledges and the ever-present giant ferns that bathed in the churning water's mist. The spray wet their faces as they scaled a steep moss- covered escarpment, stopping only long enough for Peter to catch his breath. He felt grateful for the moisture-laden clouds that drifted effortlessly overhead, cooling the mountain range and his body.

By midday, they stood high on the mountainside overlooking a vast unspoiled wilderness of emerald green to the west. Virgin rain forest stretched out for hundreds of square miles under white clouds. The clouds floated low overhead, occasionally brushing the mountain faces. Their movement gave Peter the sensation of the Earth rushing through space, and he often held on to rock outcroppings to steady himself. Chan welcomed the wind, greeting it first with gentle words, then by playfully throwing his arms wide with his deep inhalations. Not to be outdone, Peter joined in the fun, expanding his bruised chest as best he could, and throwing his arms out in an exaggerated manner. Chan looked at him in bewilderment as if he were quite insane, then laughed with unabated joy.

Lying on the smooth rock precipice, they watched the clouds drift by overhead. Although Peter ached and his wounds burned from the strenuous climb, it had felt good to exercise. Now, it felt equally good to rest. After a short catnap, he sat up, intrigued by the wilderness that stretched out as far as the eye could see.

"What lies in that direction, Chan?"

Chan looked thoughtfully at the scene. "You do not recognize your home."

Peter only smiled, knowing he could not possibly remember such a thing.

"It is the Forbidden Jungle."

"Forbidden to whom?"

"To all who enter."

Chan seemed reluctant to speak more of it. They grew quiet while Peter pondered Chan's cryptic words. He had heard of the area before. Jazmin had spoken of superstitions held by the natives living on its borders.

Jazmin had told him the story of a Mexican army that had disappeared while attempting to cross a vast area of some twelve hundred square miles during the Mexican Revolution of 1910. As the story went, General Felix Diaz led his army of revolutionaries into those remote mountains to flee the Federal troops. He had intended to cross the mountains, and intersect the railroad running between the towns of San Jerónimo and Guatemala City to make his escape. But the general never reached Guatemala, or the railroad, and his entire army of three thousand troops vanished without a trace.

"Do you see the spirit of the tree?" Chan pointed. "It likes you, and has come out to look at you."

Peter studied the tree for several minutes, wanting to give the exercise a good try, but he saw nothing unusual, and shook his head.

"When you see the edge of light around objects, you will know you are on the path of knowledge. People, animals, trees; all things have this light. The light is a teacher. It says we see the world with a clear mind." Chan paused to sniff the air, then continued. "The trees are your allies. They will protect you. Someday you will hear their voices."

"You actually hear their voices?"

Chan waved his hand casually. "*Sí, sí.*"

"How often?"

"All the time. I think they like to talk more than me. Sometimes they talk so much, I cannot hear anything else."

Chan stood and cupped his hands on either side of his mouth and yelled into the forest. "Would everyone be quiet so my friend, Sitting Raven, and I can talk?"

Chan buckled over with laughter, in obvious glee over his antics. "Oh my, I am very funny, no?"

Peter grinned. "*Sí, Señor.* You are a very funny man."

Chan put his hand to his ear as if listening. Holding this position, he turned and whispered conspiratorially into Peter's ear. "Our forest friends say they will try to be quiet for us."

Chan closed his eyes and leaned back against the rock ledge behind them. Peter could only guess at Chan's level of seriousness. Would the forest really be quiet? Then in apparent recognition of his doubts, Chan opened one eye. "*Sí,* the jungle will help you if you ask."

"How do you know these things, Chan? No one else seems to know them."

"We cannot know the trees, or the wind. We can only feel their power and truth. You must allow them to show you."

Chan smiled and shut his eyes. Peter watched the clouds continue their journey overhead. Gently and gracefully, they lulled him into their fluid world until his attention was totally fixed on their motion. Then the massive clouds collided with the mountains one at a time. They appeared solid and tangible like castles in the sky, but as they reached the towering mountain range, they broke up, clashing with rock and tree, rolling up and over the sharp summit like the ocean surf hitting a rocky shore.

Subtly at first, Peter became aware of the gentle, steady motion of the earth as it turned on its axis and floated through space. He drifted into the clouds' dreamy, ever-changing world. It seemed they were encouraging him to join them. Practicing his deep breathing, he inhaled their delicate scent, absorbing their energy and life. Then, unexpectedly, his ears popped and everything became quiet. Barely noticing the transition, he found himself floating with the clouds.

In a most tangible way, the wind pushed him from behind and then came rushing by, turning, spinning, and rolling him in its wake. He danced with the wind and flirted with the trees, gently caressing and teasing their branches and leaves. He smelled the clouds' inner moisture as he rose and fell through the atmosphere. The wind played with him, tumbling and twirling him one way and then another, fast and slow, rising and falling like a silent roller coaster. He played with grace and abandon in the warm tropical currents, soaring through the air without thought between heaven and Earth. But it wasn't Peter the clouds played with. Peter had become the clouds, become the consciousness of the clouds, become the dance.

All too soon, his ears popped again and he found himself back on the hard rock, stiff and disoriented. Chan lay nearby, perfectly still, eyes closed, the picture of contentment. Peter studied the old shaman's long dark hair falling casually over his white tunic, and thought of the raven that had shone blue-black in the sunlight.

"You danced with our cloud friends?" Chan asked, eyes still closed. Surprised, Peter looked at Chan in wonder, still digesting his experience. Chan sat up, stretched, and turned toward him.

"Very good." Chan's nod of approval was almost imperceptible. "The cloud people like you. *Sí,* very good. You are remembering."

Lightheaded and detached, Peter took out the gourd of water he carried and drank from it. He understood what real freedom meant now, and why Chan resisted the reservations so.

"*Now* you remember," Chan said.

They were quiet while Peter absorbed his experience with the clouds. He wanted to hold the memory, but the emotion of remembering was fleeting, and to attempt to grasp it was to lose it.

He lay back down and closed his eyes. For the first time since floating with the clouds, he became aware of the birds' and monkeys' cries again. Peter realized he had not heard any sound from the jungle since Chan had asked the spirits of the jungle to be silent. But he could not remember whether he had simply blanked it out, or if the creatures had remained silent.

"Chan?" he whispered.

Chan stirred and tilted his head in Peter's direction. Peter pointed toward the jungle. "Did the jungle just start making noises again, or was I just not hearing it earlier?"

Chan stretched, cracked his back, rolled up slowly, and tilted his head toward the clouds. He cast a bewildered glance at Peter. "How would I know?" He pointed skyward with his chin. "I was up there."

Peter took several deep breaths. Somehow, reality in Lacandón country seemed to be ruled by Chan, with the help of the jungle spirits. Suddenly, that became more acceptable to Peter. The cloud spirits had danced with him, and now he wanted more. The child within him had been reborn.

"How can I learn to see this light you say is around the trees?"

Chan lay back down and answered Peter's question with his eyes shut. "Your question is good, Sitting Raven. I wondered when you were going to ask it. To see Spirit is good." He sighed deeply and rubbed his face. "We have two minds. One thinks, the other knows. The mind that knows goes back many lifetimes. This is the mind of the one heart, of all things: the trees, the plants, the clouds, the rivers, the mountains. The more time you spend with this mind, the more you will see Spirit around you. Your color will improve—less monkey poop."

Peter looked to see if Chan would break into laughter, but his mood seemed contemplative and sober.

"How can I tell when I hear my knowing mind?" he asked.

"It is a quiet voice. *Sí*, quiet, but very smart." Still lying down, Chan put his finger to his lips. "One must be quiet to hear it." He cocked his head as though listening, then nodded as if hearing a confirmation. "*Sí*, let this voice guide you through the jungle, my friend."

"A voice or a feeling?"

"Today you *feel*, but later you will *hear* its voice."

"Earlier, you said we need a clear mind to see. What exactly is a clear mind?"

Chan lay quietly for several minutes, pondering it, or listening for the answer. Peter had become accustomed to these pauses.

"No distractions," Chan finally said. "No distractions, no wants, no opinions, no beliefs, no nothing . . ." Opening one eye, Chan leaned toward Peter as if he intended to whisper some deep secret into his ear. "Clear your mind, and the quiet voice can speak a few words to you. Then you are free of fear. Today our cloud friends came to help you. When we see self in everything in the jungle, what is left to fear?"

"But how can you think about those who are trying to take your land away without fearing them?"

"I know their fears. I have known them many lifetimes. They always want the same thing," Chan sighed. "Their lesson is the same today as yesterday, and many lifetimes ago. *Sí*, I know them well. Only their names and faces change."

"What do these people want?"

"Power, but one cannot steal power."

"Wait a minute. People have stolen power throughout history. Entire nations, including yours, have been conquered and plundered of their wealth and power, leaving people helpless and in poverty."

Chan waved this notion away. "They take only the illusion of power."

"Who are these people that want to take your land?"

"The same people who ruled over it before. They are from *Na-Bolom*." Chan's words shot through him like a sword, causing him to buckle over and clench his chest. Seeing his distress, Chan walked the few paces to where he lay and placed his hands over Peter's heart. Under Chan's warm and soothing hands, Peter's pain began to disappear.

"Your body does not like that name," Chan said, chuckling through his words.

"Apparently not," Peter gasped.

"Rulers of the Jaguar Empire learned to use Spirit of Darkness. Jaguar spirit is a good teacher, but its knowledge was used for a dark purpose."

"Do I . . ." Peter stopped to breathe, "stand in their way?"

"For a long, long time." Chan nodded as he studied the scars that showed through Peter's sweat-soaked T-shirt.

Peter looked down at the scars, and then back at Chan. "I thought the jaguar was on my side."

"Those who use the power of the jaguar use the power against you. They tried to get to your heart again. They know you are here."

Peter shivered. "Who were these jaguar people?"

"Do you not remember?"

"Oh no." Peter shook his head. "I know where this conversation is going, and you're not taking me there again."

"Do not be frightened, Sitting Raven. You are not ready to go there."

"Not today. Or ever. Having my heart pulled out of my chest once is enough for me."

"Spirit showed you something important to jolt your memory. In that life, you learned to listen to your heart. It was your greatest moment." Chan sounded almost sad as he said it.

They sat in silence for a long time, Peter staring off into the distant hills, listening to the earth as it moved through the universe, the wind whipping at their clothes. He loved soaring above the humid jungle. The mountains energized him. For the first time in weeks, he could breathe freely again.

Breaking the silence, Peter asked, "How do we prepare to know Spirit?"

"We must make a new body. Change the vibration of the mind."

Gazing across the tangled sea of treetops, Peter reflected on Chan's words. Chan was preparing his body. But for what? What would be expected of him?

Na-Bolom, he thought. Once again, his body shivered involuntarily. Some distance to the north, an isolated thundercloud hovered, dark and menacing. Unlike the other clouds around it, this one reached down to the earth, raining in a violent downpour.

Another thought hit him and he glanced at the shaman, who was still lying down with closed eyes. "Chan, is that a storm cloud in the distance, or is it smoke?"

With eyes still shut, Chan did not move or answer right away. Finally, in a soft voice he said, "Do you see only smoke? Do you not see the spirits of our village rising with its ashes?"

In stunned silence, Peter studied the menacing cloud of smoke. "My God. They're burning your village!"

There was no immediate danger to the tribe. It was the old village that was on fire. But the reality of Chan's predictions had come to life. There was indeed an unseen danger lurking out there. Jazmin had said the old village was some fifty miles away, and as he studied the ashen cloud, he determined it could easily be that distance.

Chan continued to lie motionless, eyes closed. He never looked in the direction of the smoke. Soon Peter too looked away.

"Come," Chan said, standing up. "*Vamos*."

CHAPTER 14

Chan and Peter descended the steep cliff, retracing their path across the meadows and creeks, back into the thick underbrush of the valley.

Hours later, Peter felt a deep hunger eating away at his stomach as they approached the campsite. Long shadows formed in the waning light, and his heart warmed when they caught sight of a campfire and Jazmin's concerned face.

"¿*Como estas, amorcito?* I missed you . . ."

"Another incredible day. Yesterday opened my mind; today opened my eyes."

"It must have been important. What happened?"

"We saw a fire."

"Farmers in Lacandón territory are always burning new fields. They—"

"No," Peter said. "It was the village. Chan said he saw the spirits of the village going up in smoke." His face turned grave as he cradled Jazmin's face in his hands and watched her turn pale. "I'm sorry."

"Are you sure?"

"That's what Chan said."

"What does it mean?"

"Obviously someone doesn't want the tribe around. Maybe they just want to keep them tucked away deep in the jungle where they won't stir up any more trouble."

"I pray it be so," Jazmin added, crossing herself.

The next morning greeted the trio with sunshine, and after a simple meal, they started back toward the village. Sore and tired from the long trek the day before, Peter relaxed in the comfort of the canoe. The ancient forest filled them up, and no one wanted to break the spell with careless words or thoughts. Traveling upstream took most of the day, yet it was too short for Peter. He was not ready to face the tumultuous welcome from their friends.

He remembered laughing at Chan when he had expressed his desire to get away from the noise of the village. Now he understood. Having journeyed to the quiet place in his mind Chan had alluded to, the tranquil world of the village seemed intrusive.

A sound emanated from the village as they came within earshot, the steady, rhythmic beat of a drum. It called to Peter's emotions in some inexplicable way. "What's going on in the village?" he asked.

"Dancing," Chan said.

Several long startling blasts from a conch shell soared across the valley, its primordial quality echoing into the vastness of the forest.

"Jazmin, if there's anyone within fifty square miles of here searching for us, the village just gave away our location."

They both looked to Chan, who had stopped in front of them to listen to the conch's song, but he showed no concern.

"They call the gods." He turned away, and continued walking toward the camp.

Jazmin whispered to Peter. "I am sure he knows the risk."

"I certainly hope so," Peter replied, but his emotions suggested otherwise.

As they neared the village, the children made their usual rush to greet them, bobbing and dancing about in a din of chatter.

Peter stopped to look around, surprised at the new addition to the village. He recognized it as a god house, a simple, bullpen-like structure constructed of tall wooden poles set in a circle about twenty feet in diameter. Jazmin had shown him pictures of such structures. Even more surprising, a dugout canoe sat near the entry of the enclosure. He ventured it must have taken ten men several hours to haul the twelve-foot craft up from the river. When he walked up to it, he saw that it was filled with a milky white liquid. Jazmin called it *balche*, a fermented drink the Lacandón used in their sacred ceremonies. The villagers must have dragged the canoe there soon after the three of them had left, and the long process of preparing the *balche* begun immediately. It took two days for the mixture to ferment to maturity, and the men were already drinking it.

The children ran off with Jazmin toward her lab to arrange her plant specimens. Peter stayed with Chan to inspect the god house. Inside, religious paraphernalia and ornaments sat before an altar, and red circular designs with a single dot in the middle had been painted on posts. Peter sensed the great care placed in its construction and décor.

"To Lacandón this is not just a ritual house," Chan said. "Man enters here to meet the gods. It is a place of great magic."

Coming from anyone else, Peter would have been skeptical, but Chan had demonstrated his ability to take him to another world. Some men sat contemplating around the fire, while others finished making preparations. They seemed to have been awaiting Chan's arrival, and several embraced him as they entered. However, Chan's absence had obviously not discouraged them from partaking of the *balche*. Several already had difficulty staying upright. Peter wondered if he wanted to participate in the ceremony at all—he didn't handle alcohol well.

Jazmin embraced him from behind. "*Hola, amor.* I'm glad we made it back in time for the ceremony."

"It looks like they've started without us," Peter said.

"Don't feel cheated—these ceremonies often last all night."

A heavyset man in his middle years came toward them with two bowls. One held red paint, the other black. He gestured to Peter.

"This is Kayum," Jazmin said. "He wants to paint your face. It's part of the ceremony."

"Great." Peter offered Kayum a wan smile. "I'll scare the spirits right back."

"This will be wonderful. But are you up to it? You must be exhausted from hiking." Jazmin's brown eyes widened. "And the Lacandón love their *balche*."

"I'm fine." He sat on a stump so the man could paint his face. "In fact, I feel strong. That forest did something to me. Besides, I slept a lot in the canoe. I'll go light on the refreshments. Maybe we can sneak away early—I doubt they'll miss us after a few gourds of *balche*."

Jazmin gave Peter a skeptical look. She sat down next to him, stroking the scars on his chest while Kayum painted his face. He placed his hand on her thigh, and held his face forward for the artist.

"Apparently Chan isn't worried about being attacked tonight," Peter said.

"I guess not. He always has scouts out during the day. They would have warned the village."

"I suppose," he said. "So, what's the celebration about?"

"It's for you." She smiled brightly.

"Me? What? Why didn't you tell me earlier?"

Before she could answer, Chan stepped out and waved them inside. The artist put the final touches on Peter's face and Jazmin studied his new look as they stood to go in.

"I think it is a little scary, but scaring me is not what they have in mind."

"What do I look like?"

She paused. "I would say you were painted in the spirit of a cat."

"Oh, great." Peter sneered, uncomfortable with the symbology. If what Chan had in mind was calling forth the spirit of the jaguar, he wanted nothing to do with it.

As they entered the god house, Chan gestured to the area where he wanted them to sit. They took their places within the circle of men around a large fire pit. Kin sat on one side of him, Jazmin on the other. He guessed Chan intended that K'in and Jazmin act as interpreters.

"It's a man's ceremony," Jazmin explained. About twenty filled the god house, ranging in age from teenage boys to old men. "Chan has made an exception for me, but I won't participate in the ceremony."

Several children gathered at the entrance. The sweet aroma of the jungle gave way to the fire's pungent smoke as they waited for the ceremony to begin. In the distance, Peter could hear the transition from daylight to darkness as the creatures of the night began to stir in anticipation of another nocturnal feast. Bats began to dart in and out of the firelight, catching an easy meal of insects attracted to the flames as Chan stood and threw something into the fire. He began to speak, but his words were in Maya.

Peter turned to Jazmin. "What's going on?"

Jazmin conferred with K'in for a brief moment. "Food is thrown into the fire as an offering to the god *K'akoch,* the supreme creator. The ceremonial tamale, or *nahwah,* as they call it, becomes human flesh as it enters the fire, and the *atole* is transformed into sacred water. The red paint on your faces represents blood and sacrifice."

"I was afraid of that," he whispered back.

"Don't worry. Even though they still practice the Maya tradition of sacrifice, they use symbolic objects now, not people."

"I can't tell you how happy I am to hear that, especially since I'm the guest of honor."

Jazmin smiled, and patted him on the leg. "I think it will be a nice ceremony."

"Ceremony? What kind of ceremony? I thought we were just throwing a party."

Jazmin conferred with K'in again before answering Peter's question. "It is a dance."

"Good. I like dances. Do they have a name for it?"

"K'in called it the dance of the jaguar."

Peter felt a sudden chill. This would be no ordinary dance. Nothing Chan ever did was ordinary.

Everyone turned to Chan as he began a prayer in Yucatec Maya. K'in whispered in Jazmin's ear as Chan spoke, and Jazmin translated the Maya and Spanish into English for Peter.

"We ask Spirit to accept these gifts of blood and flesh, song and dance. In deep silence we come to hear your voice this night, *K'akoch*, so you will guide us. Through you all knowledge comes. We thank you for your knowledge, *K'akoch*. We will pass your wisdom on to our children. We will come to you this night, Great One, to share your peace."

Chan finished and sat down directly opposite Peter in his spot near the fire pit. Several men passed out the *balche* and handed Peter a gourd of ceremonial drink. Still thirsty from their long hike, he forgot Jazmin's warning and downed a mouthful.

The unusual drink tasted like weak, warm beer with milky undertones. Halfway down, his taste buds decided it wasn't something that belonged in his mouth, and he began to choke. Jazmin glared at him with an "I told you so" look.

After fidgeting with the tepid brew for several minutes, Peter set the gourd down with the intention of ignoring it the rest of the evening. The Lacandón men seemed to enjoy the concoction in large quantities, and it looked like the evening might deteriorate into a drunken party. Disappointed by the ordinary beginnings, Peter looked across the fire and watched Chan take a sip and pass his gourd on.

Chan rose again, and Jazmin continued to interpret. "*Hahanak'uk* speaks to us, and guards us from the darkness. He is coming. Do not be afraid. He will protect us, provide rain to water our *milpas*, and keep our enemies away."

Jazmin whispered in Peter's ear. "*Hahanak'uk* is the god of thunder and lightning. It sounds like a storm is coming. Perhaps the monsoons are going to begin."

Chan sat on his haunches, and pulled a pouch from under his tunic. He placed the mixture from the bag into the end of a long wooden pipe, then gently tapped it into place with his ring finger. After lighting the pipe, he took a short draw, then passed it to the next man. The pipe moved clockwise along the circle. The musty smell of Chan's herbs filled the air as each man inhaled and coughed from the strong mixture. They held the smoke in their lungs, their faces turning red and strained. Peter grew uneasy as the pipe worked its way closer to him. He took slow, deep breaths, assuring himself that Jazmin sat at his side should he need her. As an observer, she would not be allowed to drink the *balche,* or smoke from the ceremonial pipe.

Peter envied her as the pipe passed to K'in. K'in drew deeply on it and held in the smoke without coughing. He then handed the pipe to Peter. He acknowledged K'in's control with a nod, then anxiously studied the circle of men still choking and coughing violently, worried for his sore ribs and healing wounds.

All eyes fixed on Peter as he placed the pipe stem to his lips and drew a cautious breath. After a few seconds he exhaled and smiled, then extended the pipe to the next man. That Chan chose to sit opposite him was no accident. Chan's eyes caught Peter's, and the old shaman gestured with his chin, encouraging him to take another draw. He hesitated and glanced around again, hoping to see smiles of approval. The men only stared in stoic anticipation as he brought the pipe to his lips again and inhaled deeply. The smoke burned down his throat and into his lungs. He coughed it out immediately. Chan's dark eyes gently urged him to try again.

Jazmin's face tightened with concern and she stroked Peter's back. Bracing himself, he drew in deeply again, managing to hold the mixture in his lungs this time. The aroma of the smoking mixture was unfamiliar, but he knew there was a mild hallucinogenic in it—at least he hoped it was mild. He held it for as long as he dared, then collapsed on his side, coughing and gasping for air.

The pipe continued around the circle of men while Peter convulsed on the ground. K'in patted his back, muttering unrecognizable yet comforting Maya words. When he thought he couldn't stand more pain, his coughing stopped and he focused on his breathing. Several minutes passed before a warm, relaxed feeling began flooding his senses.

Soon the painted faces across the fire pit took on a strange, animated appearance, distorting into eerie shapes from the disturbed waves of heat and smoke. Chan began to chant in a deep, clear voice, his words suspended like leaves drifting to the ground.

K'in and Jazmin helped Peter into a sitting position. The sound seemed to calm the men, who began swaying slightly to its cadence.

Peter thought he had heard it before, perhaps from his cot, but never with this authority. There was a mournful beauty to it. Something about the song touched him, filled him with a sense of sadness, as if the earth had opened up to receive him. Though the words were Maya, he sensed their meaning and felt their sorrow as if he knew the song or recalled its ancient meaning.

Peter knew in his gut that it was a warrior's song: not about battle or of the thrill of victory past or future, but a song celebrating the warrior's soul and its long journey to awakening. He thought of the dark smoke rising from the burning village and, in that moment, realized this song was the story of the last free men to walk the earth. Raw emotion welled up inside of him and blurred his vision. He turned to look at Jazmin. She wiped a tear from moist eyes. In that moment they touched one another soul to soul, feeling the same sorrow at the warrior's lament. It was a moment he had longed for without knowing it. He wiped the tears from his face, then hers. They mingled in his hand.

When the last soaring notes left Chan's lips, a vast silence filled the air. Only the sound of the crackling fire remained. Peter gazed at the faces around the fire, and for the first time felt the overwhelming significance of their lives. Here, the primitive world collided with the twenty-first century, and sitting before him were perhaps the last truly free people in the world.

The pipe came around again, and he looked at it with trepidation. K'in held it before him, then placed it in his hand, wrapping each finger around it until he held it firmly. He drew on the pipe, and another wave of incomprehensible sensations flooded through him. As the drug coursed through his body, K'in began to whisper in his ear. The Maya words comforted him, and again he thought he understood them or somehow absorbed what K'in said. But his overpowering thought was that this mysterious, dreamlike world was beginning to feel familiar. Even the faces around the fire began to look familiar now, like old friends he had known for years. As though awakened from a long sleep, he experienced a certain communion with them. He reached out his hand to pass the pipe to the man sitting on the other side of Jazmin, but didn't remember it leaving his hand afterward.

Someone threw more food into the fire, then incense, its sweet aroma winding skyward toward the gods. He sat in a stupor for an unaccountable amount of time before he noticed some of the men moving around the fire pit. White tunics swept before him as he listened to the steady beat of drums and voices.

Consumed by the repetitive beat of the music and the dancers' movement, Peter's mind remained fixed in the moment. Everything was in motion; men and shadows dancing, arms flailing, flames leaping to the sky. The Lacandón men looked upward, gesturing to the spirits, staring with wild eyes into another world. Red-hot embers floated high into the air, disappearing into the night. Darkness quietly descended on them, but Peter didn't notice until the change was complete.

The pipe came around again. This time Peter took it and inhaled the powerful herbs without hesitation. The blast of hot smoke seared his lungs. His body and mind reeled like a string of popping firecrackers.

Peter found himself lying down, and noticed a man standing over him, filling his vision. Shadows ran across the strange man's face, but his eyes flickered in the firelight. The man's lips moved, but he couldn't make out the words, drowned out by the chanting and the shuffle of the dancers.

Several men helped Peter to his feet and nudged him forward, encouraging him to dance. He found his rhythm and soon danced around the fire with the others, watching their shadows as they glided around the perimeter of the god house. The shadows seemed to move of their own volition along the walls. The fire and chanting beckoned both shadow and flesh dancers, and they all swayed together, around and around. The dancers became a single living organism in a place where no separation existed. He felt the dancers' pain and their struggle as he moved to the rhythm of their lives. Sweat mingled with the earth, shadows merged, and they danced on.

Then only the shadows remained: running, dancing, flying across the wooden walls of the god house, darting deep into the forest. Leaping into the trees and back into the god house, the shadows soared back and forth, in and out.

Then he crouched close to the ground, running through the trees, dashing through the darkness and back into the god house, racing along its corrugated walls. Eyes flashed, lips moved, flames leapt high into the night air. Around and around he went in a seemingly inexhaustible blur. Then without fanfare, everything went silent.

Suddenly he was no longer changing his perspective, or even moving. Drawn into the red-hot embers, he became the flames of the all-consuming fire. He remained secure in that volatile world until inexplicably drawn up into the night sky to burst into a million fragments. No longer a body, he was set free.

As effortlessly as it had come, the awareness of his formless being vanished and he found himself collapsed, face down by the fire. Sweating and panting like a tired cat after a chase, he dug his fingers into the cool earth.

He felt someone covering him with something rough, but came to when he heard Chan's reassuring voice over the rustling of palm leaves. "You see through the spirit of the jaguar's eyes this night. You have become the shadow. You have become the night. Rest now. Let the Earth-spirit take you deep into her womb. She will give you her strength."

Peter listened as the last leaves covered his head; then there was only the darkness.

The leaves that kept him warm throughout the night were lifted off as he gained consciousness the next morning. Bright light assaulted his bleary eyes, then a shadow moved overhead.

Jazmin's worried face hovered over him. She shook his shoulders vigorously. "Peter? Are you okay?"

He moaned, taking a moment to assess his condition. "I guess."

His vision cleared when he looked into her eyes and then glanced at the other men asleep on the ground. They, too, had passed out around the fire pit. His muscles ached from the long night on the cool ground, but he noticed few negative after-effects from the drugs. It seemed as though the earth had absorbed the toxins from his body, leaving him clear-headed and refreshed.

With Jazmin's help, he rose slowly to his feet and looked down at himself. Only then did he realize he was naked. He gazed around the God house, searching for his clothes before he noticed Jazmin holding his t-shirt and shorts, and smiling sympathetically.

"You would have had some explaining to do if I had not been here last night to see for myself," she teased.

"Very funny." He took the clothes from her. "You don't know the half of it. I don't know what Chan put in that pipe, but I had one hell of a ride last night—a social anthropologist's dream. My head was spinning so fast I thought it would explode." He pulled on his shorts and looked queerly at Jazmin. "Come to think of it, it did explode."

Jazmin reached for him and stroked his hair. "You've been through so much since you came here." She handed him a gourd filled with one of Chan's multi-herb concoctions.

He savored the tea and its refreshing aroma, a hint of mint, as they sat on a log near the fire pit.

"Tell me what happened to you last night."

"I don't know exactly," Peter said. "After I smoked Chan's herbs I was in kind of a stupor, then I found myself going around the fire like a twister."

"How exactly do you mean?"

"It wasn't like anything I've ever experienced, as if the shadows grabbed me, and took me around with them. Strange, but I wasn't frightened."

"What did it teach you? Chan says there is always a lesson in these experiences."

"Do you remember my telling you that Chan talked about the priests who came here when he was a child? He told me they refused to ask the spirit of the plants permission before picking them, and that they had become sick because of it. At the time, it really didn't mean much to me. I never experienced anything even remotely like it before. But last night I felt Spirit inside of me." He gestured toward his face with his hands. "I saw through its eyes."

Moved by his words, Jazmin locked her arms around Peter and kissed him tenderly on the lips.

"Thank you," she whispered.

"What for?"

"For everything," she said. "For joining me in my world."

They sat, wrapped in each other's arms, absorbed in their own thoughts. Then Peter sat back to gain a better look at Jazmin's face.

"What did it look like from your perspective?"

"I saw you dance around the fire for a while, then you ran off in the dark. I was afraid for you, but when I stood up to go after you, Chan caught my attention and waved me back to my place by the fire. Eventually you came back, but you didn't have any clothes on. Your motions were rapid, like a wild man. I was afraid you were going to hurt yourself. Then you did something that really frightened me."

"What was that?"

"You walked into the fire, and stood on the hot coals." Jazmin looked perplexed. "The men did nothing to help you. Finally, you collapsed on the ground. After that the men gathered around you and covered you."

"I knew things were getting hot." Peter looked at his feet. "But my feet aren't burnt. All I really remember is the dancing. What else did you see?"

"There was something strange happening when you were outside the god house. I heard a sound. There were many sounds," she said, sipping her tea. "But this one I remember. This sound frightened me."

Peter set his hot tea down, and gave her his full attention. "Why? What kind of sound was it?"

"Well . . ." She hesitated, looking for the right words. "It was like the snarl of a leopard, or a jaguar."

CHAPTER 15

Peter slept the rest of the day and into the evening, exhausted by the journey and the dance of the jaguar. In the wee hours, he sat up in his cot, startled by a sound. He scanned the dark village through his open doorway. Though the night was serene and silent, an uneasy awareness swept through him and he gazed at the black darkness beyond the stick walls of his shelter again. At first, he saw only a white mist moving through the trees outside the village, seeping through the branches like ghosts on the prowl. Then a swift movement caught his attention. A shadow. The dark form stalked the night, making its way from hammock to hammock.

Peter reached for his gun, careful not to make any noise. Chan had instilled in him the practice of keeping everything in its proper place for easy finding, even in total darkness. The shadow picked its way among the villagers, moving closer until it reached his small enclosure. He eased his fingers over the gun's handle, released the safety, and aimed it toward the entrance of the shelter. The silent intruder pulled the door canopy aside and entered.

"*Alto*," Peter commanded.

The figure stopped and spoke in a familiar voice. "*Buenas noches.*"

Jazmin awakened with a start. "What is it, Peter?"

"It's okay, honey. It's just Chan."

He turned back to Chan, anxious and annoyed. "What are you

doing coming in here like that? I could have shot you."

"Thank you for your concern, old friend, but I was not in danger." Chan's tone was calm and direct. "Your gun is not loaded."

Peter pulled the slide action back to check the chamber. It was empty. The clip was full. He could feel the weight of the bullets. But he'd made a point of keeping a round in the chamber in case he needed to use the gun in a hurry. Chan had indeed tricked him.

"Why did you—"

"Men with guns approach."

"Oh my God." Jazmin clambered from the bed and clutched Peter's arm.

"Why did you do this, Chan?" Peter groped in the dark for his bullets. "How are we to defend ourselves without weapons?"

"Guns will not save the jungle. Guns will not save you. The clouds and trees saw this darkness coming."

"Why didn't you tell us earlier?"

"You needed a good sleep. Men come in darkness. They are serious about their task. You must hurry. Take my daughter, and go deep into the jungle."

"How can this be?" Jazmin asked, her voice shaking as they hurried to dress. "The ranchers and farmers here are superstitious about the jungle, afraid of what the darkness brings. They would not travel in here at night."

It was more a question than a statement, but it went unanswered. They grabbed their packs, and were out of the shelter in less than a minute. A light rain fell in a misty curtain when they stepped outside the hut. Already the villagers were moving quietly and efficiently out of the village.

"Are we not to go with you, Chan?" Jazmin asked, new panic evident in her voice.

"Our path leads south. You must follow the red ruby. It is time for us to say goodbye."

"But why, Chan?" she asked. "Why can't we go with you?"

"Men with guns will follow us," Chan said. "And leave you to find your way to safety. Your survival is most important. If you die, the jungle dies. Go now."

"That's preposterous," Peter blurted out. "It's you who must survive at all costs! I don't know what to do here."

"Why don't we at least talk to the men?" Jazmin said. "Maybe we could reach an understanding. They need the forest for their survival too."

"The men with guns do not come to talk, gentle daughter." Chan turned to see the villagers had vanished down the darkened path. "They come with money in their pockets."

Peter and Jazmin stood stunned for a moment, unable to respond to the certainty in Chan's voice.

"They're hired killers?" Peter asked. Chan was silent.

"Who would do such a thing?"

"Very old enemies," Chan warned with a hint of sadness in his voice. Chan held Jazmin for a long moment, then Peter. "We have said many good-byes, old friends. Do not think about this now. You have prepared all your life for this moment. Be sure in your heart you can do what Spirit has asked you to do." He spoke in low, measured tones to emphasize his words. "Listen to the calm waters flowing through your mind. Let them guide you through the jungle."

"You said to follow a red ruby," Peter whispered as loudly as he dared. "What do you mean?"

"Spirit showed me a red ruby. That is all."

The rain fell as the last of Chan's people disappeared down the trail, their white tunics vanishing completely in the night. "The clouds weep for us this night," Chan called. "Go home, my friend."

He turned and melted into the night.

Peter felt cheated by the moment, denied even a last look at the old shaman who had saved his life. "Which way do we go, Chan?" he called softly.

"You must go where they will not follow. Your path leads west through the Forbidden Jungle."

"But no one goes in there, Chan. You said so yourself."

"Hurry, Sitting Raven. The jungle is burning."

CHAPTER 16

A syrupy white fog hung on the trees and oozed through the hills, giving the night the appearance of a stalker. Peter studied the lights moving silent as death through the misty jungle. Though it was difficult to determine their distance, he sensed they were moving quickly.

Jazmin took his arm. "Peter, we must hurry. They will be here soon."

They headed in a westerly direction toward the unknown wilderness, moving at a fast pace along a vague animal trail. The moon had just set, turning the forest into a tree-studded ocean of fog. The trail became the darkest of shadows before them. With hearts racing, they stumbled along, stopping only to catch their breath and to orient themselves.

Peter started to push the button on his watch to activate its light, then thought better of it. In the black of night, even a tiny light could be seen from a great distance.

"I think we have another hour of total darkness," he said quietly. "They can use their flashlights, but we can't. If they follow us, they'll catch us for sure. Hopefully, they'll take the bait and follow the tribe. We'll be able to lose ourselves in the jungle long before they realize we've escaped. This rain should cover our tracks. I just hope Chan and the rest of the tribe can stay ahead of them—"

Gunfire erupted in the distance behind them. They dove to the ground.

"My God!" Jazmin gasped. "They are shooting."

Even more disturbing to Peter was the rat-tat-tat sound the weapons made. "Automatic weapons," he declared. "They sure as hell aren't locals. They're professionals."

"Chan said they had money in their pockets," Jazmin said, her body trembling, her voice husky with tears. "They're burning the village."

Flames shot up through the jungle canopy, high into the night sky.

"Scratch village number two." Peter rose from his crouched position and grabbed Jazmin's arm. "Let's run while we have light from the fire."

They took off at a sprint and ran along the animal trail, stopping only once to catch their breath. When they could run no more, they looked back to see the last of the flames flickering out in the distance. The darkness was complete once again, and their pace slowed.

Eventually, the faint light of early morning made the trail clear, and their careful steps turned into a steady jog. A pack of peccaries startled and ran, disappearing into the dense undergrowth. A ringtail cat scurried up a tree and into a hollow in the trunk. They heard some thrashing in a nearby thicket and froze. Peter aimed his Beretta, fingering the trigger lightly. They both breathed a sigh of relief when a large, fat tapir showed itself. When they began running again, every tree and rock began to take on the shape of a man. Moving quickly, they continually checked the trail behind them.

"Chan's plan worked," Peter said to a sweat-soaked Jazmin. Then he noticed, for the first time in the pale morning light, the T-shirt she wore—bright red, her favorite color. "You've got to get out of that shirt. You're going to stand out like a stop sign."

"Ah," she exclaimed.

Jazmin quickly unbuckled her pack and rummaged through it, producing a green blouse. Moments later, they were running again.

Hours passed before they slowed their pace to follow a stream down a ravine. Peter held his ribs, occasionally grimacing with pain, but adrenaline kept him going. The light rain had stopped, and the clouds were beginning to break up. When they stepped out on a flat rock precipice and looked down, they saw that the water no longer flowed along the ground, but dropped vertically hundreds of feet before disappearing into a deep and narrow gorge. The tumbling, splashing falls gushed into the canyon below, washing out all other sounds. Only a darkened abyss with no bottom in sight lay before them, a light mist rising from the canyon depths. Exhausted, they took off their packs and set them on the smooth rock surface. Peter picked up a stone and tossed it into the canyon. It sailed through the white mist and disappeared into the darkness. He heard nothing.

"That's one deep canyon," he said.

Jazmin gazed up and down the canyon. "There doesn't seem to be a way to get down."

"There has to be," he said. "We can take our time, skirt the rim until we find a place to climb down. Or walk around it. Those gunmen are probably miles away, standing on the edge of the Rio Jataté, wondering how the tribe slipped away from them."

"Okay, but let's keep moving." She cast him a worried look. "I have an uneasy feeling about this."

Peter reached down to pick up his backpack, and saw a movement out of the corner of his eye. He crouched down to take a better look.

People were coming: men in black fatigues and black berets.

"Get down," he whispered, pulling Jazmin by the arm.

Soon the soldiers were about a hundred yards distant, making their way down the creek bed.

"They're tracking us." Peter stayed low behind the rock shelf. "I don't think they've spotted us yet . . . come on!"

He rose to sprint into the jungle and took a step, but gunshots barked out in the same breath, first one, then a series. Bullets scattered rocks in front of him, ricocheting in every direction, forcing them to dive back to the small shelf for shelter.

"Damn! Those sons-of-bitches have us pinned down. And they're sure as hell not keen on taking prisoners."

A quick glance up the ridge revealed several soldiers scrambling to block any escape from their precarious position. More bullets ripped overhead.

"Those bastards are going to die. I'm going to kill every last one of them."

Peter raised his head above the shelf and opened fire when the soldiers came close enough for his weapon to be effective. In a panic, they dove for cover behind boulders and trees.

Peter knew he'd given away the advantage of surprise. "Still, they're not so brave when someone's shooting back. Maybe that'll slow them down long enough for us to figure a way out of here."

He grappled with his bullets, inserting them into the empty magazine of the Beretta. He glanced at Jazmin, expecting a response, but she lay mute and motionless.

"My God, Jazmin, are you okay? Have you been hit?"

"We have to jump," she whispered.

Her response left him nearly speechless. "What?"

Coming to life, she opened her eyes and looked up at him. "We must jump."

"Are you nuts?" he said, pointing toward the abyss. "That canyon's bottomless."

But as he spoke, Jazmin sprang to her feet, and ran the few steps to the edge of the cliff. Peter slammed a full clip into the Beretta and sprayed bullets into the jungle to pin down the gunmen. Looking over his shoulder, he watched as Jazmin paused, then threw herself off the edge.

"Jazmin!" Peter's anguished cry hurtled through the canyon, eerily bouncing off the walls as she dropped into the darkness. His heart stopped. All signs of life seemed to stop as well, frozen in the moment. Everything but Jazmin. But her image seemed to change, to morph into a different woman as she jumped.

No longer clad in shorts and her green blouse, he saw a native woman in colorful dress with her hands bound behind her, falling away, a violet flower coming loose from behind her ear and floating, spinning slowly into the canyon.

There was no time to question the uncanny sight as bullets slammed into the rock escarpment in front of him.

Rage filled his body. A quick backward glance revealed soldiers moving in closer. With nowhere to run, he grabbed the packs and threw them off the canyon's edge. Trembling with anger, he stood and pulled the trigger of his gun as fast as he could, cursing and firing until the gun was empty and impotent. His gunfire had temporarily silenced the soldiers. In this stolen moment, he ran to the cliffs' edge, and launched himself into the uncertain darkness. Bullets burst violently off the far canyon wall, shattering rock and throwing dust as he fell.

Peter wanted to grab onto something—anything—as he braced himself for the terrifying moment of impact, but all he could embrace was the fleeting rush of wind. Time crept forward as he descended in slow motion, leaving him to wonder if he would ever stop falling. While his life ticked away to its certain end, he wanted to pass out, to end the terror, but the adrenaline racing through him would not allow this luxury.

He hit feet first with a loud smack followed by a dull thud, instantly under water. Before he could rebound from the first impact, he hit something even harder—the bottom of a creek bed.

Peter found his feet embedded in heavy gravel. He struggled to push himself up, but couldn't feel his legs and thought he must have broken them. Fighting to orient himself, he saw a narrow band of blue sky above. The water's surface was at least eight feet above him, and it took all his strength to launch himself upward toward his next breath. His legs came back to life, and he broke the surface, gasping for air.

He had landed in a deep pool in front of the falls. But where was

Jazmin? The still waters showed no sign of her. The creek was narrow and shallow in all but the one spot where he had landed, and only their packs floated at the surface.

Turning frantically around, he explored the water's edge, not wanting to consider that she had missed the life-saving pool in her desperate leap.

He twisted and turned, terrified by his thoughts until he saw her. Jazmin lay lifeless on the edge of the pool. He swam desperately until his feet found the creek bottom.

"Oh God . . . no."

The tails of her blouse fluttered lazily in the light breeze whispering under the roar of the falls. She was dry. She had not hit the water.

He stood frozen in the chest deep water, trying to accept what he was seeing.

How can this be?

She said they would be all right. He shook his head as if to repel thoughts of her death. He moaned again, grappling for an explanation that would deny the moment.

Then the impossible happened. Her right hand slowly rose toward her head.

Peter scrambled out of the water, first swimming, then running toward her, faster than he thought possible.

"Jazmin!"

As he reached her side, he knelt and put his ear to her chest. A pulse. Her chest moved gently. Still breathing. Then he checked for lacerations, signs of internal bleeding. Nothing. Gingerly moving her onto one side, he ran his fingers down her spine. He expected the worst but detected no crushed bones, no terrible bruises.

Peter eased her onto her back. No visible injuries. How could this be?

Jazmin's eyes fluttered open, out of focus. She appeared to be looking inside her mind, trying to unscramble her thoughts.

"Jazmin, can you hear me?"

She whispered, her lips barely moving. "Peter?"

"I'm here, honey. Can you move your arms and legs?"

She groaned as she shifted one leg out from under the other. "Do you feel any pain?"

She looked at him, trying to find the answer, her voice barely audible. "I don't know."

Peter held her in his arms, grateful for the miracle of her life. "What happened?" she asked.

He stroked her face, and kissed her several times before answering. "I was hoping you could tell me. We jumped off that cliff," he said, pointing upward. "I landed in the water, but you..."

Looking up at the top of the canyon, Peter estimated it was at least a hundred fifty-foot vertical drop. As he looked up and down the twisted, narrow canyon, he realized he had landed in the only pool of water deep enough to save his life.

Taking Jazmin in his arms again, he held her for his own comfort as well as hers. Another flood of relief washed over him.

He eased Jazmin down and ran to retrieve their packs from the stream, then checked to see if everything was intact. It was—another miracle.

The soldiers were nowhere to be seen. There was no way down but to jump, and he was sure there would be no volunteers among them. Since the bottom of the canyon wasn't visible from above, Peter reasoned the soldiers would assume they had fallen to their deaths and call off the chase.

He set up camp where they were. He still worried that Jazmin might have suffered a concussion or internal injuries, but another examination revealed no signs of a head injury and no symptoms of internal distress. Somehow, it seemed she had not sustained any physical trauma. After he raised the tent on a bank of coarse sand, he did what little he could to make her comfortable inside. Then he hung his wet clothes out to dry and returned to her side. It was nearly dark before she stirred again to look up at him and squeeze his hand.

He stroked her hair, and asked the question he'd tried to answer for hours. "What made you so confident we would be okay if we threw ourselves off that cliff?"

"I heard a voice," she whispered weakly.

"A voice?"

"*Sí.*" Tears began streaming down her cheeks. "A voice said 'jump.' I knew you would jump only if I jumped first."

"Do you remember falling?"

Her voice trembled. "I heard wings," she said. "I heard wings."

Peter held her in his arms until she wept herself to sleep. When he eased away and crawled from the tent, the night was clear, with only a faint light from the waning moon keeping the shadows at bay. He dragged a log near the tent, and sat pondering their entry into the Forbidden Jungle. In his years spent in the field as a paleontologist, he'd heard many superstitions. He hadn't believed any of them. He never believed in miracles, whether the supernatural variety of angelic intervention, or the more mundane occurrences that defied the odds. There was always a rational explanation for everything. But as he gaped at the towering cliff, he felt an unsettling sensation of movement deep within himself again, another uninvited guest knocking at his rational mind.

The roar of the waterfall settled into a soothing sound that drowned out the rest of the canyon's inner world. Only the occasional distant call of a predator penetrated its walls. Peter was thankful for Chan's insight the night before. The old shaman had said they would need a good night's sleep. So true, he thought. But not even Chan had seemed to realize their enemy would be so bold as to come in the night.

The quarter moon stood directly overhead, its light softened by the humidity in the air. Now a brilliant indigo, the sky glimmered with millions of stars. Peter always felt humbled by the vastness of the night sky. He felt small and insignificant. As he breathed in the cool air, he felt more alert and refreshed than he had any right to feel. But the day had been exhausting, and his eyelids soon grew heavy and fluttered shut.

A flock of parrots squawking in the first hint of sunlight on the canyon walls startled Peter awake. "Damn it," he said, chiding himself for being so careless. The soldiers could have shot them in their sleep.

Still perched against his log, he stood, then looked in on Jazmin, chiding himself for neglecting her. She was still asleep. He had not heard her stir all night. He ran a finger over the curve of one cheek and gently shook her awake. He eased her into a sitting position and examined her eyes. Still distant, she smiled weakly and looked about, obviously disoriented.

"*Buenos días,*" she said.

"*Buenos días.* Do you think you can walk?"

She picked up a sock and began to dress, her movements slow and mechanical. He sensed her mind was troubled, but he still could not detect any sign of injury.

"Do you feel okay, honey?" He helped her out of the tent, one arm wrapped around her waist.

"I . . . I think so," she said.

He watched her closely while they had a light breakfast of the dried fruit the Lacandón women had prepared. After packing their equipment and supplies, they started down the canyon to look for a path up the steep cliffs in a direction opposite their pursuers. Jazmin was able to keep up a good pace. Relieved, Peter spoke to her often, making certain she was lucid as they moved cautiously through the canyon, alert for the sound of soldiers behind them.

They found no path to the rim of the canyon, so they followed the creek bed. Several miles downstream, the narrow canyon opened up into a valley and headed in a westerly direction. Careful not to expose themselves, they moved quickly through the wilderness, and by midday had gained several miles. They snacked on dried fruit and tubers by a shallow stream, reflecting on the events of the day before. Peter leaned against his pack to relieve his aching back, and Jazmin crouched beside him, staring at her hands.

They sat in silence for several minutes until her face clouded with confusion. "Peter? What happened yesterday?"

"You don't remember anything? The soldiers had us pinned against the canyon, and you said we had to jump. Before I could argue, you hurled yourself over the edge. You didn't even hesitate. I couldn't believe it. I was sure you'd die."

"I jumped off the cliff?" Her eyes were incredulous. "And you?"

"I jumped too, because I didn't have any choice. Either I took my chances jumping into the canyon, or dying in a gunfight. Those guys had me out-gunned. I landed in the water and thought I'd broken my legs in the creek bed—"

"You said you found me unconscious. I don't remember falling, or swimming out of the water. Did you pull me out?"

"No." Peter looked at the ground, wondering if he wanted to revisit that moment.

"Then I swam out on my own."

"No." He shook his head. "You didn't hit the water. You were on the rocks."

Jazmin's brown eyes studied his face for clues.

"Peter, I could not have landed on the rocks. That cliff was hundreds of meters high."

He heard fear rising in her voice. "I know," he said.

"Then I had to land in the water. I did not fly down."

Peter took a deep breath. "Apparently you did. Remember when I found you? Your clothing was dry. You never touched the water."

Jazmin looked dumbfounded, on the brink of tears. "Chan said the forest loved me and would take care of me, but . . ."

Peter placed an arm around her, and pulled her head over to rest on his shoulder. "You told me something yesterday that made my hair stand on end. I asked if you remembered anything from the time you leaped from the ledge." He kissed her head, and stroked her cheek. "You were emotional and started crying. Do you remember our conversation?"

"No. I remember nothing."

"You were difficult to understand, but I think you said, 'I heard wings.'"

Jazmin's face twisted, and she began to sob.

Peter wanted to kick himself. Instead, he just held her.

They continued west at a steady pace through the widening canyon, confident no one could spot them in the ever-thickening vegetation. By midday, the air had turned heavy, and the jungle became silent and motionless as if all the flora and fauna held its collective breath. Only the small white butterflies that began to appear gave them any comfort. Soon the butterflies numbered in the hundreds, fluttering from flower to flower in a silent, magical dance.

The scent of moisture alerted Jazmin's sensitive nose to a distant storm. They came to a small clearing and looked up. A black bank of clouds worked its way inland, anchored like an impenetrable wall. At first, a barely perceptible movement of air set leaves to fluttering, then a gentle swaying of branches high in the trees. Within minutes, the jungle began to tremble from a sudden invasion of cold wind.

"It is the first monsoon of the season," Jazmin said.

They stopped to orient themselves and gaze around. "Look," she whispered. "The white butterflies are gone."

"That's strange. They were here by the zillions a few minutes ago. What do you think it means?"

"It means we have only a few minutes to find shelter."

They searched for any tall, stout tree they could take shelter under as the wind increased. The turbulent sea air relieved the dankness of the jungle, and they greedily breathed it in as they ran through the forest. The chattering of birds stopped as the dark clouds advanced like a tide, blotting out the sun.

Peter slashed a path before them with his *machete*. Spotting a huge tree not far away, they sprinted toward it. Arriving at its base, he was surprised to find that the tree was much larger than he had imagined. The giant had a base nearly twelve feet in diameter and rose at least one hundred and fifty feet into the air.

He spotted a branch twice as big around as his waist, about fifteen feet from the ground. The tree's canopy would provide shelter and keep them out of reach from most predators. The storm would do the rest, keeping any soldiers who might be tracking them at bay.

Looking up, Peter found the craggy tree had easy-to-find footholds, but the strong tempest made his every move a struggle. He fought his way through the tree's branches. Gaining his objective on the large branch, then removed the hammock from his pack, tied its two ends to the branch, and threw the tarp over the branch so that it sheltered the hammock. He secured the tarp, worked his way down again, took Jazmin's hand, and helped her up. They found branches to strap their packs to, and secured them together with twine.

Jazmin swung under the tarp as powerful gusts slashed the treetops. Large branches crackled ominously to the ground, scattering debris to the whirling wind. The stout branch they sheltered under moved little in the violent wind, but the powerful gusts rocked their vulnerable hammock cocoon as they climbed into it. When they settled in, lightning began to terrorize the jungle. Within minutes, the sky closed in around them with sizzling, strobe-like flashes of light and deafening explosions of thunder.

The leading edge of the storm quickly thrust the forest floor into shadow. With each brilliant flash, the canopy lit up against a darkened sky. One bolt after another erupted around them, shattering trees and starting fires. They held their ears and screamed to relieve their fear as one brilliant crash after another blasted away at the darkness. The forest trembled under the onslaught. Stimulated by the danger and fury of the storm, they held each other in a passionate embrace.

At first, only a few large drops of rain fell. But the powerful winds gradually yielded to rain, which slapped the tarp that surrounded them with a steady staccato. Then the rhythm turned to the dull thudding of a torrential cascade. It seemed the sea had fallen from the heavens, determined to wash the land away. Peter scrambled to secure the tarp's ends together, closing the gap in their shelter. The downpour was so violent, they could barely hear each other. They clutched one another tightly again.

Despite the severity of the storm, Peter was strangely calm for the first time since entering the jungle. He felt safe, contented even, and in a profound way, in harmony with the intricate web of life around them. He wondered if there would ever again be such pristine places on Earth, where the imagination could savor the endless array of unsolved mysteries unaltered by the hand of man.

"At least no one can track us in this rain," he yelled, uncertain Jazmin could hear him as she shivered in his arms.

"I think this is some of Chan's magic," Jazmin yelled back, snuggling against him. "The soldiers will surely turn back now if they continued to hunt for us."

The day rolled slowly into night, the rain continuing in a furious torrent. There was nothing to do but stay dry and wait it out. Once the thunder moved into the distant hills, they began to relax. After an exhausting and stressful day, it took little urging to fall into a fitful sleep.

When Peter awoke his watch read 6:00 a.m.—the time he always got up at home. Old habits die hard, he figured. He peeked out of the hammock, searching the early morning light through a fog-shrouded forest. The rain still fell in a steady drone, but with a fraction of the intensity it had displayed during the night.

Peter untied the tarp from around the hammock and glanced down. Confused, he rubbed his eyes and looked again. He turned in every direction, searching for a familiar landmark. "This can't be the same place we fell asleep in last night."

Jazmin began to stir. "What is it?"

"This can't be right," he added.

Jazmin's gaze followed Peter's and her mouth dropped open.

"¡Dios mío!"

CHAPTER 17

Unable to soak up more water, the jungle had disappeared. The forest valley had transformed overnight into a flooded plain, an ocean of dark green water dotted with islands for miles in every direction. Their tree stood on a rise little more than a hundred yards in diameter.

Lifting himself up, Peter struggled out of the hammock, climbed down from the tree, and stood by the waters' edge. He took off his still-dry pants, placed them in a sheltered spot against the trunk of the tree, and waded out to check the water's depth. A few paces beyond the tree, the water reached his stomach. A red-eyed leaf frog swam by and he glared at it in frustration.

Peter looked up at Jazmin. "We can't hike through this soup. It's too deep."

"Come out of there," she called from the tree. "These waters are full of poisonous snakes."

He looked up at her, still perplexed. "How could so much water fall in just one night?"

"It is a rain forest, *mi amor*. Now come out of the water."

He hastened out of the water as she struggled out of the tree to stand at the waters' edge beside him.

With a look of concern, she brushed her hair from her face, and stared at the water as if trying to comprehend it. "They don't call it the

Forbidden Jungle for nothing, no?"

"I guess not." Peter looked up at the dense cloud cover. "It doesn't look like conditions will improve soon either."

"Not for weeks, maybe months," she added, shaking her head. "The monsoons are just starting."

"Well, the Special Forces won't be able to track us in this."

After hauling their equipment out of the tree, they set up the tarp to shelter them—the tent was too much trouble in the steady rain. They sat like stones in the downpour, cold and dejected. Unable to resolve their dilemma, Peter comforted Jazmin with a hug, kissing her damp forehead.

"Like I said before, the soldiers won't follow us in this weather, if they're following us at all. They surely can't track us now, except by air. And they can't do that until the sky clears. But how long can we survive on this tiny island?"

"Not long."

"We're live bait sitting here." Peter stood suddenly and wiped a raindrop off the tip of his nose with the back of his hand. "I'm going to have a look around. Might be a while. If you see or hear anyone, get that tarp out of sight and hide yourself."

He strapped on his *machete*, then started edging around the island. A grove of young trees had blown down in the night, their roots standing high in the air like frightened tentacles. Attached to some of the trees he found a particular vine Chan had pointed out to him, strong and useful as twine or rope.

He continued on until he spotted another jumble of fallen trees, straight and about as big around as his thigh. Some lay in the water, some on land. They looked as though they'd been dead and down for some time. He unsheathed his *machete*, and began stripping one of its branches. Several hours passed before he had them lined up side-by-side, strapped together near the water's edge.

Suddenly aware of the time, he hurried back to Jazmin. When he approached the campsite, he found everything gone. Alarmed, he drew his gun, but a quick look around revealed a new campsite hidden further back in the trees. He exhaled with relief. Jazmin had moved their gear so it wouldn't be easily discovered.

Smart girl.

She waved and ran to him. "Where have you been?" she said, concern shadowing her face. "You were gone forever."

"Sorry. I lost track of the time. I meant to come back for you. But it was time well spent." He took her hand. "Come on. I have something to show you."

Peter led her along the ridge behind the tiny island until they stood before his creation. He proudly gestured toward it. "Well, what do you think?"

"Oh," she responded, unsure what to make of the bundle of trees he had assembled. "What is it?"

"What is it?" he echoed, sucking on a blistered hand, feeling a little bruised. "A raft, of course."

Jazmin smiled weakly. "Where did you get it?"

"I made it!"

"This fast?"

"Sure." He smiled again. "The trees were already down. I just trimmed them with my *machete*, and found some vines strong enough to bind them together."

"*Bueno*, Peter, *magnifico!* Does it float?"

"Of course, it will float. I just need your help getting it into the water."

The raft measured about twelve feet long from stem to stern and five feet wide. Lashed together by thin vines, it looked more like a row of sadly displaced logs than a raft. He could hardly blame Jazmin for questioning its seaworthiness.

Grunting and struggling, they inched the ungainly craft into the water, the tail end sinking deeper and deeper into the dark green murk. Jazmin looked more doubtful as they pushed, but once it was halfway into the murky water the raft's nose bobbed up like a proud pirate ship.

"It floats!" Jazmin screamed through the rain, unable to hide her delight.

"Did you doubt me? What did you think it would do? The question is will it carry us and our equipment?"

Peter held the raft steady, and urged Jazmin aboard their new vessel. It listed heavily to one side when she climbed on, sinking near the water line. But it rose again and Jazmin stood up, shaky at first, and then with new confidence she raised her arms in triumph.

"Peter, it works!"

He rolled his eyes.

"Come aboard, mate," she said, now possessive of his handiwork.

"Okay, but you'll have to sit down first." He crawled aboard, careful not to upend the raft, and it held steady, surprising even him.

Having secured a worthy vessel, and a suitable pole, they decided to break camp, anxious to put more distance between themselves and any possible pursuers.

Peter breathed another sigh of relief when he loaded the raft and found it would hold their gear without sinking below the water line. Peter checked his compass and poled the raft west. They were on their way again.

The fog thinned as they glided along a narrow passageway. Clear sailing alternated with periods of struggle as they slipped and prodded their way through the flooded valley. As they passed into rivers drowned out by the flooding, the current picked up, and an occasional crocodile surfaced to watch them pass. Sometimes the couple drifted only a few feet above the reptiles, their leathery silhouettes as long as the raft. Snakes also became an all-too-common sight. Green, yellow, red, black, striped, solid and banded, venomous and non-venomous, they swam or hung from the trees to escape the water. River otters often darted near the raft to investigate, curiosity gleaming in their deep brown eyes as they stared at the strange, two-legged creatures floating atop the water.

Life slowed to a crawl as they moved silently through tepid waters, the jungle regulating time in a world where man had no influence. The deeper into the unknown they wandered, the more focused they became. This was no man's land, and as a necessary step toward their survival, they had to learn the rules of the land. The distractions found in the city did not exist here. The jungle had its own diversions, but these served to sharpen the senses. Where the city jarred the psyche, scattering the mind, Peter found that the jungle honed his concentration, and raised his instincts and intuitions to an art.

An endless variety of smells emanated through the jungle, pungent and pleasant, acrid and decaying, from the putrid stench of an evergreen forest immersed in water to the sweet scents of flowering vines intertwined throughout the tangled canopy. Jazmin insisted on stopping frequently to pick plants whose fruits and flowers she could identify. Some of the flowers were sweet and edible, and others she intended to dry for tea.

As the days passed, their senses awakened. Their eyes become sharper, and their hearing more acute, as they grew accustomed to subtle changes in shape, texture, color and movement. Their hearing became tuned to nuances of bird and animal calls, and the different droning sounds of flying insects. Peter's body and mind transformed in response to the vibration of the land, the way Jazmin had when she began working with the Lacandón. They had to learn, and learn quickly, to survive.

There was no stopping, no starting a fire. They stayed wet, and totally exposed to the rain while on the water. One stayed on watch while the other slept under the rainfly. They filtered the cloudy floodwater through a shirt and purified it with iodine, eating fruits from the forest canopy, and wild vegetables dug from exposed "islands."

Twisting sinuously from sunrise to sunset, the waterways of the waterlogged forest served them well. But when the rains finally began to abate and the water started to recede, they agreed to abandon the raft and continue their journey on foot.

They poled the raft to a quagmire of broken tree branches, unloaded their gear, chopped the sturdy twine that held the logs together, and sent them floating away, careful not to leave any evidence of their departure. A fine mist fell as they turned toward the mountains in the west, where the valley's low-growth forest gave way to the taller deciduous trees of the highlands.

In the beginning, their only objective was to head in a westerly direction and get as far from the Special Forces as possible. Chan had said they would not be followed through the Forbidden Jungle. It was a logical assumption. Jazmin determined that if they continued to head due west, their path would take them to the city of Tehuantepec, a small native city on the Pacific coast. The local population would be sympathetic to their cause. From there, they could call U.S. authorities and apply pressure to the Mexican government to stop the genocide of the Lacandón people.

The pine, oak, and sweet gum trees of the higher regions were a welcome change from the tangled forest below. The rain let up, and the sun glimmered occasionally through gaps overhead, but the Forbidden Jungle continued to initiate them into its harsh realities. Fast-running rivers attempted to sweep them away, and the nearly impenetrable stands of trees seemed intent on suffocating them for the intrusion. Crocodiles, thorns, insects, poisonous snakes, and mosquito-infested swamps shared their hospitality. The swarms of insects that flew into their eyes, ears, and nostrils nearly drove them to the brink of insanity. The jungle seeped into their very pores, pressing itself upon them. They drank of it, ate of it, and drew it into their bodies with each breath.

Try as they might, they could neither escape the jungle's presence nor avoid its emotion.

CHAPTER 18

Two weeks had come and gone since Peter and Jazmin had entered the Forbidden Jungle. To the west lay a vertical world of jagged mountains and narrow, horizontal valleys of tangled forests and muddy swamps. How much longer would it take to navigate this wilderness?

Though he'd regained a sense of adventure since they'd bid Chan farewell, Peter still wanted to get the hell out of the jungle, out of México. He saw no practical way to save the Lacandón or their land while they navigated this bug-infested hell. And even though his body had responded well to the physical ordeal, growing harder and tougher each day, he was losing weight again.

Jazmin lay on the ground, her head propped against her backpack. Peter lowered himself onto a moss-covered rock a few feet away. He took off his stained and crumpled cap, now a rusty color, to wipe away the grime irritating his forehead. It hung in his hand like a wet dishrag. He swatted a mosquito with it, and rubbed one of the endless welts on his legs, recalling that of the thirty million species of life on Earth, twenty-nine million were insects. He figured there was a good likelihood he would meet them all before he and Jazmin found their way out of the jungle.

"Jazmin . . ." He looked behind him out of habit to see what, if anything, was coming. His intense emotion made him lower his voice.

"Guess I don't have to tell you that this is the meanest piece of real estate I've ever wandered into. It seems to take pleasure in destroying hearts as well as bodies." He shifted his weight off a sharp edge on the rock he was sitting on, keeping his eyes on the jungle. "And one message has become very clear. This land does not want us here . . ." He measured each word emphatically. "And if we don't find our way out soon, we're not going to make it. I'd rather die quickly in a gunfight with those soldiers, than slowly out here."

"Peter! Don't say that. Chan said we needed to go this way. So, he must have known we could do it."

"Yeah, just like he knew the soldiers were coming. But he informed us just a little too late for my comfort."

"He did the best he could. That I know."

"Yes, but is that good enough?"

"You need to have faith in Chan, Peter."

"No, you need to have faith in me. Chan isn't here anymore. It's up to me to get us out of this mess."

Jazmin stared at him as if his words stung. "Yes, I need to have faith in you too, Peter. But you need to stop talking about dying, and focus on getting us out of here."

He immediately regretted his anger. "Okay, fair enough."

"Then let's get going, *mi amor*. I don't like this area, and I don't think it likes me either." She stepped forward without giving him her usual caress.

Their waning determination took them to a clearing on a hillside where a large fallen tree lay. They made camp and spent the night. Rising early, more refreshed than the previous day, they readied their packs after eating their usual breakfast of fruit. Gray clouds piled high in the atmosphere, holding their moisture, and a hint of blue sky showed between them. While a day without rain should have brought a sense of comfort, they edged around the campsite like nervous animals.

"We haven't seen any signs of soldiers for weeks," Peter said. "The rains washed away all our tracks, so it's impossible anyone could track us. Chan said no one would follow us here, but I feel watched." He looked around uneasily. "I just can't put my finger on it."

He gazed with concern at Jazmin's soiled clothing, tangled hair, and worried expression. Her deeply tanned arms and legs were badly scratched and bruised, and he wondered how much longer she could bear the endless hiking. The fear of being hunted by man and beast, and the strong possibility they would never get home again had taken a toll on them.

Jazmin surveyed the area as she spoke. "Did we do something wrong? Is there something we have not thought of?"

"I don't know. Maybe," he said, searching his mind. "I had a strange dream last night."

"A dream?"

"I've had them almost every night since we left the village, though I don't always tell you about them." He gave a casual shrug. "They're generally more like nightmares. But this one was vivid." He scanned the area again. "And it keeps popping back into my head."

Jazmin's tone took on an intense seriousness. "What happened?"

Peter scratched his forehead, and made a swipe at an insect buzzing around his head. "It was nighttime in the dream, but I could see quite well even though it was pretty dark, like there was a full moon. I was moving through the jungle, looking for something. Finally, I came upon a small camp. A man sat on a fallen tree, looking at the night. A tent stood at one side of him. Somehow, I knew someone was sleeping inside the tent. The man had a rifle leaning up against the tree next to him. At first, I thought he was a black man, but when I got closer, I could see he had darkened his face like a commando." Peter looked up at her. "That's about it."

Jazmin stopped chewing her food and stared at him.

"I remember red hot coals still glowing where they made a fire," he added as an afterthought. "I could even smell it."

He looked to her for a response, but she simply looked at him with an air of disbelief.

"Peter," she whispered, her voice husky, urgent. "You know you are a dreamer. Chan showed you. He taught you to dream. You were seeing, Peter, *seeing*! Spirit showed you something important."

"I suppose you're right," he said, feeling more uncomfortable by the moment.

"Can you remember anything else?"

"Not really. It just seemed like an odd perspective."

"What do you mean?"

"I was very close to the ground, even when I was moving."

Unable to contain herself anymore, Jazmin stood and took Peter's head in her hands.

"A jaguar's eyesight is six times more powerful than a man's. You told me that. *Dios mío*, Peter, there wasn't a full moon. You were looking through the eyes of a jaguar. Chan told you the jaguar is your ally. You weren't crawling on the ground. You were stalking those men. The spirit of the jaguar was showing us the soldiers."

Peter jerked upright as if he'd been hit in the back. "How could I be so stupid? Come on. Let's get the hell out of here."

They collected their packs and hiked away from their camp as fast as they could manage. When they had covered several miles, they stopped to rest and think. It was impossible anyone could have tracked them, but their instincts suggested otherwise. They huddled uneasily in a thicket of trees, still sensing danger. As if verifying their fears, an unnatural hush settled over the forest, making the tension palpable.

Suddenly one of the saplings in front of them exploded, sending fragments of bark and splinters in every direction. Peter fell backward, taking Jazmin with him as he tumbled to the ground. Overhead, branches and leaves erupted into shreds in a shower of bullets, peppering them with debris as they hugged the ground. Bullets struck trees with a dull thud, bursting through their trunks, while others whistled overhead.

"I think my dream just caught up with us," Peter yelled, his voice hoarse. "Are you okay?" He glanced into Jazmin's terror-filled eyes.

"*Sí,*" she said.

"They're shooting from long range. They probably have scopes. Let's get out of here. Keep down below the brush."

Signaling Jazmin with a nod, they rose together, keeping low to the ground, packs in hand. They scrambled for the cover of a thickly wooded area, trees bursting around them. Bullets whizzed by like angry bees, some kicking up dirt at their feet, others ricocheting off rocks and trees. Reaching the shadows of an old-growth forest, they sprinted toward a giant evergreen and threw themselves behind it.

"Are you okay?" Peter asked again between breaths.

"I think so."

"Well, our intuition was right, if not a little late." His breath came in spurts. "Sorry, I should have discussed my dreams sooner . . . How the hell did they find us? It doesn't make sense. They must have spotted us by plane through a break in the clouds and parachuted in."

"We haven't heard any planes," Jazmin argued. "If we did not hear them, they couldn't have seen us down here."

"I know. I can't figure it out." The hair on his arms rose as he looked around for hidden eyes.

"What are we going to do, Peter?"

"Run. We can't stand them off. And they obviously aren't interested in getting too close now that they know I have a gun. But we don't have a chance in a shoot-out with them. We'll have to run for it, but where?"

"Chan always told me to turn to the trees at times of uncertainty," Jazmin said. "I'm feeling much uncertainty now."

Peter looked at her in disbelief, and slid the action back on his gun to chamber a round. More bullets sang through the brush, some hitting the large tree they hid behind with a dull smack. "Are you sure this is a good time for a meditation?"

Jazmin ignored him and stayed silent.

"At least their bullets can't penetrate this old tree," he added. His only thought was to get as far away from those snipers as he could. Even if he could lure them in close, he wouldn't stand a chance against men with rifles. Besides, these were trained soldiers, probably the very best the Mexican army could produce.

The valley below would provide the fastest passage, but its sparse vegetation offered little cover. Going down there didn't appear to be an option. Only the higher elevations offered protection and a chance to escape.

Jazmin closed her eyes and pressed her forehead against the trunk of the large old evergreen while he watched and waited.

Peter was tempted to interrupt her after the rifle fire stopped. His instincts told him to run. The snipers must be on the move, coming in closer. Seconds turned into minutes as he listened and watched. The jungle was quiet too, as if listening. If the soldiers were moving, they did so silently. Growing impatient, he turned to hurry Jazmin. But she was already standing, facing him with a calm that seemed out of place.

"Come on." He reached out for her hand. "We have to get out of here."

She hesitated. "We need to go down into the valley and cross the marshlands."

"That's crazy. We'll be exposed to their rifles down there. They're accurate to several hundred yards. Besides, we might get trapped in the swamps."

"Peter, that's what the tree spirit told me to do."

He recognized the look of determination on her face. There was no time for argument.

They took off, darting from tree to tree. On a ridge they spooked a coyote from its den—it stared at them for a moment, then disappeared into the forest. Working their way down a craggy ravine leading to the valley floor, they quickly surveyed the area. Peter's only thought was to get out of rifle range, as far away from the snipers as possible. He looked around to gauge the contours of the land to see how it lay for a defensive retreat. He decided he'd been right. It was hopeless. Just as he feared, the thinly wooded valley floor consisted of a marshy mangrove swamp on the verge of drying up. It offered little cover.

He pointed the way and they sprinted across the vast expanse of land a hundred yards before stopping in a grove of thin trees. They caught their breath, casting glances behind them. The only thing he saw was a mud turtle, which had stuck its head up out of the muck to see what was running by.

"Do you see them?" Jazmin asked.

"No. Maybe they didn't see us come down that ridge. Let's hope not, because this ground is getting softer. We can't run through this stuff."

Just then, rifle shots whistled through the air and hit the ground around them.

Running on adrenaline across the uncertain terrain, their footing became less stable with each stride. The ground began to feel less like terra firma and more like an arboreal sponge waiting to suck them up. Peter cursed himself for letting Jazmin talk him into dropping into the valley. There was no place to hide, and no defensive position from which to stand and fight. He sprinted a few paces ahead of her, scanning the area for a suitable shelter. The ground suddenly gave way, sending him chest deep into a liquid quagmire.

He yelled in a panic as he struggled to remove his pack. "Stop, Jazmin—quicksand!"

She looked at him, obviously trying to comprehend the situation.

He was sure it looked like the earth had sprung to life and was swallowing him up.

"Here, take my pack," he pleaded, tossing it toward her. "Find a large branch…" He panted as he sunk up to his neck. "Something I can grab onto." His eyes widened with terror as he appealed to her for help.

Jazmin reached out for the pack, grabbed it, then retreated a few yards from the uncertain ground.

"Now find a branch. Quick!"

She looked frantically around, ran a few paces toward some brush, hesitated, and started back toward Peter, holding only a twig.

His face flushed and veins stood out in his neck. "Find a branch—a big branch," he yelled, groping for the Spanish word. His voice shook with fear and fury. "Something big . . . *grande* . . . *madera*. Something big enough to hold me!"

Jazmin froze, more confused than ever, then she burst into tears. Panic overwhelmed Peter as he watched her fall apart. He was halfway up his neck in quicksand when Jazmin threw herself on the soft ground. Clutching handfuls of wet earth, she began crawling toward him. His hopes for survival vanished as she inched her way along the uncertain surface, the ridiculous twig clenched in her teeth. Peter accepted his fate with a deep breath. If the quicksand didn't kill him, the soldiers surely would. There was no point in struggling now.

"They're telling me to give you this," Jazmin sobbed.

His heart went out to her. When she came close enough, she tossed her small offering to him. Now up to his chin in quicksand, his arms scrunched high around his head, Peter stretched out for it, keeping his gaze on her tear-filled eyes.

"I love you," he said, thinking it was the last thing he would ever say to her.

About to go under, he stopped struggling. He would surrender to the hopeless situation with dignity. Her hand touched his and he took the stick without looking at it, still holding his gaze on her. She was the last thing he ever wanted to see.

But Jazmin's face took on a new resolve. "Peter," she said softly, but with urgency. "I know what this is now. You will be able to breathe through this reed."

Peter looked at the object in his hand for the first time. What he had mistaken for a twig was actually a hollow reed an inch in diameter, and about fifteen inches in length. His heart surged with new hope.

"You're right. Hide yourself," he said. "When you're sure the soldiers are gone, drag a fallen tree branch over to me and help pull me out. Go!" Jazmin's eyes widened with a renewed hope as she wriggled back to solid ground. As soon as she disappeared into a thicket of young saplings, he saw another movement out of the corner of his eye.

Three men in black uniforms wearing bandoliers of ammunition slung over their shoulders entered the clearing, rifles pointing forward. Their heads turned rapidly from side to side. Moving fast, the soldiers headed straight toward him. Peter clamped the reed tightly in his mouth and tilted his head back as the insidious mud completely engulfed him. His world turned black and silent.

He instinctively struggled to keep his head up at first, then gave into the mud. When he realized he could actually breathe through the reed, he calmed down enough to slow his racing heart. As he continued to sink, fear and helplessness overcame his fragile composure, and he began to struggle toward the surface again. He heard nothing. No footsteps, no gunfire, no voices, only the sickening silence. Suddenly his left foot touched something, then his right. Firm ground. His head was just inches below the surface and he had stopped sinking. He could still breathe. Now, if only he could deal with his urge to panic.

Concentrate, he told himself. Focus on breathing smoothly.

Long tortuous minutes rolled by, with the hollow reed the only thing keeping him alive. A claustrophobic panic returned to overcome him again as the seconds turned to minutes and the minutes to eternity. Keep breathing, he told himself. Focus. Don't panic. He heard nothing. No footsteps, no gunfire, no voices, only a sickening silence.

Standing on the tips of his toes in a world devoid of light and sound, he prayed for Jazmin and for himself. If she died, he would die too. It was as simple as that. He would die where no one would ever find him. And Jazmin would have little chance of survival without him. She couldn't fend off the soldiers, and she wasn't efficient with the *machete*. They needed each other to stay alive.

As the minutes rolled by, the questions came at him harder. *Am I alone? If she's alive, will she be able to pull me out of this hell? How long can I last?*

The quicksand pressed in on his ears, nostrils, and chest. Panic hit him again. He started to struggle. Chan's words washed over him and he held onto them. "If you die, the jungle will die too."

Help me, he heard himself say. He focused on the sound of his breath passing in and out of his body through the hollow reed.

He stood in that smothering place for what seemed an eternity.

Then he detected a movement. Something above him. A hand was groping for his head. In a burst of adrenaline, he pushed up with all his strength, felt his hands come out of the muck. He grabbed someone's hand and struggled to bring his head to the surface. At first, the pressure of the mud was too strong. Then he felt a stick wedging in beside him, and the mud released him a little. He inched his way upward.

Slapping his hand around on the surface, he found a large branch above him. He grabbed it for his very life, and with a heave he felt in his gut, he pushed his head out of the thick mud. Spitting the reed from his mouth, he pulled a full breath of air into his lungs. Anxious hands wiped his eyes clean. Expecting to see the barrel of a gun, Peter opened his eyes. Instead of an angry soldier, his eyes took in the most beautiful sight, one he would remember always. Jazmin lay prone across the large branch he grasped, looking directly into his eyes.

They clung to one another, heads touching, in a moment where they could summon no more strength. Unable to speak after the strain of their combined effort, they simply looked into one another's eyes.

"What happened?" Peter finally whispered. He fought for air with the pressure of the quicksand still pressing against his chest. "Where are the soldiers?"

"The jungle took them," she said, trembling. Tears streamed down her cheeks. "They ran into the quicksand. They cried out for help, but I could not help them. It happened so fast. It was terrible."

Glancing around, he saw a black beret on the quicksand just a dozen feet away, its fierce image of a black jaguar slowly sinking into the dark, putrefying mud.

CHAPTER 19

Blue sky occasionally shone through the formless gray cloud cover, promising a change in the dreary weather. Exhausted to the limits of their endurance, Peter and Jazmin stopped when they found a small creek. They edged forward to the water, alert to any sights and sounds betraying the peaceful scene, then dropped their packs. The water was sweet and clear, and they drank with abandon.

They followed the familiar sound of a splashing waterfall to an emerald green pool that reflected the forest canopy, large enough for both to bathe in. Without speaking, they crawled into the refreshing water in their soiled clothes, dunking their heads under to rinse their hair clean of the swamp's muddy slime. They soaked the stench of sweat and quicksand away, as well as the day's frightening memories. Lying motionless in the shallow pool, they allowed the cool water to soothe and heal them.

In a gentle dance that played to the wind's music, a multitude of leaves from various trees of the canopy rained down around them. Some of the leaves twirled frantically as though they tried to catch and hold the wind, while others swung in wide, easy arcs toward the ground.

"The trees are silent," Jazmin said in a soft voice. "As if they have withdrawn, and want to be alone. They are not sorrowful, just quiet."

Peter felt it too. The silence was restful and complete. As he lay submerged in the water, he caught himself wondering if the trees knew of the morning's drama. He'd become a disciple of the trees! No longer did he question the reality of their consciousness. The jungle had transformed him, converted him to its ways. He searched in vain for the old Peter, his old attitudes, but they had faded away. The danger Chan had spoken of was real. The spirits of the jungle had whispered their wisdom in Jazmin's ear. Without a doubt, the trees had saved their lives. And the spirit of the jaguar was undeniably inside of him now. This was not just some crazy shaman's reality, but his own.

He thought about how the soldiers had tracked the two of them under such impossible conditions. The jaguar's image wouldn't leave his mind, nor would what Chan had said about *Na-Bolom*. The consciousness in the House of the Jaguar had been reawakened in him. And in some inexplicable way, the soldiers were connected to the jaguar, somehow emerging from a dark Maya past. They had followed him through the eyes of the jaguar. There was no other way they could have tracked them through the swamps. It had to be the jaguar.

Darkened clouds drifted by, but no rain fell. Unseen birds chirped and screeched, rejoicing around the meadow. The primrose vines' tubular-shaped flowers cascaded down the rocks above them in a river of violet.

After soaking their soiled clothing for several hours, Jazmin beat the shorts and shirts on a smooth stone at the water's edge, then hung them on the branches of nearby trees. She lay down on a large flat rock to drift away with the clouds. With no rain to hinder the process, they would have clean, dry clothes the following day. Peter pitched the tent, then returned to the creek, letting the water carry away his physical and emotional impurities, as Chan had taught him. Neither one of them spoke.

Intuition told them there were no more soldiers chasing them, at least for the moment. The day had given them some difficult lessons. From now on, they would pay attention to their inner voices. The price of ignoring them was too high. And Peter vowed never to disregard his dreams again.

Leaving the water, he walked to where Jazmin lay. Kneeling at her side, he stroked her hair and studied her face.

"Jazmin, I know you would have saved those men if it were possible." She did not respond. It was too soon to talk. She would discuss it when she was ready. He lay down next to her, and stroked her gently until he fell asleep.

Peter awoke to an overcast sky. Shivering, he retrieved dry clothes from their packs, and woke Jazmin. They organized their equipment and finished setting up camp. When twilight descended, they ate a quick meal of fruit and retired to the tent, still too exhausted to talk. They curled up in each other's arms, and immediately fell asleep.

Peter awoke with a sudden jerk in the middle of the night. Jazmin was trembling. He tightened his arm around her as disturbing convulsions of grief worked their way through her body. She refused to speak, even to look at him. He stroked her hair until she quieted and fell asleep. He fell into a dreamless sleep, only to be awakened again by her sobs. Despite a difficult night, they both managed to get some rest by the time daylight returned.

Peter opened his eyes to bird calls, and to the silhouette of an ant brigade moving across the illumined tent's exterior. He watched sleepily for several minutes before he realized their significance. Jazmin lay asleep, with her back turned toward him. He braced himself on an elbow to peer at her face, still puffy and tense from crying. He unzipped the door of the tent and gazed upward, smiling. White cotton-ball clouds stretched to the horizon, highlighting an azure sky.

Jazmin stirred, then looked up at him, brushing tangled hair from her scratched and weathered face. She motioned him back to her.

"The sun is shining," he said as they held each other.

"Ah, *sí, mi amor*. The jungle is at peace with us this day."

I think you're right. Tell you what," Peter said. "Let's have a hot meal and a cup of your favorite tea."

"Really?" Jazmin's face brightened.

"Sure. Why not? There's no danger now. We'll build a fire, and finish drying our clothes and gear."

"*Sí, sí*, okay," she agreed.

The jungle came alive with sound as he collected wood and built a fire. Jazmin prepared her favorite tea to the harmonies of a troop of monkeys.

"It's a mixture Chan taught me," she said, as she handed Peter his cup. "He said it relieves stress."

Peter sniffed the pungent tea, and laughed. "It's about time we had some, then. Leave it to Chan to have the perfect remedy for every situation."

They raised their cups in a toast. "To life," Peter said. "I feel a new appreciation for it. We overcame death yesterday."

Jazmin touched her tin cup to his, but remained silent for a few minutes. "It feels funny to say this after all we have been through these past weeks," she murmured. "I don't know if I could ever leave the jungle for long again. It's become so much a part of me. Or I've become a part of it."

Peter nearly choked on his tea, and stared at her with his mouth open. Rather than look at him, Jazmin studied her cup as if it were a crystal ball. "It's difficult for me to express my feelings about this, Peter, but in the deepest sense I feel that if the jungle dies, I'll die too."

"Chan said much the same thing."

"I know we need to find our way out of this place. But the Lacandón forest is wonderful. When we went to Chan's sacred forest, I sat against one of the huge trees, praying for guidance. I felt the desire to focus my attention on a tree in front of me. I was looking at this particular tree when an indescribable sense of peace and calm enveloped me. That peace has stayed with me ever since." Jazmin raised her eyes and looked intently into his face to make sure he was listening.

He nodded slowly. "Strange, isn't it? I felt it too."

"But it wasn't just an emotion. I closed my eyes, and when I opened them again, there was an odd movement running up and down the tree, like ripples of water reflecting sunlight. I was looking into another world. As I watched the light and movement around the tree, I began to sense its life force moving through me. At that same moment I lost all connection to my body and merged with the tree's energy . . . Is this making any sense to you?"

"I think I have an idea what you felt."

"I watched the light for some time. Then another movement caught my attention, but I turned too quickly, and it disappeared." Jazmin shrugged, eyes wide with the surprise she had felt that day. "I think I frightened it. After a few seconds, I saw a similar movement, only in a different spot. This time I turned my head slowly in the direction of the movement, and the image stayed. I found myself gazing at a wispy, transparent form emerging from one of the trees. Peter, it wasn't just energy emanating from the tree," she exclaimed. "This was an entity, a conscious being, and it was looking at me."

Peter reflected on her story, remembering *his* experience with the trees and later with the clouds.

"It looked like fog," Jazmin continued, "and it appeared to be curious about me. Then I noticed other entities observing me from a greater distance. I felt no fear of them, only the same curiosity they showed me. There was a certain naiveté about them, innocence, but also a deep wisdom. They were timid, Peter. When I looked at them directly, they would go back in the trees and hide. But ever since that day I've heard their voices."

"Like yesterday?"

"Yes. Do you think I'm crazy?"

"Of course." He smiled. "That goes without saying. Remember how afraid I was for my sanity after my first experience?" He pushed back his hat and rubbed his face, embarrassed by the memory. "It was just too weird and shocking at first, but now..."

He shook his head. "As far as those little voices in your head go..." He leaned forward to emphasize his words. "I don't know where they come from. Maybe it's the trees speaking to you, maybe something else. All I know is those little voices you heard yesterday saved our butts. So, any time a little voice wants to talk to you, that's just fine with me."

Jazmin grinned, and pulled his cap down over his eyes.

Smoke from the campfire swirled around them, repelling flying insects. The early morning dew sparkled like diamonds on the meadow's tall grass, and a flock of slender black birds with flowing yellow tails flew overhead. Peter brought them to Jazmin's attention, and they watched until the brilliant birds vanished from sight. They relished their first hot meal in weeks—fried fruit and seeds—and when their stomachs were full, they leaned against a log and basked in the sun while the gentle breezes and heat from the fire dried their clothes.

Peter found his thoughts turning back to serious issues. "Who is behind all this?"

Jazmin furrowed her brow and stared into the fire. "Mexican Special Forces. You know that."

"I'm still stunned that the Mexican government actually sent Special Forces to assassinate us. But *who* exactly would order this?"

Jazmin's face flushed with anger. "I have been suspicious of the government all along, but I never thought they would go this far."

"Someone high up in the Mexican government must have their hand in the logging company's pockets," he mused.

The photo of President José Aguilar in the México City newspaper came to mind once more. *El Presidénte.* It seemed the man's dark shadow loomed over them. He must be involved. The soldiers had tracked them through the eyes of the jaguar. It was simple, yet untenable, and the only explanation that made any sense. Peter shook his head in wonder. He was way too new to this game.

After breakfast, they returned to the creek to bathe, allowing the water and the rays of sun penetrating the canopy to do their healing work.

"The trees here are wonderful." Jazmin stood up, and shook water off the curves of her sleek, tan body. Aroused, Peter admired every inch and longed to make love to her. But a dark oppressive energy hung over him, working on his emotions. At first, he thought the obstacle was the trauma of the jaguar attack and his injuries. Then, the pressures brought on by the Special Forces' pursuit. Now he knew there was something else.

Jazmin slipped back into her khaki shorts and green blouse, dry from the morning sun. His longing stare turned to frustration, and he looked away. She was just as alluring with her clothes on. She gathered up their clothes, folded them carefully, and placed them with precision into their packs. Peter spent the afternoon cleaning his gun and equipment, sharpening the *machete*, and hunting. He hadn't eaten meat in weeks and he longed for it, but he still didn't dare to fire his gun. He soon returned empty-handed. Jazmin scoured the area for food they could eat on the run.

The next morning, before the sun greeted the eastern horizon, they filled their gourds and canteens with the healing waters of the creek, and continued westward. Black vultures with silver-edged wings wheeled overhead. Heavy with moisture, the air began to cool as they moved through the thickening forest.

The longer they stayed in the jungle, the more they learned of its secrets, and the sharper their senses became. Though their diet was spartan, they became stronger, their bodies finely tuned. Rather than wearing them down, the jungle now served to keep them strong. While each day presented challenges, they kept their minds sharp and bodies alert. Each movement was carefully considered, each step thoughtfully planted. They could ill afford a serious injury, for even a small cut might become inflamed with a life-threatening infection.

Life had become a meditation on survival.

CHAPTER 20

Peter watched with fascination as a small flock of snowy egrets moved in a thin white line above the valley like a school of fish in a crystal-clear ocean. The morning had dawned bright and clear, but the valley below lay in sheets of white haze not yet burned off by the sun. Everything appeared normal, save for the valley's jagged hills protruding through the haze. Their symmetry was uncharacteristic of any they had seen before. Small and uniform, the hills seemed at odds with the terrain, lying in the lower areas of the valley where the runoff would be greatest. Because anything new or unusual was cause for concern, they studied the terrain carefully.

They ate the oily nuts of the coquito palm and considered their options while resting on the crest of a rugged mountain range where they had spent the night.

"Are you getting used to their oily taste?" Jazmin asked.

He took his eyes off the valley and nodded, but breakfast wasn't the thing occupying his thoughts.

The jaguar haunted his dreams with regularity, pacing back and forth before him. He always awoke at the same moment in the dream—when the large cat stopped its restless pacing and turned its fiery gaze on him. He tired of waking up in the middle of the night, sweat beading up on his face. This morning his dream was even more vivid than ever. The big cat had seemed even more agitated. "There's something strange about this area," Peter said, in a subdued voice. "I can feel it."

Jazmin stopped chewing, concerned by his statement, and even more concerned by his tone. "What is the matter, Peter?"

"I don't know exactly, but I have a bad feeling about this valley. The darkness I feel here is stronger than ever."

"I have a bad feeling about this place too," she said, scooting closer to him. "But I don't know why."

He placed an arm around her waist. "I wish we had more to go on than two bad feelings."

"What do you think? Is this valley making us feel this way?"

Peter took his sweat-stained cap off his head and flipped the moisture from his brow with one finger, still searching the shadows below. "It could be anything: a rabid animal, malaria mosquitoes, a dangerous cliff, quicksand . . ."

She sighed. "Oh, please, Spirit, not quicksand again."

"I don't think they're going to show us that trick again, honey." He kissed her gently on the top of her head. "But something's bothering me. Chan sent us here for a reason, and I don't think it was simply to evade the soldiers. Say . . ." For the first time during their travels through the Forbidden Forest, Peter heard a subtle, unexplainable beat, like that of a drum. He sat up sharply as the drumbeat raised in volume. "Do you hear that?"

"No, what?" she asked, startled by the sudden alarm in his voice. "What is it? What do you hear?"

"I just have the strange impression that I hear something. He listened again. "Like distant drumming."

Jazmin closed her eyes and listened, barely breathing. Several minutes passed before she turned to him and shook her head. She hadn't heard it. The sound faded, and he stood and listened more carefully. Again, he recognized the barely discernible beat of a drum.

"There it is again. Don't you hear it?"

"I don't hear anything. And you are scaring me." She tightened her lips and added in an accusing voice, "Just how long have you been hearing this sound?"

"I don't really know. The sound is so vague that I wasn't sure I was really hearing anything."

Jazmin looked at him through narrowed eyes. "We agreed to share our intuitive feelings and experiences." She bit her lip and glared at him before glancing away.

They had. This definitely fell into that category. "I'm sorry. It was almost subconscious."

Jazmin stirred uneasily. "I guess I've been holding back too."

He raised his eyebrows, his lips rounded in a perfect circle. "Oh?"

"Yes. See that large fern-like tree over there?"

He looked at her pointed finger, then at the plant.

"That's a sacred reed-mace," she explained. "It's a living fossil that dates back to the Mesozoic era. It shouldn't be here. I think I've seen several other plants from that same era . . . they're not supposed to exist anymore either. Not for millions of years—this area is covered with plants that are tens of millions of years old! If only I had my lab . . ."

Peter turned his back to her and looked out across the valley. "I'm not sure I want to stick around that long." He turned toward her again, his face grim. "So why didn't you say something to me before?"

"I guess I couldn't work up so much enthusiasm for it at the time."

Peter studied her face for a moment, and knew that wasn't the entire reason. He pulled his compass from a pocket at the front of his pack.

"I don't like it, either. We're in for something strange. Spirit is calling us once again."

"I don't know if I'm ready for another challenge," Jazmin complained.

He pocketed the compass and pointed past the hills into the valley, then touched his forefinger on a point on the map. "This valley gives us the quickest access to the west, and to a town of any size. The weather's in our favor. The lowlands are drying up, and there's no storm on the horizon."

He gazed at the landscape, then at his blistered hands, relishing the opportunity to rest them. The terrain sloped gently into the valley and the dense canopy of mature trees suggested moderate to light underbrush. That meant easy hiking, with little need for a *machete*.

Jazmin winced. "I'm sorry, *amorcito*. I'm confused. This place scares me, but I'm scared to leave it, too."

He ran a hand through his hair. "Now I'm getting butterflies in my gut. I don't know what to think."

"Peter, we should sit and wait for a sign that will set our minds at ease."

"Okay. We wait."

The sun came up over the odd hills, comforting and warming them while they waited for a sign.

After sitting awhile, Peter looked at Jazmin and raised his eyebrows.

Jazmin shrugged. "I'm not getting anything."

"I didn't get anything either. I don't trust this place, but I think we should head through this valley as quickly as possible."

He lifted his pack onto his shoulders. "Let's get this over with."

"Peter," she protested.

He turned and walked away. She kicked at a tree, threw her hands up, and followed. The piercing call of a hawk sliced through the canopy. She looked up at a large red hawk circling directly overhead and repeated something Chan had said: "Hawk is a hunter. It flies between the worlds. When it circles above you, it offers you its keen eyes. Stay watchful. It will help you see into this world, and into the world of Spirit."

Peter stopped for a moment and turned around to face Jazmin. "It won't take us more than half a day to cross the valley floor if we don't stop to rest and eat. We'll be on the other side by dark."

"Okay, but stay alert, and tell me if you feel anything unusual."

They negotiated the slope, picking their way through brush and boulders. Soon they found an animal trail and followed it, watchful for any clues that might explain away their apprehension. The mood of the land seemed subdued. Within an hour, they were deep within the darkened forest of the valley. As Peter expected, the going was easy, and he kept his *machete* sheathed.

"Odd, aren't they?" Jazmin said as they approached the first of the series of small hills they had studied from the ridge.

They stopped to wait for an impression. Still nothing. But as they came closer, the reason for the strange shapes became obvious. Comprised of rock overgrown with vegetation, the hills reached up to a height of four to six stories and tiered back symmetrically, forming four equal sides.

"Pyramids," she said, looking up at an imposing edifice.

"I guess that explains some things." He gazed around cautiously and pointed ahead of them. "Looks like there are more structures down this corridor. Let's have a look around."

"Okay," she whispered. "But be careful. We don't know what this is, and I still have a bad feeling about it."

He felt a heaviness pressing in on him as they continued down the worn cobblestone road that appeared to be a major corridor into the city.

The scene before them would have inspired jubilation under other circumstances, but they viewed it now with grim fascination. The structures they passed appeared solemn in their abandonment. As if holding their collective breath, the ruins seemed to wait patiently for man's exiled memories to rekindle their grand expression. There was something disturbing in their stillness, something dark and familiar. Jazmin took his arm, and held him close.

Peter wondered what name they had given this city. Whatever it was, it had long been placed among the names of many forgotten things, forever erased from memory. As they continued along the silent walkways, a name crept into his mind and body, a name Peter did not want to hear. It bumped around his subconscious mind with an urgency hard to ignore, harder still to accept. For the moment, he pushed away the emotion and the name.

They came upon more buildings rising high into the forest canopy. A series of tall stone steps led to a rock wall that paralleled the cobblestone corridor. They climbed up and walked along it to better view the area. Intimidating deities of serpents and jaguars, carved into rain-weathered stone, stood out along the many walls and structures, intertwined with the tangled roots and vines of the jungle. The city stood nearly intact, as if indifferent to the passage of time.

Farther down the corridor, several monoliths lined the pathway. Some stood erect, while others leaned precariously to one side. The towering sculptures rose ten feet above the ground, intricately carved with images of animal deities, human figures, and ancient inscriptions.

Peter brushed a hand across the deeply carved details of one of the sculptures. "These giant stone stelae can tell us volumes about the people who lived here. There's a story on each one of these slabs."

"Terrible stories," Jazmin added.

Peter turned and looked at her. He studied her ashen face, wondering what dark memories she felt. "We've discovered an entire Maya city." He tried to sound excited.

"It's so beautiful," Jazmin said. "So frightening. These people must have had terrible nightmares."

"I'm afraid we would too if we stayed the night."

She turned to face him, her face clouding up. "Surely we will not spend the night *here*?"

"That's not in my plans, but I'd like to have a better look around before we leave."

She stared at him, uncertain. "Just be careful, Peter."

They wandered carefully through the ancient grounds to a grand courtyard, scanning everything around them. Half the size of a football field, its perimeter was walled on all four sides. He picked a place to rest, removed his backpack, and set it down on the overgrown plaza floor. Kneeling to adjust one of the shoulder harnesses cutting into his arm, he caught a fleeting image.

He removed his cap, wiped his eyes with the soiled sleeve of his shirt, and then looked again at the cracked and tarnished steps and serpentine walls that wavered uncertainly around the large plaza. Incongruous, the moment had passed quickly, but for a millisecond, he thought he saw the plaza as it might have looked in its prime.

Freshly whitewashed walls with terraced gardens had meandered around the well-manicured plaza. In that fleeting moment, the grounds had been flat and even, with a few well-placed trees along its perimeter. And on the side where they now stood, the ground was paved with white rock that provided a smooth surface on which to walk.

He glanced at Jazmin, wondering if she had noticed anything, but she had stopped to study a giant fern tree nearby. He removed his *machete* from its sheath and dug into the soft earth. An inch or two down, he hit something hard. He cleared away some of the grassy soil, and revealed a smooth rock floor of tarnished white rock, the same rock he'd seen a moment ago in his vision.

"My God," he whispered to himself. A shudder registered through his body. He stood to survey the area again, taking several deep breaths to calm his racing heart.

"Are you okay?" Jazmin asked, walking over to him. "You look pale."

"Sure, I just got a little chill is all."

"A little chill?" She wiped the sweat from her forehead with the back of her hand. "It is very warm to be having chills, no?"

"I guess."

"Peter, this city is giving me more than chills. It is scaring me. Even the trees here are silent and dark. I think we need to keep moving."

"Well, I'm not going to let some dilapidated pile of rubble scare me off," Peter stated with a bravado that sounded foolish.

He helped Jazmin take her pack off and looked into her eyes, which sparkled in the midday light despite her fear. He extended his arms to her.

"Let's dance," he said, hoping to push their fears away.

"Dance?" she asked, her jaw hanging slack. "Here?"

"Yes. It's a dance floor."

"A dance floor?"

"Yes. I think so. So, let's dance."

"Right now?"

"It's the only time there is. Come on. You told me you liked dancing. How about a two-step? Do you remember it?"

"*Sí.*" She relented, offering him a tentative hand, looking more worried than pleased.

The grounds were still surprisingly level as they moved over the grassy surface of the courtyard that once gleamed white with stone. They glided around, turning and spinning, and Jazmin's frown soon transformed to a radiant smile.

They fell into a comfortable rhythm, and soon heard their own laughter echoing across the courtyard. Peter found himself humming a beautiful tune. Like a waltz, simple, yet moving.

"Where do you know that song from?" Jazmin asked. "It sounds familiar."

Peter thought for a moment before answering. "I don't know. I don't remember ever hearing it."

As he hummed his tune, he began to realize that he sang to the sound of strange instruments that had inexplicably come alive in his mind. The haunting sounds were like nothing he had ever heard before.

Primitive yet delicate, the music pulled him deeper into its dreamy world. He glanced down at the grounds of the courtyard and saw a finely cut floor of polished rock once again. Blinking hard, he looked up at another surprise. They were not alone.

The courtyard was filled with hundreds of people dancing to the music's rhythm. They wore brightly colored tunics and knee-length skirts, necklaces and earrings of shell, gold, and green jade that sparkled in the evening's torchlight. They seemed unaware of him and Jazmin, or perhaps they were simply preoccupied with themselves.

He wondered if Jazmin could see them too, and looked down to whisper to her. But another beautiful native woman with jet-black hair and high cheekbones stood before him, her arms entwined in his. Her complexion was dark, her skin silky smooth, and her long black hair intricately woven with pink seashells and multicolored beads. Behind one ear lay a violet bougainvillea flower. With a shy smile, she glanced up at him, her eyes a familiar deep brown, and then quickly looked away.

In an instant, the image was gone, the spell broken. Peter stopped dead in his tracks. He looked at Jazmin's familiar face. Though one face had faded into the other, the two women's eyes were the same. He stared at her uncertainly.

Jazmin dropped her hands and stood back to study his face. "What's happening, Peter? What is wrong? Are you okay?"

"I'm fine." He rubbed his face. "Just dizzy."

They walked to one of the rock benches that still lined the courtyard walls and sat. Peter tried to make sense of the visions. Jazmin continued to study him, her face filled with concern.

"This city needs to be left alone. I don't think we can dance away this darkness." She squeezed his hand. "But I feel gratitude for your effort."

"You're probably right," he said. "This place is bringing up a lot of emotion for me. We'd better get out of here."

"That is fine with me."

They made their way across the grounds and into a smaller courtyard, passing through a dome-shaped entrance. Something odd arose on the far side of the courtyard. Like a delicate translucent curtain, it cast a pale white sheen against the trees. As they edged forward, the series of hazy, cloud-like veils floating in the trees became clearer.

"Spider webs," Peter said.

The webs stopped them in their tracks. The hauntingly beautiful designs rose twenty feet into the trees' branches, spanning the far end of courtyard. Like giant cones, the webs rose from a point on the ground, and increased in diameter until they attached themselves high in the branches fifteen to twenty feet up. Transfixed by the strange shapes, they stared until they remembered to look up into the dark recesses of the trees for the webs' residents.

Peter approached them, thumbed one of the translucent white webs and jumped back as the webs erupted with hundreds of scurrying black and white spiders. Jazmin screamed.

"I'll take this as our invitation to leave," he said. Peter noticed a narrow trail through the cone-shaped spires. He squeezed Jazmin's hand and walked a short way in, noting a courtyard wall with a gateway not far away.

"The shortest way out is only another twenty or thirty paces from here, through that gate." He motioned toward the opening in the courtyard wall. "The webs are spaced a few feet apart at the bottom. If we move slowly, I think we can walk around them instead of going back through the courtyard."

Jazmin folded her arms across her chest, and cast him an uncertain look. "I feel like a long walk. I have heard of these spiders. These are Funnel Web spiders, and they are very poisonous, no?"

"I think that's an Australian spider you're thinking of."

"*Sí*. Maybe you are right. I hope so."

"Yeah, me too. Come on," Peter said, suddenly impatient. "We'll walk right under them, and they won't even know we're here."

Jazmin hesitated. "Okay. But I don't like it."

They started through the milky white maze of webs, almost tiptoeing, their eyes cast upward. The channel was easily maneuvered at first, but the closer they came to the gate the narrower their path and the denser the webs became. They edged sideways until the sticky white webs narrowed to a gap too small to walk through.

"I think it is time to turn around," Jazmin whispered.

"The passageway through the wall is only a couple of yards in front of us." He slowly drew his *machete*.

"I'm not sure that's a good idea, Peter."

"Don't worry. I sharpened the *machete* this morning. The blade will sever the bottom of the webs and leave the spiders high in the trees wondering what happened."

Jazmin grimaced. "Oh, Peter."

He raised the two-foot-long blade to shoulder height, and braced himself. "Get ready to run."

Swinging the *machete* through the webs directly in front of them, he lurched forward into the vacant space with Jazmin hanging on to his free arm. But the webs proved sticky and clung tenaciously to the blade. The *machete* pulled sharply on the webs and the tree branches shook violently over their heads. Before he could make a second pass with the blade, a shower of spiders rained upon them.

He swore and she screamed. They feverishly swatted at the spiders while they ran for the gate, *machete* flying. With every slash of the blade, a new shower of hairy vermin fell upon them. The large spiders made their way into their short-sleeved shirts, shorts, and sandals. He burst through the gateway in a blur of steel, spiders, and webs, and tore his clothes off, all the while batting at the host of angry spiders. Peter threw the *machete* down to use both hands, gyrating around in a circle and swiping spiders off. Suddenly he felt a sharp pain at his heel and winced. The back of his foot was covered in blood. He had bumped into the sharp blade of the long knife. Grabbing his foot with one hand, he continued swatting spiders with the other, while Jazmin danced about wildly trying to shake the spiders out of her hair.

Finally freeing herself of spiders, Jazmin ran to Peter and knocked the last of the spiders off him. They stood for a moment in a daze, panting as the spiders scurried away. Jazmin helped him to a low wall where they sat and listened to their hearts pound. He squeezed his foot with both hands to staunch the trickle of blood.

Recovering her composure, Jazmin wiped tears from her face. "Is it bad?"

"How would I know? It hurts like hell." He grimaced, then his face softened. "You okay?"

"I think so. That really scared me," she added. "Let me look at your heel."

He moved his hand from the laceration and blood ran freely from the wound. Jazmin ran to her pack and pulled out their first aid kit. She cleaned the wound with hydrogen peroxide and, when the bubbles subsided, inspected it carefully. The cut went to the bone.

She met his gaze with a worried look. "It looks like it only grazed the tendon. I think you'll be able to walk in a few days."

Peter grunted, stood on his good foot, and slowly put pressure on the wounded heel. He grimaced again. An ominous whisper buzzed through the trees. They both knew they would spend the night in the ancient city.

Jazmin poured more peroxide over the wound, then applied pressure. When the bleeding subsided, she bandaged the foot so he could get his sandal back on. He swore at himself for being so clumsy.

"Peter, don't be so hard on yourself," she scolded. "It will heal quickly. Besides, it is obvious this place does not want us to leave."

"What's that supposed to mean?" He tried to stand on his injured foot again.

"You should know by now that we didn't just stumble into this city. Spirit guided us here, and into those webs, just as surely as we were guided into that quicksand the other day. Spirit wants us here, and now we have to stay."

"I'm not sure that makes me feel any better."

"We don't have much choice," Jazmin said as she ran her fingers through her hair.

Peter felt like a sight, sitting naked with cobwebs in his hair, wounded again. Then it became clear to him. Chan hadn't sent them fleeing from danger. He had sent them into it, into this dark and ancient chasm where panthers hid in the shadows and time forgot to move forward.

He had sent them to *Na-Bolom*. "Damn him, anyway," Peter said.

"Damn who?"

"Chan!"

"Peter! Why do you say that?"

"He sent us in here, and you know it."

"Well, I guess he did. So, this is where we are supposed to be."

"Yeah, maybe. But I don't like it."

"Me neither." She sat next to him and laid her head on his shoulder. "But it could be worse. Those spiders could have been deadly poisonous."

"How do you know they're not?"

"Look at your bites," she said. "The poison should be running through our bodies by now, and all we have are small welts."

She was right. A deadly poison would make them ill, causing nausea at the very least. These bites were not unlike numerous others they had received during their weeks in the jungle—worse than some, less serious than others. The *machete* had inflicted the real damage.

"I suspect that is why they swarm their prey in such large numbers," Jazmin said. "Their poison is not strong. Perhaps we've been bitten so many times now we've developed some immunity."

"Now, that's a fine example of deductive thinking, Sherlock," he said.

Jazmin walked around the perimeter of the courtyard looking for a suitable campsite while Peter attempted to make himself comfortable.

His heel was turning black and blue, and painful. Chan had called spiders "the weavers of dreams." What did they mean to weave for him this night? His thoughts veered back to the images he saw in the plaza and the scars over his heart left by an angry cat. As he stroked the scars, he heard words pound in his ears like a bass drum: *Na-Bolom, Na-Bolom.*

A pain ripped into Peter's midsection like a well-aimed fist. He bent over, holding his stomach as the ominous name rumbled through his body again. *Na-Bolom*, the House of the Jaguar. He had come back . . . been brought back. And now he was its captive. It had called him back, tricked him . . . but why?

He hadn't mentioned the visions to Jazmin. How could he? She was already scared to death of the place. She felt the ominous energy too, but they were calling *him*, not her, just as Chan said. "The jungle calls you."

Peter pulled himself up on the crumbling rock wall, hugging his stomach, trying to keep at bay the feeling of a condemned man awaiting his execution.

He tried to recompose himself as Jazmin returned. She suggested they spend the night atop one of the pyramids, high above the crawling insects and nocturnal predators roaming the jungle floor. They chose a small temple at one side of the plaza, tall enough to offer some safety, low enough that he could climb the steep staircase.

They collected their packs, crossed the plaza, and stood at the foot of the temple. Peter half crawled, half walked up the steps while Jazmin went ahead to drop her pack at the top, then returned for his. She hefted his heavy pack up the stairs, but still managed to beat him to the top.

At the top level, Peter surveyed the smooth rock floor. He immediately spotted a solitary limestone sculpture sitting on the far side of the landing. A male figure reclined on its back, legs drawn up. The head was turned to the side, facing him. As soon as his eyes glanced at the strange statue, pain ripped through his heart. He clutched at his chest and fell to his knees in agony.

"Peter, what's wrong?"

He rolled onto his back, his lungs heaving for air.

Panic-stricken, Jazmin bolted to him and knelt at his side. "What's wrong, Peter?"

"Don't know," he gasped. "My heart . . ."

She held his head and looked into his face, terrified.

He took several deep breaths, still fighting for air. "Don't worry . . ." He tried to assure her, stroking feebly at her down-turned lips. "I won't leave you alone in this place."

As suddenly as the pain had come on, it passed and he began to relax in her arms. Soon the color that had drained from his face started to return. Jazmin helped him into a sitting position, fussing over him.

"Whew. I'm fine now," he said.

Jazmin raised an eyebrow.

"Hey," he said, pointing to his heart. "I'm in good shape. I've never had heart problems before." His eyes roamed the scene before them. "It's this city. The moment I laid eyes on that altar, I felt a pain like a knife stabbing through my heart . . . What's with this place? I've been here before. I'm sure of it now."

"Why do you say that?" She looked at him as though she already knew the answer.

"When we were in the plaza, I flashed on the grounds as they looked when the city was occupied. Just a flicker of an image at first. I wasn't sure at the time if it was real or not, but the images kept coming."

"Peter, why didn't you tell me?"

He hesitated, knowing he had betrayed their pact of full disclosure once again. "Well, everything happened so fast. I didn't want to spook you more than you already were."

She suddenly rose up from her knees to confront him, nearly screaming. "That's against our pact, Peter. We speak of these things. Everything we think, feel, or see!"

He pulled away, jarred by her anger. Again, he felt like an idiot. "I know. I'm sorry. I was just trying to protect you from reading too much into these things."

"In our situation, I'm not sure I appreciate that," she fired back. "It does not help to keep things from me." She lowered her voice and looked hard into his eyes. "We've talked about this, Peter. Promise me you won't do it again."

He nodded in agreement. "Okay, I think that's a good idea."

She walked over to the altar and pointed to the reclining figure, a touch of anger still in her voice. "Tell me what this is all about. What does this represent to you?"

"It's a sacrificial altar where they cut out the hearts of their victims."

Her dark eyes went wide with apprehension. "Yes, I know about these figures. Do you think this was the place you saw in your vision that night around the fire?"

"I'd say that's a pretty good guess, based on the reaction I just had."

"But why would they want you here again?"

"Maybe they didn't get it right the first time," he said cryptically.

"Don't talk that way, Peter. You're scaring me."

He stood and limped the few steps to her and held out his arms. "I'm sorry. I guess I'm more than a little scared too."

"So, what else have you not told me?" she asked, folding her arms across her chest.

"Not much. Only that today wasn't the first time we danced together in that plaza."

Jazmin studied his face. "What do you mean?"

"I looked down at you when we danced in the plaza," he continued. "Your face was different, but I knew it was you."

"The tune you were humming," Jazmin said. "It sounded familiar to me."

"It was from this city, *Na-Bolom*. I'm sure of it. You're remembering too."

"How do you know its name? *Na-Bolom*?"

"Chan spoke of it when were atop the mountain in the tribe's sacred forest." The flat, open pinnacle of the pyramid commanded a three-hundred-sixty-degree view. He took Jazmin's hand and they walked around the temple, gazing out onto the city below.

"We were communicating so well before we came into this valley. What happened, Peter? Why did we start holding back?"

"I don't know. I suspect there were many secrets kept around here long ago. This was not a safe place."

The sky turned burnt orange, then a fiery red, as the sun began to set. Awestruck by the city's grandeur, they shared their speculation about how it must have looked and how it must have felt to have lived in it hundreds of years ago.

"Think of the hidden treasures lying around here just waiting to be discovered," he mused.

"How can you think of treasure hunting at a time like this?" Jazmin vented, still upset. "We have only been here a few hours, and you are already hurt. Now it is getting dark, and we have to spend the night in this monument of gloom and await our fate. Who knows what awaits us tonight."

"Well, if I wasn't feeling uneasy before, I sure am now. Thanks for the pep talk."

"I'm scared . . ." Jazmin's voice rose. "As soon as we walked into this place we became caught in its web. The symbology frightens me."

He nodded. "It frightens me too, sweetheart, but we promised to stay positive. How about we give it another try? As you pointed out, the spiders didn't hurt us, and the cut on my heel isn't as serious as we feared."

She opened her arms to him this time, and they held one another.

Despite his bravado, he felt the firm pressure of cold fingers gripping his heart as the sun's last rays faded and the world around them began to darken.

"I'm not worried about the spirits of the jungle, Peter. I'm worried about the presence here. This city was filled with pain and suffering. We both felt it when we crossed that ridge this morning."

"So, you think this place has a consciousness separate from the rest of the jungle?"

"*Sí*. You know it does. Everything here is old." She waved her arms around, pointing as she spoke. "The flora dates back to the dinosaur age. This energy has been here forever. It's dark and full of pain."

He frowned. "I'm especially thrilled at the prospect of spending the night here now."

"I'm sorry," she said, embracing him again. "I am not being very strong."

"It's okay. I didn't mean to insult you . . . but if this ghost town is going to have me for dinner, I want to see who's coming so I can give them a piece of my mind. Why don't you collect as much firewood as you can while I set up camp? We'll keep the dark, and maybe even the spirits, at bay through the night."

"Okay," Jazmin agreed. She picked up the *machete*, eager to go on the offensive.

"Just stay within eyesight," he called out after her. "And be careful with that *machete*."

Jazmin flashed a brave smile, and headed down the steps. She gathered dead branches, broke them up with the *machete*, then stacked the kindling at the base of the temple. After several trips up and down the steps, she stacked enough wood to keep the fire going throughout the night. Peter made a fire ring with chunks of rock and mortar atop the temple, lit the dry grass, and blew on it until it smoldered into flame, gradually adding bigger kindling as the fire grew. He added pieces of rotting logs until the firelight illuminated the area.

They took comfort in the light and warmth, but their hearts sank as they watched a wispy sky turn from soft gray to cold black. It would be dark until the quarter moon rose to light the night. Left only with their imaginations and the shadows that darted over the treetops and into the courtyard below, they huddled together and fed the fire.

"Why don't you try and get some sleep?" Peter suggested, stroking Jazmin's head as they stared into the fire.

"Sleep? Here?" She looked surprised at his suggestion. "I would have to be dead tired to sleep in this creepy place."

"I wish you wouldn't use that term right now," Peter said.

She smiled weakly. "Sorry."

By the time stars began to appear through the sparse cloud cover, Jazmin's head leaned heavily against his shoulder. Then she worked her way into a comfortable position, her head securely on his leg. She nodded a few times, then fell into a deep sleep.

Peter stroked her head and whispered, "I won't leave you here alone, my love. I won't leave you."

He could only pray it was true.

CHAPTER 21

Someone once said that nothing so penetrates the soul of man as absolute darkness. Peter understood that now as he watched the play of firelight and shadows atop the ancient pyramid. He stoked the fire, but as it flared, the jungle only closed in around him in response.

Jazmin showed no signs of awakening, though he secretly hoped for her company. He considered waking her, but she was exhausted, both emotionally and physically. They had traversed the steep, heavily wooded mountains surrounding the valley all day only to descend into the dark uncertainty of this ancient city.

His blistered hands and throbbing heel still demanded attention, but his mind remained focused on *Na-Bolom*. He thought about the woman who had danced with him in the plaza, how her shy, downcast eyes had unexpectedly turned upward to look into his. Radiant eyes, so utterly familiar. Had they been lovers? Husband and wife?

When Jazmin had leaped from the edge of the canyon weeks ago, he'd had a vague impression of her as a native woman, with hands bound by twine behind her. He'd seen her from the back and caught only a fleeting glimpse of her lovely profile. The last thing he'd remembered was the violet flower floating from behind her ear, twirling down into the abyss. The woman in the plaza had worn a violet bougainvillea. He'd untangled the bougainvillea from Jazmin's hair, and gently twirled it in his fingers.

Chan said he had saved her life once. Maybe so, but not in his vision at the canyon. Chan had also predicted Jazmin would have the opportunity to save him. She'd saved his life in the swamp. Apparently, their score was even but the thought gave him little comfort while surrounded by the darkness of *Na-Bolom*.

He recalled his vision of the people dancing in the plaza, and tried to recreate the image of the woman with the violet flower in her hair, but his eyes grew heavy. Carefully slipping away from her, he stood to avoid the urge to sleep. He had to stay alert.

Drawing his gun, he pulled back on the action to check the chamber for a bullet, then returned it to his holster. He smiled at the absurdity of trying to defend himself from the spirits of the city with a handgun.

Peter hobbled around the fire, fed it again, and peered out into the darkness, averting his eyes from the sacrificial altar. The malevolent city seemed to draw closer, and the structures wavered in the firelight. Then a flicker of light below the temple startled him.

He pulled the gun from its holster, clicked the safety off, and looked again. He spun around. He fought to adjust his eyes to the darkness, and began to make out a pair of golden-green eyes, then another.

Illuminated by the fire's glow, several pairs of iridescent eyes stared back at him. The strange firelight and the two-legged creature standing atop the tall structure had sparked the curiosity of the forest's nocturnal creatures. Peter set the safety back on the Beretta and returned it to his holster.

As the night wore on, he identified coatimundis, ring-tailed cats, striped skunks, porcupine, and rare nocturnal monkeys. They darted a little way up the pyramid to get a closer look, and when their curiosity was satisfied, scurried off in search of an evening meal.

After the parade of animals had come and gone, a strange-looking creature crept up the steps of the pyramid. With its long tail and quick legs, it looked like a cross between a fat cat and a small monkey. Peter recognized it as a kinkajou, another rare mammal peculiar to the jungles of Chiapas. The animal had likely never seen a human before, and sensed he was no threat. It boldly came within a few feet of him. Glad for the distraction, he studied its odd form until it too scurried back into the darkness.

The nocturnal creatures were so prevalent, it was unlikely any large predators prowled the area. He sat down next to Jazmin again and relaxed a notch. She continued sleeping soundly at his side. The dancing flames of the fire soon carried his thoughts off again into the city's hidden past. What had happened to the people that once lived in this grand metropolis? It was obviously a thriving center of commerce. Why were its grand structures so well preserved, and how had it escaped the notice of scientists and treasure seekers? Even the jungle seemed reluctant to intrude itself upon its ancient walls.

As the night deepened, more immediate questions began to press themselves upon him. Why had they been led to *Na-Bolom*, then prevented from leaving? What was in store for them this night? What was the dark presence they both felt? He had managed to push away his negative emotions by day, but as the night deepened, he found he could no longer resist their dark calls.

The distant drumming he'd heard all day caught his attention again. He shook his head. Was he going mad? After all, Jazmin had not heard it. Weeks of wandering the jungle could push a man to the edge.

Now even the firelight seemed to conspire with the drumming, pulsating to the drum's cadence. He wanted to look away. The light held no sense of safety for him now. But Chan had challenged him to face his fears. He was tired of running. He chose instead to examine his emotions, to flow with them, to immerse himself in the pulse of the flames.

The fire danced and flickered, leaping high into the night sky with the beat of the drums. Peter merged his mind with the flames, and soon images appeared within the yellow and blue flashes. Unclear at first, they began to take shape. He stared harder, fascinated by the strange twisting shapes. As his mind became absorbed by the flames, his head and heart seemed to pulse to the drums' rhythm too. The fire came to life in a tapestry of color and motion, stretching and morphing into people.

Dark-skinned people in brightly colored costumes undulated in unison to the pulsations of the drumbeat and flames. He felt enchanted by their movements. Faces void of emotion, they stared ahead as if in a trance. He hadn't noticed the transition at first, but now they were all around him. He began to lose cognizance of the present and future—he became the past. The scene before him became a part of him, and he a part of it.

The mesmerizing dancers were all men. He studied their dark faces, prominent noses, unusual clothing, and striking ornamentation. Lavish costumes of exotic animal skins and colorful baubles of jade and shell filled his senses. The frightening necklaces of jaguar teeth and brightly-colored feathered headdresses all fought for his attention, but it was the intricately painted faces that fascinated him most, magnificent designs that transformed them into frightening beasts.

His growing awareness told him they were not dancing for show. The objects in their hands, and fastened to their arms—lances and plumed banners with exotic feathers, obsidian tipped clubs, painted tortoiseshell shields—told another story. These weren't entertainers. They were warriors. Willing his head to turn, he stared down the long line of men, and only then did he gain a broader visual perspective. The lines of lavishly arrayed warriors numbered in the hundreds. A dozen rows deep, their ranks ran for a hundred yards before disappearing into the brush.

This was not just a band of warriors, but a vast army preparing for battle. They believed their beauty and color would bring them power. Deep in his soul, Peter knew they were right. He saw their power, felt it draw him closer. Never was an army so seductive and alluring in its raw grace and power.

Peter walked through their ranks, yet they seemed not to notice. A particularly striking warrior caught his attention and he stopped to gaze into his eyes. The warrior's headdress was adorned with the brilliant green and red feathers of the *quetzal*, his muscular chest covered in a black draping, the skin of a black jaguar. Tarnished white claws hung from his necklace, sharply contrasted against the deep black fur. Keenly focused, the muscular man radiated a seasoned warrior's confidence.

Suddenly the warrior in black shifted his focus and gazed directly back at Peter. Somehow, this ancient man intuited his presence. Startled, he tried to pull away, but the warrior's piercing black eyes grabbed him with surprising force. His mind pushed and pulled, fighting to unlock his eyes from the warrior's, but to no avail. Peter soon realized the futility of his struggle and stopped resisting. As he relaxed, his panic subsided, and he allowed the warrior to pull him deeper into his world. This dreamy, shadowy dimension surrounding the warrior felt vile and, although desperate to escape it, he allowed the warrior's emotions to penetrate his consciousness.

"Have I given up? No," Peter heard himself say, struggling again to free himself.

The warrior's pupils began to change. Peter followed their movement as they morphed into irregular forms, then into the haunting shape of jaguars. The stealthy cat paced back and forth hypnotically against the warrior's nut-brown irises. Then the jaguar stopped and looked at him, its yellow eyes ablaze.

Peter's revulsion of the image registered in the pit of his stomach, and his heart pounded the rhythm of his fear as he returned the jaguar's stare. *I must face this darkness,* he thought, trembling before the haunting eyes.

He felt the warrior's power over him, but there was great sadness in this power, a familiar sadness, cold and ancient. He trembled at this pain, this place of sorrow. He wanted to hold his stomach, but his hands couldn't find his body. Overcome with emotion, he tried again to shut his eyes, to turn his head away, move his body, anything to resist the gaze. But the piercing eyes remained locked on his.

Then he heard a voice rise up like a gale beyond the warriors' battle lines. "The spirit of darkness no longer serves me."

In a fleeting moment of awareness, Peter sensed weakness—even desperation—in the steely gaze. He realized that the spirit of darkness *needed* him.

This darkness needs me, he thought. *But I do not need it.*

Peter experienced a sudden glimmer of confidence. A tiny light in the jaguar's eyes flashed like a beacon, warm and full of hope and strength. Peter suddenly felt full of hope, even joy. He wanted to celebrate. No longer did the jaguar evoke fear within him. Then the jaguar simply turned away.

Once again, Peter found himself looking into the eyes of the ancient warrior in black. But something within those eyes had shifted. Light and joy surrounded him. "We are free," a voice chanted within. "We are free at last."

The Maya warrior still stood before him, but the pain in his face had vanished. The jaguar's image no longer appeared in his eyes. In a place words could not touch, he caressed Peter's soul. In that moment, Peter felt their deep bond, their long brotherhood. But now the time had come to say farewell and the warrior embraced Peter's essence with the overwhelming love of one warrior for another.

After one last look, the warrior in black took a long, deep breath, arched his head back, and with his muscular chest heaving upward, yelled so loud that Peter's ears rang. The intense sound penetrated his brain, blurring the warrior's image. Piercing beyond measure, the cry fractured the sights and sounds around him into a confused state of fragmented images. Unable to make sense of the scrambled sensory input, Peter heard himself gasp and he reached for something to hold on to.

Then everything stopped, and there was only the fire atop the pyramid, its dying embers no longer dancing with the warriors. The scream echoed through Peter's mind a moment longer as he found himself staring into the fire's ashes. Sweat beaded up on his face, his heart throbbed, and his chest heaved with the effort of drawing oxygen into his lungs.

He took several deep breaths to clear his head, and shivered in the cool morning air. As his mind became fully conscious, he watched the single point of light within the dying embers blow out, and within that last wisp of smoke, the fleeting image of a black jaguar drifted to the heavens.

The first rays of dawn lit the surrounding peaks, turning them gold. The morning sky began to erase the stars, and the ancient city became visible again. It seemed odd to Peter that Jazmin still slept at his side, unaware the world had changed. He looked on the city with fresh eyes. No longer did he fear it. In fact, his heart now went out to it.

The city was an old friend. He had lived, loved, and died here. While life had been brutal and frightening then, it was also filled with great joy and beauty, with endless mysteries. A part of him would miss it, and he longed to see it as it had been. His heart filled with sadness, knowing he would soon say goodbye for the last time. Deep inside his soul, he knew he would never return. For the first time since their arrival in the valley, he no longer heard the sound of distant drumming. The city's heartbeat had stopped. For a moment, he wondered what that meant. It seemed odd, as though the city had died, had finally been laid to rest . . .

Peter stood and walked to the pyramid's edge.

He reacquainted himself with the city's ancient walls, structures, and frightening deities of stone that no longer threatened. Gazing over the treetops to the pyramid on the great plaza's far side, he realized it was not so long ago that the great city had thrived. It was only because life had changed so dramatically in the last two or three centuries that people could no longer relate to its way of life. He smiled inwardly, knowing this was how people had lived for tens of thousands of years. It saddened him to know how civilization had become isolated from its roots in nature, estranged from the ancient spirit within its bones.

Peter returned to Jazmin's side, and sat again, assessing his vision of the warriors. Gradually, he became aware of an intruder and his relaxed feeling dissipated. The jungle had nurtured his awareness and he knew the signs well. Someone or something was watching him. He rotated his head to look to the far side of the landing and found his target. A black jaguar waited in a crouch, its yellow eyes glaring.

The cat was too close, just a few yards away, to dare draw his gun or move. To awaken Jazmin would risk alarming both her and the animal. The jaguar's muscles rippled under the smooth black sheen of fur around its neck and shoulders, a reminder of its terrible strength and speed. Peter and the jaguar remained frozen, eyes fixed on one another.

This was the language of the jungle. It was a bad sign. The powerful predator showed no fear of him. That was clear from the cat's eyes and its casual yet alert stance. The animal's cold stare sent chills through Peter's body, but he continued to sit absolutely still.

The jaguar rose into a low crouch, edged forward a few paces, paused uncertainly, and then took another step. Peter's heart began to pound and he made the conscious effort to breathe, remaining motionless, eyes fixed on the creature. Another step. The animal was careful, cautious, but grew bolder with each step.

Questions raced through Peter's mind: *Why is it here? What does it want? Why didn't it attack when my head was turned? Is it simply taunting me before it tears me apart?*

Then he remembered Chan's words: "*Bolom* is a part of you now. Do not fear it. The spirit of *bolom* is your ally." He prayed it might be so as the animal took another step forward. Taking another deep breath, he coaxed his body to relax. The jaguar hesitated, then stood from its crouch and moved forward again.

Peter looked up as the animal boldly came face-to-face with him. The big cat paused and looked into his eyes. He steadied himself and returned its stare. The deep yellow eyes seemed to move closer until they were all he could see. The cat was nearly touching noses with him. Peter's body shook, his mind too tinged with fear to determine the animal's intent.

Peter held his breath. He didn't dare flinch as the jaguar brushed by, leaning heavily against him for a moment, then padding past. He was nearly knocked over by its weight.

Turning, the huge cat came up against him once more, this time from behind. It paused, then silently moved past him and back to the far side of the landing where it first appeared. The jaguar turned to look at him again. They observed one another in silence for several moments. Peter began to breathe easier again.

Faint at first, a shiver ran through the earth, passing from the mountains on one side of the valley in a ripple that entered the city like a python. Peter shifted his gaze from the jaguar and peered in the direction of the sound. Another more pronounced tremor moved from mountain to valley. He turned back to the jaguar, but it was gone.

"What is that?" Jazmin yawned, coming to life. "I heard something."

Peter forced himself to exhale evenly. "The ground's shaking . . ." He shot to his feet, and pulled Jazmin to hers.

A third tremor sent a car-sized block of stone toppling down the steps, landing with a shudder at the temple's base.

Jazmin watched, mesmerized by the movement.

"Come on!" Peter yelled. "We've got to get out of here." His heel wound no longer slowed him down as a heavy rush of adrenaline brushed aside his pain.

The pyramid shook with amazing force. He grabbed his pack and *machete*, and started down the trembling steps of the temple, Jazmin close behind. She caught up halfway down the stairs, picking up a compass that spilled from the open pockets of Peter's pack.

At the bottom of the pyramid, they headed for the open plaza on the forest floor, sprinting down the ancient avenue in a race for their lives.

"*¿Que pasa?*" Jazmin yelled over the deafening rumble of the quake. "Yesterday they wouldn't let us leave. Now they are throwing us out?"

"I'll try to explain later—if we live long enough," he yelled, but she could not hear him over the roar.

The earth shook violently as they ran, sending great blocks of stone from the temples and monuments crumbling to the ground. Giant rocks carved and set in place centuries before tumbled into trees and walls, smashing them with a tremendous roar.

As they dashed between the giant stone monuments, the towering stelae lining the road teetered precariously, then as if on cue, toppled to the earth with ear-shattering explosions. Peter and Jazmin stumbled to the ground, picked themselves up, and continued running hand-in-hand. Everywhere stones and trees fell along their path.

Jazmin tumbled to the ground, tripping again over a rolling boulder.

He screamed above the earthquake's thunder as he picked her up. "Are you hurt?"

"I don't care!"

Her point registered. It was run or die. Nothing else mattered.

They raced down the open corridor as trees vibrated and peeled up from the earth, their roots like hands grasping for safety. The quaking serpent rippled beneath them, crumbling everything in its path. Before they reached the gate, a tree toppled over the rattling entrance. They scurried through the debris of the gate and into an open meadow, gasping for breath. Another tremor sent them to the ground. They held one another while the earth swayed beneath them, rolling and shifting like an angry sea.

Peter covered their heads with his arms as the earth continued to rip itself apart. Nothing in his experience had prepared him for such an event. It was the first time in his life he could not depend on the earth to support him. He and Jazmin only had one another to hold, absorbing the earth's upheavals with their bodies.

Then the thunder subsided, and the quake ended as suddenly as it had begun. Their world became absolutely silent.

They lay gasping on the ground, too shocked to speak, too dizzy to stand. Jazmin loosened her grip on Peter. Her face flushed from running and from fear. She looked as if she wanted to say something. At first, her mouth moved, but the words didn't come out. Her face flushed with fear as she finally managed to speak.

"I think you really angered the gods this time, *mi amigo*."

CHAPTER 22

Peter's and Jazmin's clothing and equipment lay strewn across the ground like so much discarded trash. Shirts, shorts, undergarments, tent, food, utensils—all looked forlorn in the dawn's unforgiving light, spilled from hands and unsecured packs as they dashed the last desperate yards into the open meadow.

Now the peace was complete, but when Peter tried to say something, he couldn't put his thoughts together. The quake had juggled their minds as well as their bodies.

Finally, he steadied himself and got to his feet to begin the process of gathering and repacking their belongings. His mind wandered from warrior to jaguar to earthquake, trying to make sense of the events. Everything had happened so quickly he couldn't assimilate it.

Jazmin remained on the ground, silent, attempting to pull her emotions together. When she finally sat up, she rubbed her badly bruised shinbone, then started to cry.

He rushed over to hold her. "Are you all right?"

She gently turned away. He understood. She simply needed time to release the terror of the morning on her own terms.

Once their packs were reassembled, they hefted them onto their backs and started wearily down the worn cobblestone road leading away from the city. Bruised, battered, and emotionally spent, both hobbled now. They would not be able to travel far. It seemed Jazmin had been right. The city was finished with them, and in a grand style, had encouraged them to leave.

Negotiating this terrain was relatively easy, requiring little use of the *machete*. Occasionally a light tremor vibrated under them, a mere reminder of the violent quake. Shaken from jungle homes, wildlife showed itself everywhere. Monkeys, ringtail cats, a porcupine, and even a rarely seen nocturnal margay crossed their path. An hour into their trek, they approached a large depression in the earth and stopped to investigate.

About a hundred feet across, fifty feet down and perfectly round, the great depression formed a natural swimming hole with sheer limestone walls that plummeted straight down into a crystal-clear pool.

Peter glanced at Jazmin and smiled for the first time that day. "Wow, a sinkhole. Does that ever look inviting. It must connect to the underground water table."

"It is a *cenote*."

"Right," he said, remembering the Spanish translation of the Yucatec Maya term for the formation. "I've seen them in the Yucatan peninsula, but I didn't know any existed here."

"I doubt anyone knows."

"This must have been the public swimming hole for the community. I'll bet there are steps around here somewhere."

They removed their packs and walked around the hole, surveying its deep recesses and aquamarine water until they spotted the man-made steps, carved into the rock. Though cracked and overgrown with gnarled broadleaf trees and bright green moss, they were still usable.

The adrenaline rush of the morning had worn off and their bodies now began to pulse with pain. The *cenote* area looked like a good place for a campsite.

They cautiously made their way down to the water, Peter limping on his injured heel, Jazmin's shin purple and painful. The healing water would soothe their injuries and they both needed a good bath. Discarding their clothes, they splashed their way into the cool water. The sun hovered high in the sky, lifting their spirits while the water removed the tension from their bodies.

After a relaxing swim, they stood in the water, their arms wrapped around each other. Jazmin studied Peter's scratched and weathered face to discern his thoughts.

"What happened back in the city? Is it possible those ruins just coincidentally crumbled to the ground this morning after standing for hundreds of years? Or did our being there affect it somehow?"

He kissed her lightly on the lips. "No, it wasn't a coincidence. Something incredible happened last night. I had a vision."

Jazmin listened intently as he related a detailed account, describing the Maya army, the jaguar of his dreams, and the warrior in black.

"What does it all mean, Peter?"

"I don't know exactly."

"Well," she said. "*Your* presence certainly had an impact on the city—a mortal impact."

Peter grinned. "Yeah, I just hope they don't make us rebuild the damn thing."

Jazmin grinned back. "I think you accomplished what you were sent there to do. The spirits of that city called us there because they wanted our help. Chan said you had an appointment with the jungle. Now a great weight has been lifted from the land. I can feel it. The trees seem lighter this morning."

They continued holding one another, the clear blue water lapping at their waists in sparkling waves. Peter took in the scent of her hair and skin, then pulled away to admire her firm breasts, which seemed to be begging for his attention.

"I feel better too," he added, "much better."

"Me too, *amorcito*."

"There's one other thing I have to tell you. I saw a jaguar."

"The jaguar in your vision?"

"No—well, yes. A real jaguar. After I came out of my trance and cleared my head, I looked over my shoulder to the far side of the temple. A magnificent black jaguar stood at the top of the stairs."

Jazmin pulled away from Peter, and he studied her with a lust he had not felt since he had entered the jungle months ago.

"What did it do?" She gazed back at him, sensing his newfound interest in her.

"It just sat there at first. It held no fear of me, and I thought it was there to kill me. It stalked me, slowly creeping up with its belly close to the ground, and then stood face to face with me. I almost had a heart attack when it brushed up against me like a housecat. Then the earthquake started, and it was gone."

"Why do you suppose the jaguar did that?"

"It seemed to be making up to me, or thanking me, or both. I think it was the same animal that attacked me. Chan said someone had sent it to me. Maybe I freed it from the House of the Jaguar."

"And I slept through the whole thing?"

"Yep."

"I wonder what it all means." Jazmin shook her lustrous hair out in the warm sun, like a Maya queen.

"A lot of things," he said, wading closer to her. "For one, it means the dark cloud hanging over that city, and over me, is gone."

Unable to resist Jazmin any more, Peter lifted her out of the water and onto the sun-drenched rim of the *cenote*.

CHAPTER 23

The rains had ceased altogether after Peter and Jazmin crested the last mountain range, which now lay far behind them. The arid region they found themselves in had received only light amounts of rainfall during the monsoons, judging by the dry, grassy hillsides, sandy creek beds, and lack of thick undergrowth among the trees.

After several days in the new valley, they struggled to find enough water to sustain themselves. While dying in the Forbidden Jungle due to dehydration would have seemed preposterous a few days earlier, their gourds were nearly empty now, and the prospect of finding a spring, creek, or lake looked bleak.

"Jazmin, Tehuantepec is somewhere west of us along the coast."

"Let's hope we haven't veered too far north or south, *mi amor*."

He took out his compass. "The valley we're in has led us west, but now it's turning south."

They would have to decide whether to climb the steep Sierra Madres to the west or continue through the valley. While the valley offered a dim prospect of finding a stream or lake, it would take them miles away from their destination. On the other hand, climbing the mountains would be strenuous, and they would quickly use up what little water they had. With little idea of what water, if any, they would encounter on the other side, they stopped to consider their options. Exhausted, they laid their packs and weary bodies to rest in the shade of a giant tropical cedar overlooking a dry creek bed of smooth rock and gravel. By now, it was a matter of habit to sit and clear their minds in times of indecision. Leaning against the cedar's trunk, they tuned into the heartbeat of the forest. The gentle trill of a bird in the distance accompanied the soft rustle of leaves blowing in the treetops.

As they listened, Jazmin began to see an image in her mind's eye. "Spirit is showing me something. I'm just not sure what it is. It looks like a dry wash, similar to the one below us." She paused and opened her eyes wider. "In fact, it is this very wash." She looked down at the narrow ravine with confusion. "But why Spirit is showing me this, I do not know."

Peter stood and walked down to the wash, studying the intricate shapes in the rocks, looking for any depressions that might hold water. The first one he came to was shallow, only a few inches deep, and dry. Looking up, he saw a series of the formations running along the creek bed, all too shallow to hold water, but something about them caught his attention—a distinct uniformity that his trained eyes could not ignore. Four rows of depressions ran a hundred feet or more down the wash. He looked back down at the one under his feet.

"Jazmin, come look." His voice filled with enthusiasm. "I see what Spirit is showing us."

She ran over, alert to his excited voice and anxious for a long drink. She looked at the depression and gasped.

"Dinosaur tracks!"

"Yes. Aren't they magnificent?"

"*Sí . . .*" Her voice trailed off, sounding more disappointed than excited.

Two sets of prints ran down the wash, side-by-side. Peter identified one set as belonging to large bipedal predator, the other a plant eater. The predator's prints were massive and heavily clawed, while the plant eater's prints were rounded with blunt claws.

"This was some kind of a tyrannosaurid," he said, pointing at the smaller prints. "Look. They run clearly all the way down the creek bed. This is the finest set of tracks I've ever seen." He shook his head. The larger tracks were about two feet long and nearly as wide, the other set slightly smaller.

"The larger prints," he said, "are probably from a member of the duckbill family of dinosaurs. You can see that the predator is following the larger creature. Wow. These tracks can teach volumes about these creature's habits."

"What do they tell you?" Jazmin tried to sound enthusiastic as she licked her parched lips.

He spoke as he walked down the line of tracks, estimating the distance between them as he went along. "They can tell us how fast each animal was running, the length of their strides, the size and weight of each animal—all kinds of things. Here the depth of the toes of each track, and their distance apart, tells us these two creatures were running at a high speed. They also suggest with a fair degree of certainty that the predator was chasing the other creature. In fact, they strongly argue that this animal"—he pointed to a smaller print—"was a very aggressive hunter that relied on speed and cunning to catch its prey."

Jazmin cringed. "So this big, mean animal could run fast too?"

"That's exactly what these tracks suggest. But I'll need to take some measurements and photos, then do a little calculating first. How about we set up camp, and spend the night?"

"Peter, we're out of water," she said, exasperated. "Don't you think we ought to find water before we do anything else?"

"Sure, go ahead," he said, already involved as he studied the claw marks of a large print.

Jazmin looked puzzled. "Don't you think it is odd?"

"What?"

"That Spirit led us to these tracks when we were asking for water and directions?"

He nodded, distracted by his work. She gave him a hopeless look, then walked off to scout the area for water. Sometime later, she came back with a shirt full of ripe fruit, but no water. They eagerly ate the fruit, happy to consume the moisture.

"I just spent an hour looking for water," Jazmin said, "and couldn't even find a drop of dew on a leaf. This fruit will get us through the day, but right now I would trade these dinosaur tracks for a cool drink of water in the blink of my eye." She looked at Peter, then down at the tracks with a look of disgust on her face.

"What? You'd trade my dinosaur tracks for a drink of water? This blasphemy will not go unpunished!" He jumped up.

She screamed, and ran down the creek bed laughing as he chased her, cursing like a drunken sailor.

"May the pox be on you, girl! How dare you think of trading my dinosaur tracks for mere water?"

He caught up to her where the tracks disappeared into the sand, and tackled her lightly on the soft ground. They wrestled, laughing and rolling in the sand, then lay exhausted from their effort, staring up into the forest canopy.

"This sand is so nice and cool," she said, enjoying the moment.

A slight breeze caressed the leaves of the upper canopy, coaxing the two weary travelers into a restful state. He smiled, realizing it was the first time they had played since entering the jungle. It was a good sign.

Several tranquil minutes passed before a noise caught his attention. Startled, he sat up to find Jazmin digging in the sand with her bare hands.

"What are you doing?"

"This sand is cool and deep. That means water."

"Of course! And with this rock beneath it, there's a good chance it's holding more water."

He joined her with a passion that surprised him. They dug like dogs on a frenzied hunt, clawing into the sand until the hole was several feet deep. The deeper the hole, the wetter the sand became, until they brought sand out in big fistfuls and a muddy seep of water formed. They dug deeper. Once the water pooled up on the surface of the hole, he took his shirt off and filtered the murky water through it. They drank from it, splashed one another, then lay breathless in the cool sand wrapped in one another's arms.

After foraging for food and enjoying a large meal, they spent the evening with full stomachs, enjoying the gourds of boiled water at their side. Gazing at the River of Flowers in the cloudless sky through the netting of the tent, they felt more relaxed and safer than on any other night of their journey.

CHAPTER 24

Peter awakened to the dim pre-dawn light illuminating the tent. Daunted by the haunting red eyes that interrupted his slumber, he knew he would not return to sleep though it was some time before sunrise.

He inhaled deeply to clear his head, wondering why menacing eyes still stalked his dreams. Since his encounter with the warrior and the jaguar in *Na-Bolom,* he had hoped the eyes were gone for good. But it was not the jaguar that had returned. These eyes were different. Was the sudden reappearance of the nightmare connected with the tracks in the ravine?

He crawled to the tent's entrance, unzipped the flap, and peered out. A yellowish light gleamed high up on the mountain peaks, penetrating a heavy fog that hung lazily on the trees, obscuring much of the forest. He looked forward to the day, and felt his excitement about the tracks grow, anticipating a day spent reacquainting himself with old friends.

Slipping a badly stained shirt over his head, he exited the tent and padded barefoot down the solid rock surface toward the tracks. The sweet morning air was pungent with the scent of pines and damp green grass. The cool rock soothed his bruised feet as he walked along the creek bed, worn away by endless years of water rushing over its surface. He made his way to a particularly fine set of prints near the middle of the row, and sat next to them.

He felt strangely at home in these mountains and their ancient forest. Looking back in time a hundred million years teased at his imagination. Little had changed in eons. The ferns, palms, conifers, and grasses he gazed at were virtually identical to their ancient ancestors. For now, his world no longer existed. He and Jazmin were visitors to the past.

He placed his feet in the middle of one of the giant prints to cool his toes, remembering how Chan had instilled in him the need to keep his feet in direct contact with the earth. He chided himself for not doing it more often. It was inexplicably satisfying. He wanted to be in touch with the Great Mother in this situation. As far back as he could remember, the desire to understand dinosaurs had directed and dominated his life. Now that he'd taken all the necessary measurements and photographs of the tracks, he wanted to relax and become better acquainted with them.

He traced the ridges of the ancient predator's giant imprint with his toes as he studied the terrain. Though much of the vegetation was the same, the geography was different when the two dinosaurs ran through it. The mountains had just begun to lift from the sea, forming the tail end of the Sierra Madres. The valley would have been significantly flatter, with a thin veil of standing water covering its surface. The land that formed the creek bed would have stretched to the horizon. After the water evaporated, the mud would have dried and hardened quickly to preserve the tracks, which meant a rapid climate change. Fewer trees would have grown in the receding and dying mangrove swamp, and flowering plants had not yet evolved.

Peter studied the hills, watching the fog drifting through the trees as beautiful blue and green dragonflies swarmed around him. They reminded him that they were also present when the two dinosaurs raced along this bank. Letting his imagination run, he studied the forest's ancient beauty, then the long line of tracks. He tried to imagine the moment the giant plant-eater and sprinting predator set down their footprints, a long-forgotten drama.

Soaring overhead, a frigate bird caught his attention. It turned in the cloud-laden sky, banking easily, its forked tail sailing gracefully behind as it rose higher on the warm tropical currents. It was the first Peter had seen in a long time.

Something about the bird, its primitive tail and pointed, crooked wings, looked out of place, perhaps out of time. As he gazed through the silhouettes of hovering dragonflies, memories began to stir deep inside him, lulling him into a trance-like state. The exotic bird soared high overhead, then slowly, effortlessly, back over the mountains and out of sight.

He studied the billowing clouds as they turned pink and orange, then golden in the morning light. Then he noticed the frigate bird circling back from the mountain. It became a meditation for him, gliding through the air in dark contrast to the puffy white cumulus clouds. As the bird neared, its silhouette seemed different. Still high overhead, it tilted to one side and began a steep descent.

Larger than he'd assumed, it no longer appeared to be the same bird. Like the other, this one was a glider, but beyond that, there were few similarities. What he thought to be the forked tail of the frigate turned out not to be a tail at all, but a pair of thin legs extending backward behind the bird's torso. The legs worked like a rudder in the wind as it soared closer. And a large, elongated head protruded back to a point.

It's huge, he thought. *What the hell is it?*

As it drew closer, the less familiar it became, its shadow rippling over the trees like a low-flying airplane. Peter's heart raced when it dawned on him that it wasn't a bird at all. He estimated the creature's wingspan to be at least twenty feet from tip-to-tip.

My God, it's a Pteranodon!

Fear overcame curiosity when the flying reptile dove down upon him like an oversized bat and tried to snag him with its massive claws. He threw himself flat on the ground as the giant reptile passed just inches overhead, the wind generated by its huge wings hitting him with a smack and raising dust all around.

When the dust cleared and Peter raised his head, he could see a vast wetland stretched out before him. There were no tracks, no mountains, no campsite, and no Jazmin, and yet the incongruity of it did not occur to him. Instead, he sniffed the air, gaining a vivid mental picture of the environment. His awareness was no longer contained in a human body. Nor was he laying on the ground—he was a *Corythosaurus* in motion.

Sensing danger, Peter slowed his pace and lifted his head high to sniff the troubling air, his camel-like snout wavering anxiously in the wind. His keen sense of smell detected a hundred different scents, including the iron-laced smell of blood. Swinging his massive neck around to an injured rear leg, he licked at it.

But what interested the plant eater most was the scent of an animal approaching from the thick jungle behind him. Most of the odors held no concern, but this single scent demanded his attention. Something stirred in a nearby thicket, and Peter instinctively froze, continuing to sample the plethora of scents arising from the hot and humid jungle.

To Peter's right, a herd of twenty-five or more giant sauropods were crossing the savanna, their long necks craning high into the cloud-plumed sky. Like whales in a pond, their massive bodies rose some fifty feet above the landscape, dwarfing everything around them. They stopped to see what caused the large herds of rhino-like ceratopsids grazing nearby to stir and bellow in defiance. Craning their long necks high into the cloud-plumed sky, the sauropods studied Peter, the solitary *Corythosaurus*.

From its hiding place in a thicket, a giant predator burst forth, its two powerful hind legs crashing through thick undergrowth.

Peter bolted into the open plain of the wetlands, hoping to outpace this horrific predator, but his injured leg slowed his pace.

The *Tyrannosaur* stopped short of the clearing, pausing in the trees only a couple of hundred yards away—too close for safety. Then the powerful dinosaur thundered out onto the savanna, ignoring the angry herds of ceratopsids already tightly packed into their defensive circles. Weighing more than a ton, the predator sent panic through every creature on the plain. It wasn't just the animal's size that caused such consternation, or its powerful jaws, which could tear twenty pounds from its prey in a single bite. Intelligence and an aggressive attitude combined with speed and endurance set this one apart. No other tyrannosaurid had greater ability to run down a *Corythosaurus* across an open plain, and this one seemed intent on doing just that.

Peter kept a constant eye on the monster predator, and took little notice of the great herds of frightened animals stampeding nearby as he fled, sending muddy water shooting out in all directions. Flying reptiles with ten-foot wingspans soared overhead, anticipating their next meal as predator and prey dashed across the open savanna, mile after mile. One herd after another of grazing dinosaurs scattered before them, leaving a clear trail ahead. Peter fought for each breath, his aching lungs adding to the pain of his injured leg, which grew more severe with each step.

With quick, unrelenting strides, the *Tyrannosaur* gained on Peter, then overtook him. Fierce red eyes sent spasms of terror through his gut as the giant predator drew to his side. The predator grimaced, taunting his helpless prey.

Like a bull, the *Tyrannosaur* lunged at Peter, narrowly missing, then dropped back to rip his flanks with deadly razor teeth. In the next powerful lunge, it knocked him off his feet. Claws like grappling hooks slashed at his vulnerable back and flanks, opening long running gashes. Peter kicked his legs and swung his powerful tail from side-to-side in a desperate effort to dislodge the predator, but this only increased the spray of blood from his wounds.

Peter began to thrash in the mud, kicking his legs and swinging his powerful tail from side to side in a desperate effort to dislodge the *Tyrannosaur*. The intensity of their struggle threw mud, blood, and flesh in every direction. The determined predator bellowed a deafening roar as its claws and fangs slashed deeply into his vulnerable neck.

Then in a moment that seemed detached from the scene, peace filtered through Peter's exhausted awareness, and with the clarity of a still mind, he accepted his fate. A final strained inhalation gurgled through his massive lungs before his vision darkened, then dissolved altogether.

Peter suddenly lay in the forest breathing hard as a sickening rush to his abdomen hailed a new awareness in him. He felt as if he were falling. His ears popped abruptly and with that, the jungle came to life around him. He was back in human form, though suspended in time and space, unable to fully comprehend his circumstances.

Who am I? What am I? Man or animal?

Peter looked down at his trembling body with a sense of relief. *Human . . . and still alive.* But nothing looked familiar. Disoriented, he buried his face in his hands. The transition was disturbing, too quick. Then, the familiar sound of a bipedal creature moving toward him nearly stopped his heart.

CHAPTER 25

Peter looked with blurry eyes in the direction of the sound, struggling to his hands and knees. *Not again,* he thought.

Rather than the expected claws and fangs, he saw Jazmin wielding a large stick, running toward him, ready to do battle with some unknown adversary. Her naked body was covered only by her long, dark hair that fell around her face and shoulders in trailing wisps. She glanced about, tensed with excitement, expecting a fight. When no opponent appeared, she looked back to him.

"*¡Dios mío!* . . . Where is the danger? What happened? How did you get down here?"

He looked around, then looked at the ground. "I don't know, exactly."

"Are you all right, Peter?"

"I think so." He attempted to stand, stumbled, and sat back down. "Just feel a little chewed on is all."

"You scared me nearly to death!" she said, still scanning the bushes around him. "I was deeply asleep when I heard your scream." She frowned at him. "What were you screaming about?"

"I had an . . . episode," he huffed. "You know. One of those dinosaur episodes I told you about."

She knelt over him and hugged him, her nipples brushing his cheek. Peter held on to her, reassured, feeling his heart pound against her body. As he relaxed, he began to chuckle.

She pulled away to look into his eyes. "Why do you laugh?

"You're quite the jungle woman, running down here naked with that big stick of yours. You looked like Tarzan's Jane. And now I feel like a little kid with those beautiful tatas in my face."

Jazmin giggled, and collapsed beside him. He looked into her eyes.

"It's good to be human again." He ran a hand through Jazmin's hair and kissed her passionately. "Chan was right. It's much better being human. I'm sorry I scared you."

She pulled back and looked at him, her eyes weary. "You couldn't help it, Peter. It must have been terrifying. For some reason, you have to go through this. You're gaining something valuable from these visions, or the spirits of the jungle would stop showing them to you."

He sighed. "I guess. But I'm sure tired of being eaten by that damn overgrown lizard. That thing's been stalking me since Denver."

"Denver?"

"Yes. The skull of that very *Tyrannosaur* is in my office at the museum as we speak. I've worked on it for months. I'm sure this was the same animal that came to life in the lab the day K'in called me."

"Really! It came to life?"

"Sort of. Its eyes appeared to me. They looked exactly like the eyes on the predator that just ripped the guts out of me."

Jazmin cringed. "Oh, Peter."

"Damn thing scared the hell out of me. It obviously had something on its mind in Denver. Then it chased me through the jungle while I was recovering from my wounds in the village. Now we stumble on these tracks. I'm just getting the hang of this supernatural stuff, but I'm sure of one thing—that skull led us to these tracks."

"I don't understand."

"That makes two of us," he said, glancing at the tracks. "What could be so important about my experiencing an event that occurred a hundred million years ago? One thing I learned for certain is that *Tyrannosaurs* ran like the wind, just as I predicted. But that's hardly important on a cosmic level."

They fell silent, letting their thoughts dissolve into the songs of exotic birds. The birds seemed to be everywhere, singing their glorious melodies to the new morning.

"Are you sure you're okay?" Jazmin asked.

"I'm fine. I don't seem to have injured myself. How are you doing? Getting lost in the wilderness with a madman must be pretty scary."

"Peter, you're the sanest man I know," she said, holding his face in her hands. "You've been through more than most people could bear, but you are dealing with it so well."

"Thanks." Peter touched her cheek. "I needed to hear that."

"You are welcome, *mi amor*," she said softy. "How did it happen this morning?"

"I saw the eyes of the *Tyrannosaur* again in my dreams this morning. I woke up and couldn't get back to sleep. I got up, and came down to the tracks. One minute I was sitting in one of the tracks meditating, with dragonflies all around me, and the next minute I was in the Cretaceous period running for my life—the usual." He grinned.

"Gatekeepers," she muttered.

"What?"

"Chan mentioned that dragonflies are the gatekeepers of the past."

"Interesting. Their wings have the patterns of dinosaur skin."

"The Lacandón say they have dragon spirits," Jazmin said. "They are masters of the air and water as well as the land, so it is thought the dragonfly can take us to other worlds."

"It makes sense. Dragonflies have been around for the whole show. They were here when dinosaurs roamed the earth, and they're still here today. In some form or another they've been present for a couple hundred million years."

Peter stood on shaky legs with Jazmin's help and they turned back up the ravine, following the ancient trackway. Halfway up, he stopped. Something else about the prints caught his attention.

"Jazmin! These larger prints . . . look at them. The right foot indentation isn't *nearly* as deep as the left. This creature was favoring its right rear foot. Do you see it?"

"*Sí, sí* . . . So?"

Peter kneeled into a crouch to run his hand over the track, then looked up at Jazmin. "I was limping as I ran from the tyrannosaurus."

Her mouth hung open. "Are you saying you were the creature that left these prints?"

"Yes. At least I think so. Chan said my experiences were more than mere dreams. I believe him now. I felt the mud between my toes...smelled a hundred different scents. I could even smell my own blood as . . . that," he said, pointing to one of the predator's tracks, "started eating me."

"Oh, Peter, that's horrifying. No wonder you were frightened. Was this the same dream you had before?"

He nodded his head. "Only longer this time, with more detail. It was terrifying, but at the same time exhilarating..." His voice trailed off as he stared at the tracks.

"What's wrong?"

"Chan. He kept asking me who I was. I really don't know anymore." He took a deep breath. "I guess I never did. All I know is I'm more than this guy called Peter."

They contemplated the tracks and all the mysteries these implied a while longer, then climbed back up the ravine to the campsite. Jazmin prepared a light breakfast of breadnut, guava, and mamey, while Peter mulled over more details of the dinosaur chase.

"I remember seeing the reflection of my head and face in the water when I stopped to drink in the savanna. It was the same image I saw in my first vision—a *Corythosaurus*—a type of duckbill dinosaur with a large wedge on top of its head. I described them to you before. Do you remember what they look like?"

"I think so."

"As I crossed this great open plain, herds of magnificent dinosaurs roamed for as far as the eye could see. They were migrating, apparently. A herd of giant sauropods roamed to my right. Their necks must have reached fifty feet into the air when they saw that *Tyrannosaurus*." Peter reflected for a moment. "Wow, what a sight."

"It must have been amazing, *mi amor*."

"You know, if we could find some of those sauropod tracks, it would establish, at least in my mind, that what I experienced this morning really happened right here on this very spot."

"Sauropod tracks here? Spirit would have to guide us to them if we are to have any hope of finding them," Jazmin said. "Assuming those creatures even left tracks."

"It's a long shot. But we'll most likely never come back here again. Besides, Spirit went way out of the way to get me this far. There's something more to this than meets the eye. So, how about we give it a try?"

"Okay," she said, sighing as she stood. "It must be important."

They loaded their daypacks with the bare essentials necessary for a morning's hike, and started down the tracks, pausing at their water hole, where the rock ran under the sand.

"We ran for miles, but the conditions weren't right to lay down tracks until we came to the mud flat, where the ground was soft and wet. So, this was the general area where I saw the sauropods."

They continued down the ravine another hundred yards, then turned in a northerly direction where he had seen the plant eaters. Cutting their way through the thick brush with his *machete*, they arrived at the base of a vermilion cliff towering nearly a hundred feet above them. "This is hopeless." Peter looked up the cliff face. "We won't find anything here in this thick vegetation. There isn't any exposed rock."

Jazmin stroked his back, seeing his disappointment. "Why don't we climb the cliff? We can cool down in the breeze up there while we look around and have our lunch."

Higher ground sounded like a good alternative to the hot, buggy brush. They picked their way up the steep rock wall and soon stood on a plateau rim overlooking the jungle. A green paradise spread out before them like a lush carpet, but to Peter's disappointment, the outlying area revealed little exposed rock.

"This doesn't look too promising," he said.

But as he looked around at the steep face of the cliff they had just climbed, he noticed an unusual depression. Pointing down at a slab of exposed rock, he called out, and they stared together at a large depression in the rock. It was irregular, about two feet in diameter and four inches deep.

Peter immediately recognized it—a giant sauropod track. He hadn't expected to find one on the vertical bluff, high above the valley, but the earth had been shifting, rising from the valley for tens of millions of years. There was only one track, but that was enough.

"This is it," he said. "My God, this is really the place I saw in my vision." His face remained impassive.

Jazmin looked at him, and frowned. His reaction surprised both of them. He should have been happy, elated even, but he wasn't. The implications of the sauropod track, along with those below in the creek bed, were staggering. What should have been the joy of discovery turned out to be something else, something deeply disturbing.

Troubling thoughts raced through his consciousness. No longer did he live one life, but several lives . . . maybe more. How many more episodes would he have? And how would he control them? Could he control them?

Jazmin read his mind, giving him an impish grin. "I love you no matter what kind of animal you are."

He took her small hand in his and held it tenderly against his rough, unshaven cheek. "Thank you," he said, appreciating her humor as well as her effort to understand. He knew he would go crazy if he couldn't share his feelings and experiences with her. "Thank you for joining me in my world—one of them, anyway."

"I am happy to return the favor, *mi amor*."

They sat in the warm sunshine and reflected upon their discovery. "What is it all about, Peter?"

"What?"

"What are these tracks and those frightening visions of yours all about?"

He thought for a moment. "Chan was always asking me who I am. Well, I still don't have an answer. But I do know I'm more than Peter Campbell, or a dinosaur, or a Maya. I experienced these lives, and probably many more, but they do not define me. We are much more than the sum of our experiences, or lives."

After a short rest, they headed back to camp and began preparations to leave. They were packed and ready to go by mid-afternoon, with plenty of water and daylight left.

They stood in the wash and gazed upon the trackway one more time, thanking Spirit for leading them to the life-sustaining water. With gourds filled, they turned away from another chapter in their lives, heading for the mountains to the west.

"Jazmin, you didn't happen to see a frigate bird flying around here this morning, did you?"

She laughed. "Of course not. They're a shore bird. You won't see any frigate birds around here."

CHAPTER 26

Peter wiped his hand across his forehead before the sweat stung his eyes. Like a giant sauna, the jungle languished under the hot sun, exuding a steamy tropical perspiration even the dense canopy could not cool. "These trees are suffocating me," he said.

"It is awfully hot," Jazmin agreed as she let her pack fall to the ground. "But it is not the trees' fault."

"It may just be my imagination," he retorted, "but it seems this jungle produces either too much, or too little water, and we're either fleeing from it or dying for the lack of it."

Their gourds were nearly empty again. They had followed the monkeys, who knew where food rich in moisture could be found, but the wise primates left little to their desperate relatives. After three days of climbing and working their way through the dense jungle, they found themselves surrounded by a deep canyon. Exhausted and worried, Jazmin looked at him with swollen lips. "Do you know which way to go?"

He glanced at her. "Not really. It's hard to follow the sun through this heavy canopy." He took the compass out of his pack and opened the brass covering.

"I cannot keep this up much longer," she added, licking her parched lips. "We only have a few sips of water left."

He looked at the compass, closed it, and placed it back in his pack without comment. Jazmin looked at him, expecting some direction, but none came.

"What does your compass say?"

"It says we're lost."

Jazmin looked on the verge of tears. He balled his fist into his shorts pocket. Unbelievable, getting lost a second time. He could think of nothing to say that would console her.

"As uncertain as we are, we haven't asked Spirit for help today," Jazmin added. "What has happened to us?"

"I guess we aren't desperate enough."

"Well, I'm desperate enough now." Her tone exuded anger. "And I am not going another step until we receive guidance. Chan sent us here because we had the ability to listen to the spirits of the jungle and survive. Very few have survived this jungle. Even those professional soldiers were swallowed up by it. They had no chance, and neither do we if we don't listen to its voice. Every time we set off without Spirit's guidance, something has gone wrong."

"That's the pattern," he agreed, inspecting his worn sandals and bruised feet. "You're right. But after all we've gone through, I felt we'd get through the rest of the journey without much trouble."

Jazmin shot him a look of disbelief. He slumped against his pack, ignoring her gaze. They weren't going anywhere until she was good and ready. And it didn't matter, because he had no idea which way to proceed anyway.

They eased into quiet contemplation, breathing the stagnant air as the incessant mosquitoes, flies, and myriad other insects buzzed around their faces. But even they lost interest as the couple tuned deeper into Spirit. The world seemed to hold its breath, and the jungle became quiet with the exception of an intermittent call of a distant bird. They sat for well over an hour before Peter stirred and glanced at Jazmin. She opened her eyes and smiled and he rejoiced to see her that way.

"The trees here are very soothing."

"Getting anything?"

"No," she said. "But I feel better. You?"

Peter shook his head and settled against his pack again, trying not to think about their predicament.

His mind drifted to a tranquil image of Chan. He thought to ask Chan for help, but was distracted by a wasp flying past his head. The high-pitched drone of insects usually irritated him, but this time he focused his full attention on it rather than ignoring the sound. He tried to imagine what the tiny insect was feeling, what it sensed, what attracted the bug to him. The sound deepened. Far away at first, it became louder and louder until he feared an imminent attack by a giant insect. He flinched and opened his eyes, confronted not by the world's largest insect, but by the world's smallest bird.

A tiny hummingbird hovered in front of his face, displaying a soft gray chest and a crimson red throat that cast a jewel-like sparkle where the sun struck it. Peter drank in the spectacle, as fascinated by the bird as it was by him. He slowly turned his head to one side, expecting the bird to fly away; but the bird stayed directly in front of his face. He rotated his head in the other direction. Again, the bird moved with him in a synchronistic dance, hovering a mere foot from his face.

"Are your eyes open?" he whispered.

Jazmin stirred. "Hmm?"

"Open your eyes."

Her eyes opened, and she caught her breath. Peter rotated his head from side to side. Again, the bird followed.

"It's a ruby throat," Jazmin whispered, excitement palpable in her voice. "I think it is trying to tell you something."

"What did you call it?"

"A ruby throat. Ruby-throated hummingbird."

Ruby. "Do you remember Chan mentioning a ruby? It was the last thing he said the night the village was attacked."

"Yes. He said it would lead us out of darkness." Jazmin studied the hummingbird for a moment as it hovered in front of Peter. Suddenly she sprang to her feet, startling the bird. Its wings beat faster, accelerating as it pulled back a few inches.

"Peter, get up. The hummingbird is going to show us the way out of here. Hurry. It has waited for us to see the obvious."

"Damn, why didn't I think of that?"

"You would have, *amor*." She touched his arm tenderly, and gave him a hand to pull himself up. "I saw Chan's face when we sat down and I asked him for help."

When Peter stood, the hummingbird flew into a nearby tree and perched on a branch. They shouldered their packs and waited for the tiny bird to fly. It looked at them as if wondering what they wanted. Five minutes passed. The hummingbird began to preen itself.

Peter glanced at Jazmin. "Did someone forget to clue the bird into the master plan?"

Just as he spoke, the little bird took flight.

Jazmin grabbed her pack. "Peter! Let's go."

They ran to catch up, hoping for glimpses of its radiant body as they thrashed through the underbrush, but the green back of the tiny bird kept it well hidden. Trying to keep track of the little speedster in the thick jungle proved to be a hopeless task. When they emerged in a clearing, they stopped to look for it, but the hummingbird was nowhere in sight.

"This can't be right." Peter wiped the sweat out of his eyes with his T-shirt. "We're going back the way we came."

"So? We're lost," Jazmin said.

"Okay. Point made."

The hummingbird seemed to come from nowhere, reappearing directly in front of Peter's face, then dove into the thicket ahead of them. They ran after it, searching the trees, but the hummingbird was just too small and swift to track. After a short distance, they stumbled upon an animal trail. It was easy to follow and with few options at hand, they chose to follow it. The little bird was nowhere to be seen.

After several hours, the trail began to ascend into what seemed to be another impassable canyon. But as they came closer to a cliff, Peter spied a way up the canyon wall. There was no trail, but the rocky cliff could be traversed. Climbing hand and foot, they crawled up the steep incline. Peter reached the top first and sniffed the air curiously. He smiled and reached to help Jazmin up the last few feet.

"Smell it?"

"¡Sí, sí!" She smiled back. "Sea water!"

They ran to an overlook facing west. In the distance loomed the glassy, blue-green surface of the Pacific Ocean, a sight they had labored for so many difficult weeks to reach. Jazmin jumped into Peter's arms. "Chan said we could do it."

Then they turned and faced east, toward the jungle. The jungle seemed reluctant to let them leave after it had accepted them. Like a jealous, petulant child, it had made their lives as difficult as possible when they were nearly out of sight.

Jazmin said a prayer to the spirits of the jungle, thanking them for the gifts of courage and endurance, and for saving them from certain death. "Our ordeal is over, but my heart will remain with the jungle," she said, tears in her eyes.

Relieved to be free of the jungle, Peter glanced at her, chastened by her pain. He realized they truly did owe their lives to the forest, and that they must return the favor.

They sat to relish the cool ocean breeze playing on the ridge, teasing their hair and caressing their faces. But they still needed fresh water and would have to keep moving.

Several miles in the distance, thatched roofs stood amidst the thinning stands of trees, and beyond those, the barely discernible markings of a town. Peter pointed out the shimmer of a river in the afternoon light, coursing its way through the green valley into the bay beyond. "It must be the Rio Tehuantepec."

"*Sí, sí,* Peter. Finally, we will meet the Cloud People."

"The Cloud People?"

"*Sí.* This is what they are called."

CHAPTER 27

As the Tehuantepec River wound its way to the sea, great cumulus clouds billowed overhead, dwarfing the enormous shade trees and the picturesque city of old adobe buildings and thatched huts lining its shore A few miles upriver from the Pacific Ocean, the quaint metropolis merged with the lush tropical jungle sheltering it from the constant winds blowing inland from the Gulf of Tehuantepec.

Peter felt his tension drop away as they hiked along the river valley. Cool ocean breezes supplanted the unbearable heat of the inner jungle as they moved along a well-worn path. Unlike the stagnant air of the interior, the shore air was sweet and fresh. So peaceful and picturesque was the land that they found themselves seduced into a feeling of safety and security.

Is this too good to be true? Peter's thought dissolved into the most pressing urgency of the day—finding water.

Peter and Jazmin came to the first of several small villages along the way and spotted an old well in the *zocalo*, the village square, where a tiny native woman strained to crank a wooden bucket up to the surface. Children watched nearby as she struggled with the rickety old crank. Peter pointed her out, and they picked up their pace. When they arrived at the well, he offered to help, turning the wooden-handled crank to bring the leaky bucket up to the top in record time. The old woman thanked him in her native tongue and offered them water. They scooped it from the bucket with eager hands, not waiting to fill their gourds. Water had never tasted so good.

"Pure Spirit," Jazmin said, as he splashed water over his sweaty head.

The landscape lulled them like a drug into its carefree mood, their morning anxieties evaporating in the midday sun. People waved and smiled as they passed through the surrounding farmland. Dogs barked and chickens scurried away as cicadas beat their wings in a high-pitched chorus from the trees.

Several times along their path, excited children ran to greet them, unafraid of the tattered strangers. They asked many questions, very few that he or even Jazmin understood. Few people visited the outskirts of the city, and no one ever came through from the jungle.

They passed one village after another bordered by large groves of coconut trees filled with ripened fruit. The cool tropical breeze blew lazily through the large palm fronds, adding to the serenity of the landscape. Jazmin smiled at the waving trees. The wind ruffled the surface of the river as they walked along its banks. When they stood at the outskirts of Tehuantepec, the air became fragrant with the sweet aroma of flowers.

Dense tropical gardens lined the streets and walkways with red, yellow, purple, and pink flowers. Papaya, mango, banana, coconut, *zapote*, and other fruit trees stood in abundance in the endless gardens that greeted them outside every home and business. Intoxicated by the sweet aroma and beautiful people, Jazmin smiled at him and took his hand.

"This reminds me so much of my home. How would you like to live in México?" she asked, teasing him.

"Actually, it looks pretty good to me right now," he said, hugging her. The Tehuantepec River divided the city in half, and they soon came to a proud old bridge of finely cut rock that spanned the river in a series of graceful arches. They made their way across the bridge and entered the heart of the city, where gaily-dressed natives strolled along the walkways laughing and calling out greetings to one another. Within the heart of the quaint city, the women dressed more fashionably than those on the outskirts of town, making Jazmin feel more self-conscious. They had stood out in their rags in the villages along the way, but now they looked like beggars. Jazmin's finest red T-shirt, which she had used only to sleep in, now showed a dirty brown, and her khaki shorts were stained beyond hope. Peter's shorts and shirts had fared even worse. All their clothes had been torn and mended countless times.

"We need to get to the market and buy some clothes," Jazmin whispered.

He nodded in agreement, and stopped to look for the little money he had brought. Digging through his pack, he discovered the bills he had brought into the jungle with him were now half-rotted away and stained beyond recognition.

"A fresh change of clothes would be great," he said, holding back the bad news, not wanting to disappoint her. "Perhaps we could work a trade in the square?"

Many of the women wore embroidered flower designs and lace ruffles lining their skirts and blouses. Colorful headdresses, bright ribbon, and flowers completed their festive attire, mimicking the beauty of the land. Everywhere dense tropical gardens grew behind vine-covered walls, each nook and cranny spilling forth with flowers.

"This is beautiful beyond anything I've ever seen in México, or anywhere for that matter," Jazmin said with a sigh. "It is amazing, but the spirits of the jungle also live right here in the heart of the city." She smiled and squeezed his hand. "The trees are so happy."

Homes of adobe and rock with tiled roofs and balconies overflowing with flowers beckoned passersby to stop and admire. Color, texture, and fragrance dazzled their senses.

"The locals seem to be getting ready for a festival," Jazmin said.

"Apparently," he said, taking in the spectacle. "There's something unusual about this town. What is it about this place?"

228

She nodded her head. "It is so relaxed, and everything is so beautiful, a city of flowers, a Zapotec city."

"Maybe that's why we haven't seen policemen, or *Federales*."

"Or a man." Jazmin stopped, and placed her arm around his waist. "I better keep an eye on you. You may be the only available man in town."

"You might be right," he added. "I've seen only a few younger boys, and one or two old men leading donkeys through town."

Women walked in pairs casually down the main promenade with a confidence they had not witnessed elsewhere in México. The town's serene ambience was tangible. Instinct told them they were safe and secure here.

They inhaled deeply of the salty breeze from the bay and continued walking, passing burros lumbering placidly along the cobblestone lanes, weighted down with enormous loads that hid most of their humble frames except hooves and ears. The burros' burdens of sugar cane, pottery, brightly colored textiles, *guaraches*, hemp, and occasionally a stout *señora*, were all headed to market.

On a hill towering over the town stood a splendid old adobe church with patched walls and a cracked bell in its tower. Peter imagined a Spanish cannon had shattered its walls in some long-forgotten revolution. As if stepping back in time a hundred years or more, old churches and adobe homes stood elegantly along the way, quietly whispering their long history of romance and conflict. The air was thick with the sights and sounds of a city rich in history. The language spoken was the native Zapotec, with an occasional Spanish name thrown in for those things introduced by the European cultures. This was a Native American town with indigenous traditions and beliefs still intact.

"It would be difficult to find a town anywhere in the world more beautiful than this," Jazmin said, as they strolled along the main street like tourists. "It is so much like my home. The people are so peaceful and warm, their spirits full of life and love."

"Yeah, but we don't want to expose ourselves unnecessarily," Peter said, interrupting her reverie. "There may be *Federales* looking for us here."

"I guess you are right." She looked at him with a long face. "But they look like such nice people."

He rolled his eyes. Keeping Jazmin from socializing was like trying to herd cats. She loved people, and they were naturally attracted to her. Staying hidden in this town would be difficult, as there were few tourists.

They entered a large square, passing merchants selling food and handmade products. Peter's stomach growled at the sight and scents of mounds of *chilés*, sweet peppers, onions, sugar cane, mangoes, and an endless array of other fruits and vegetables he could not identify. In one area of the market, sticky cactus candy and a plethora of bakery goods begged to be purchased. The aromas were particularly inviting—even painful—to hungry stomachs.

Jazmin's eyes lit up. "I'm starving. Let's buy some fruit and vegetables and maybe a sweet roll to eat somewhere quiet."

Peter cringed. The only trade item they still possessed was his *machete*, and it wasn't worth much. "We have a slight problem."

"What?"

"The money in my pack rotted away." Peter knew this was the last thing Jazmin wanted to hear. At least they could forage for food in the jungle.

Jazmin's large brown eyes began to fill with tears. "I thought our struggle was over. Isn't everything supposed to be better now?"

Peter wrapped an arm around her. They had hiked a dozen miles since the break of day. Physical exhaustion and their fear of encountering *Federales* in town were driving them to the limits of their endurance. They needed food and rest and they needed it soon. The only thing keeping Peter in motion was his concern for Jazmin. He had to think of something fast.

"We just need to get to a phone. Once we get in touch with someone, we can have them wire money."

"Okay, *amorcito*."

The first order of business was finding a telephone. They had some uncooked vegetables they could get by on until they found a way to buy or barter for food. Curious eyes followed their progress as they passed the market stalls, but no one spoke to them.

They made their way past the many vendors with their *serapes* and *piñatas*, *machetes*, leather goods, ceramics, baskets, and weavings to a wide sidewalk that led to an intersection with a quiet, narrow walkway winding into some low hills along the river. They stopped to admire the elegant homes built around inviting patios perfumed with flowers. The homes suggested peace and intimacy in the tradition of the country *rancho* where the stranger was always welcome. But under the circumstances, they could take nothing for granted. They hesitated and looked into each other's eyes, tired, disoriented, and unsure which direction to go.

Jazmin wrapped her arms around Peter and began to cry. They allowed themselves a moment of vulnerability as they caressed one another, oblivious to passersby. In the jungle, they had learned well the importance of letting their emotions run their course. Pent-up fear had driven them to exhaustion more than once, nearly killing them, and they knew now to allow their bodies to release fear and anxiety so they could adapt to a higher vibration. It was an important moment; one that would allow them to regroup.

After the long embrace, they looked around, surprised by the stares of a dozen women and twice as many children with long, sorrowful faces, showing apparent empathy for them. Flushing, Peter and Jazmin smiled and greeted the women, then picked up their packs to move on. This simple action caused sudden excitement and a flurry of chatter in the Zapotec tongue.

"*¿Que pasa?*" Peter whispered.

"I'm not sure," Jazmin whispered back. "But their dialect is close to my own." She paused to listen. "They're talking about our torn and soiled clothing."

"They're not used to seeing Americans either."

"I think it's more than that, *amor*. They talk as though they expected to see us."

"How can that be?"

One of the ladies spoke reassuring words, taking Jazmin by the arm and ushering her down the narrow walkway, leaving Peter to bring their packs. Too tired to resist, she turned to glance back at him with a look of resignation.

Peter picked up their packs, and scrambled to follow. "Where do you suppose they're taking us?" he asked over the women's chatter. "Do you think it's safe?"

"*Caro mio*," she replied. "If you think these women are dangerous you have been in the jungle too long."

Peter just shrugged, realizing Jazmin and the women had already established a mutual trust. They soon arrived at the bottom of a flight of ornate tile stairs leading up to a home. The excitement in the women's voices increased as they ascended the steps and entered the house through a large handcrafted wooden door. A short hallway paved with Saltillo tile opened to a spacious room with stucco walls. Locally made pigskin chairs and tables were scattered about on the famous Zapotec rugs, for which these people were best known. At the far end of the room, French doors opened onto a verandah enclosed by a wrought-iron railing intertwined with hot pink and lavender bougainvillea. Peter and Jazmin glanced around, instinctively taking in the room's details, surprised by the simple yet lavish surroundings.

Three ladies ushered Jazmin into a smaller room, followed closely by the other women, still chattering with excitement. One woman returned to the large room with a stack of neatly folded clothes. She held out her arms to Peter and presented them. The joy she exuded overcame any apprehension that he felt, and he graciously accepted her offering. She pointed to a room, and pushed him toward the door like a mother encouraging a child.

Peter took his time to crawl out of the soiled, shredded clothes that had served him so well during the months they'd spent in the jungle. They looked unacceptable next to the clean clothes. To his delight, he discovered that not only did the new clothes fit, he truly liked the simple cotton pants and tunics of the peasantry—unpretentious, comfortable, and appropriate for blending into a crowd.

He stepped out of his room, and found the women had gathered again in the common area of the house. They voiced their approval in Zapotec and with hand gestures. One beautiful woman caught Peter's eye. After looking twice, he realized it was Jazmin. He didn't recognize her in colorful full-length native dress, so accustomed was he to her khaki shorts and simple T-shirts. She could have passed for a young Tehuantepec woman, except that she stood a full six inches taller than most of them.

"You look stunning."

"And you, *Señor*," Jazmin replied with a curtsy.

The women and children crowding the room stood quietly, looking self-conscious. They apparently spoke little or no Spanish, and not one seemed to be a natural leader. After an awkward silence, one of the children farted, and the tension turned into hysterical laughter. Soon, everyone in the room was talking again.

"Do you know what's going on?" Peter asked Jazmin above the chatter. "I have no idea," she answered, smiling broadly. "But are they not wonderful?"

"Yes. And I can't believe these clothes fit. Seems odd, as if they expected us."

Tropical fruit drinks in colorful glassware from Oaxaca were passed out among the many guests, officially getting the party underway. Jazmin looked puzzled as a commotion at the door turned everyone's heads. A young woman in an embroidered cotton dress ushered an older woman inside somewhat ceremoniously. Full-bodied with a round yet attractive face, the matron radiated inner beauty with an air of authority. Spotting Peter, she approached without hesitation, arms outstretched, speaking in flawless Spanish.

"*Buenas tardes, Señor* Campbell. I am Rosa. Welcome to my home."

Peter looked at her in astonishment, returning her hug. "How do you know my name?" He felt a sudden tightness in his chest.

"Word travels quickly in the jungle," she said, offering him her hand. "But where is the beautiful *Señorita* Jazmin?"

Jazmin stepped forward and Rosa's eyes filled with tears as she embraced her.

"My poor child," Rosa said with great emotion, as if Jazmin were a long-lost daughter whom she had given up for dead. Several sniffles could be heard as Rosa continued to hug and kiss Jazmin, and to stroke her matted hair.

"My poor child," she repeated, looking into Jazmin's eyes. "You look terrible. Your face is scratched and your hair tangled. How did you ever survive that jungle, and those treacherous soldiers?"

Jazmin shot a look at Peter. "Rosa, thank you so much for your concern, but how do you know about us?"

"We received news of your journey through the Forbidden Jungle from San Cristóbal." Rosa's rapid speech reflected her excitement. "Word was passed from village to village until it reached Tehuantepec. They said you would go west, and that men with guns were chasing you. We feared for you, my child. We did not think you would survive. No one survives the Forbidden Jungle. The Mother Mary herself blessed you. We know because we prayed to her every day. It is a miracle. Imagine our excitement to hear of you this morning."

Rosa crossed herself tearfully, and all the women in the room followed suit. Jazmin crossed herself too, then took Rosa by the arms, and looked her square in the eyes.

"You have heard from San Cristóbal?"

"*Sí,*" Rosa replied.

"Are the Lacandón people alive and safe?"

"They were alive when we last heard of their plight, but they were still pursued by those murderers. It has been many weeks now. I am sorry my child, this is all we know. They are in our prayers."

Jazmin sighed. "Hopefully the forest will protect them until we can call the embassy, and stop this terrible crime."

"What day of the week is it, Rosa?" Peter asked, anxious to make contact with the authorities.

"It is Sunday."

"We won't be able to reach anyone at the consulate today," Peter said.

Some of the women busied themselves about the house as Rosa led Peter and Jazmin to a tiled patio overlooking a spacious courtyard. Huge shade trees canopied the entire area, and flowers hung in profusion from every balcony. A large fountain spraying arcs of water stood in the middle of the square surrounded by red, yellow, and purple flowers. The water could scarcely be heard over the many chattering parrots in the surrounding trees. Several people waved at them from the courtyard and other balconies.

Jazmin took Peter's hand. "We have friends here. It's almost as though I am back home. I never suspected a place like this existed. The town is so beautiful." She turned to Rosa. "Rosa, we thought the entire city was preparing for a celebration because the people are so beautifully dressed."

"Yes, we have been preparing for a celebration in honor of our special guests."

"Who are you expecting?"

Rosa laughed and translated to the women still hovering nearby. They laughed too, holding their hands over their mouths.

"You are our honored guests."

Jazmin looked at Peter in bewilderment.

"You just said you thought we were dead until word of our arrival came this morning," Jazmin said.

"No, no. Several days ago, a little bird told us you would come."

Rosa laughed and told the other women what she said. They smiled in amusement.

"Yolima had a dream," Rosa continued. "Yolima is a dreamer, and always she is right. In her dream, she saw a little hummingbird. The hummingbird was you. When she was hanging out her laundry early yesterday morning, the little hummingbird from her dream hovered near her and she knew you would arrive soon."

"What did the hummingbird look like, Rosa?" Jazmin asked.

Rosa glanced at an attractive young woman still on the verandah and asked her something in their native tongue. Peter guessed the girl to be in her late teens. Her eyes shone like black pearls, accenting her glossy, jet-black hair. A verbal exchange with a great deal of hand gestures ensued, then Rosa turned back to Jazmin to translate. "It was very small and green…and on its throat was a red mark the color of our beautiful bougainvillea."

Jazmin and Peter gazed at one another. The hummingbird had truly played a larger part in their lives than they had ever imagined possible. As Chan had predicted, there was no understanding the jungle, only experiencing it.

With a curious smile on her face, Rosa led them back into the house, down a hallway past several bedrooms, and into a large, beautifully tiled bathroom. Richly colored deep blue and yellow tile adorned both wall and floor. The large white porcelain tub filled with steaming hot water at the center of the room caught Peter and Jazmin's attention. Lavender bougainvillea floated on the water, exuding a fragrant aroma. Two large candles sat below the tub, keeping the water warm. Peter noticed the room had no plumbing, so the water had to have been brought up by hand. He looked at the tub of water with longing as Jazmin hugged their hostess.

"*Muchas gracias, Señora*," Jazmin said, smiling as broadly as her cracked lips allowed. "We have not had a bath in days."

"Thank Spirit for a tub big enough to fit the two of us," he whispered to Jazmin, "because I don't feel too chivalrous right now."

The women ushered themselves out of the bathroom and without hesitation, Jazmin and Peter disrobed and slid into the soothing hot water.

For several minutes they bathed silently, floating their aching bodies in the deep bath. Jazmin began toying with the shampoo sitting on a tiled shelf next to the tub, then worked up a fine lather and massaged it into her hair, while Peter simply dissolved into the warm suds.

"Nothing could feel any better than this," he mumbled, then dunked his head under the bubbles. Jazmin ran a foot along one of the scars on his chest, then along his arm.

"Hmm," she murmured. "Are you sure this isn't one of those trick dreams of yours? This is too good to be real."

"Hell, I don't know. What do I know from real anymore?"

"If it is, don't wake me up for a while. Okay?"

"You're on."

After their long-overdue bath, Peter sat and watched Jazmin towel herself off. The sexual attraction he'd had just a tantalizing taste of during their weeks in the jungle flared inside him. Jazmin's sleek, tan body glistened with moisture, and even with her many scratches and bruises, her womanhood was striking. As Peter dried her back, he kissed her tenderly on the neck. She turned to face him, lovely as he had ever seen her. She looked deeply into his eyes, sensing the change. Some electric current that had been held dormant between them was suddenly alive. Her eyes caressed and teased him, and for the first time in weeks, Peter wanted her desperately.

He ran his hands over her smooth moist skin, gently caressing her. Her breathing heightened, threatening to overtake her, as he led her to the bed and gently laid her on the fine cotton sheets.

"Oh, Peter," she moaned, unable to hide her passion.

He started to caress her when someone knocked on their bedroom door. "Please, would our honored guests join us for dinner?" Rosa called.

They looked at one another, wondering if their hostess's timing could have been any worse. But they were guests, and their hunger for food every bit as great as their hunger for one another.

With grudging motions, they slipped from the bed and into their new clothes, making their way to the main living quarters of Rosa's home. Oddly, no one was there, so they headed toward the murmur of hushed voices on the veranda. Suddenly, a hundred people greeted them from below with cheers. Peter nearly knocked Jazmin off her feet as he turned and started to run from the unexpected uproar. Pleased at his surprise, the crowd below clapped and cheered, laughing and crowing at his astonishment.

Peter waved and smiled weakly at the crowd. "I've come to hate surprises," he muttered."

"What fun," Jazmin said, beaming down at the colorful gathering. "These people are so much like my own. They love to celebrate life."

Paper lanterns lit the darkening courtyard with an array of color, and *piñatas* hung in the trees just out of reach of the excited children. A colorful assortment of food lined a row of portable tables. Musicians began strumming guitars, bowing fiddles, and blowing trumpets. The party was underway.

Peter turned to Jazmin and managed another weak smile. "Well, it doesn't look like we'll be getting to bed anytime soon."

"It will be okay, *mi amor*. We are starving. We will eat, then disappear."

Peter looked at her with skepticism, knowing they were the guests of honor and that the average *Méxicano* could party all night. He could only hope the Native population was more conservative than their Mexican counterparts.

"I am famished," he acknowledged, inhaling the many fine aromas drifting through the air.

"These people are very good cooks," Jazmin said, smiling. "They live to cook."

Rosa appeared at their side to introduce them. Their many hosts and hostesses greeted them like old friends. One after another, the people embraced their guests like long-lost cousins, but the only thing on Peter's mind was the food on the courtyard's far side. They greeted more people as they made their way to the steaming, colorful platters and bowls of food arranged on a long plank table.

Peter ate with abandon, relishing the many sensational aromas and flavors. Jazmin selected her food cautiously; careful to pick lightly cooked vegetarian entrées, a difficult task considering most of the women felt it their personal duty to fatten up the two half-starved fugitives that very evening. Jazmin tried to explain her eating habits, but the women only shook their heads in bewilderment, pressing their shrimp-filled tortillas, steamed mussels, chicken enchiladas, and other delicacies in huge helpings onto her plate.

Rosa expressed particular distress at Jazmin's fussy diet. "Eat more," she pleaded throughout the evening, convinced they could not have found enough food to sustain themselves in the jungle. The partygoers offered food at every opportunity, and while Jazmin managed to say "no, thank you" throughout the evening, Peter continued to eat.

Though still outnumbered by women, the Tehuantepec men finally made an appearance. Dressed in their finest well-fitted slacks, smart felt hats with flat rims, and colorfully embroidered vests, they made a fine complement to the ladies. Proud and handsome, they exhibited the dark and leathery weathered look of hard-working peasants.

"Where were all the men today?" Peter asked Rosa after toasting the Mother Mary with several men.

"Oh," she said, gesturing with a wide sweep of her hand, looking a little tipsy. "We send them off to the fields to work. God gave us men to work the fields, and help us make babies, but we do not need them in town. Only women understand the business of running a town. Life is much more peaceful this way."

Peter turned to Jazmin and smiled. "Well, that explains that."

"See what a town of emancipated women can do given the chance?" Jazmin said, beaming mischievously. "This is the most beautiful city in all of México."

"Can't argue with that," Peter replied, toasting life with his male cohorts. "This must be the only city in history governed by women. No wonder they walk the streets with such pride and confidence."

While well-mannered and gentle in speech, the Zapotec men felt it their unbridled privilege to get Peter drunk. They offered beer, wine, and tequila in generous amounts. He refused all offers at first, then finally gave in and accepted a glass of beer. After taking several polite sips, he listened to his sensitive stomach and quietly discarded his drink in the nearest flowerpot. This strategy worked for the first few rounds, but as the evening wore on, the men handed more drinks to him, and offered more toasts. Eventually, the small sips began to mount up. The musicians seemed to play louder and faster with each round, and the people danced in greater and greater animation until Peter located Jazmin and ushered her away to make their way around the courtyard.

"We are underdressed," Jazmin despaired, looking with longing at the beautifully attired women. "I would love some dresses and skirts and blouses like the ones here this evening."

"Well," Peter replied, "right now, I would be content just to lie on a clean bed with you."

"That sounds wonderful." She smiled, kissing him passionately. "Why don't we disappear into the crowd?"

Making their way through the crowd of revelers proved more difficult than they had hoped. A head taller than most of the men, Peter stood out from the crowd. Everyone wanted to toast his heroic deeds as the couple passed through the celebration.

Hours later, Peter teetered sideways as Jazmin and several other ladies shored him upright up the staircase and into their room. A full midnight moon hovered directly overhead, its brilliance softened by the humid night air. With barely enough strength to undress, they crawled into the bed's luxuriously soft cotton sheets. "I don't feel so good," Peter said as his head hit the pillow.

The night air drifted through the bedroom, caressing their bare bodies as they snuggled. From the courtyard below, they could still hear music and the fading sounds of laughter.

CHAPTER 28

The first thing Peter heard at dawn was an army of birds chattering beyond the balcony doors—the trill of grackles, the soft keening of mourning doves, and the shriek of parrots.

He became aware of Jazmin in his arms, and the sweet aroma of flowers drifting into the bedroom. They had slept like the dead. He eased his head from side-to-side, blinking to test what damage the night's celebration had caused, and found himself surprisingly clear-headed. His lean, fit body had recovered quickly from the exhausting march into town and the effects of alcohol. A sound sleep in a soft bed with clean sheets had served him well. What a difference to feel rested, strong, and safe again.

He pulled Jazmin closer, nuzzling her hair to draw in her scent, sweet in the manner of the early morning forest, when dew still trembled on leaf and twig. Amazing what a little shampoo and warm water could do. He ran his hand over her sleek body and thick, silky hair, languishing in the delicate scent of her supple skin. Was it a coincidence her parents had named her after a plant with such a sweet aroma?

He kissed her tenderly in the hollow area just below the ear, then on her earlobe. His free hand drifted to her stomach, then to her breasts, gently teasing and caressing her nipples erect. She moaned in a murmur, her desire coming to life, and began pushing gently against him, inviting his caresses. "*Mi amor*," she whispered.

His hands continued to do their magic. Her breathing quickened, and her hips pulsated to the easy rhythm of his hand. Turning her head toward him, she pushed her lips hard into his, allowing their tongues to entwine, and then pressed closer still.

Their bodies moved with a new awareness, absorbed in one another, alive with sensation, pleasing, teasing, panting. The large wooden frame of the bed began to creak under their weight. Jazmin cried out softly at first, careful not to awaken their hosts. But having waited for this moment so long, she soon gave into his steady rhythm and cried out her joy. The bed shuddered, the headboard hitting the adobe wall with a steady thud, then all was quiet except the chatter of birds beyond the balcony. Spent and satisfied, they lay entwined in each other's arms.

Jazmin fondled Peter's hair, studying his dark, weathered face and deep blue eyes. "We're feeling *much* better this morning," she teased.

He laughed, and she glowed from deep within herself, squeezing him tightly.

Peter kissed her again, tenderly this time.

"Yeah, last night wasn't one of my better nights."

"Your eyes have changed," she said. "Their color is deeper, more radiant. The jungle has healed you from the darkness of your past."

"Maybe."

"If you want my diagnosis, you've made a complete recovery."

"Thanks, Doc. I'd almost forgotten how wonderful life can feel."

"Mm! It is better than ever."

Peter rolled over, and picked up his watch from the dresser: 5:05 a.m.—jungle time. During all the weeks in the jungle, they had become accustomed to rising before sunrise, when the air was cool and the insects less active. The American consulate wouldn't open until 8:00 a.m. Plenty of time to find a phone.

He shut his eyes and thought about the dark emotions he had carried through the jungle. Although his dark fear had dissipated after the events in *Na-Bolom*, his uneasiness still lingered. Why? Then a name popped into his mind.

José Aguilar. El Presidente was not through with him.

Peter watched as Jazmin crawled out of bed, slipped on Rosa's simple cotton robe, and stepped out onto the small balcony facing the courtyard. Many unseen birds called from the large jacaranda trees that filled the courtyard with deep shade and a carpet of lavender blossoms. A movement below caught her attention. Several party guests were still asleep, passed out in the flowerbeds along the walls of the courtyard.

"There are still people down there." She turned to him, and pointed below the balcony.

He smiled. Jazmin observed the trees' branches swaying almost imperceptibly in the morning breeze. It seemed to Peter as if the trees were gently calling to her. She stroked one of the leaves, and spoke softly to it. He sat up and looked closer, thinking he could almost see the love flow from her into the tree. The jungle had changed her as well, strengthening the love already manifest in her. She turned her radiant face toward Peter and held him in her gaze. Her eyes sparkled like smoked glass in the morning light. His soul bathed in them, transfixed by their beauty.

Several minutes eased by before he stood, smoothly placing one leg at a time into his pants before finding his way to the adjoining bathroom. He detoured to the door leading into the common room where several ladies lay asleep on couches and floor, and then looked back at Jazmin. She seemed to be in peaceful meditation. So solid and tangible was the moment, it seemed nothing could disturb the peace, but something did.

Jazmin spun around suddenly, and locked eyes with him. He knew the look on her face well, immediately recognizing it. The trees must have warned her of something. Like a deer sensing danger, she stood motionless on the balcony, obviously listening to her inner voice. He asked her with hand movements where the danger was. She indicated she did not know with a slight shake of her head. He looked across the room to where his gun lay hidden under the mattress, and began stepping across the bathroom, but it was too late.

Screams followed a loud commotion at the front door, stopping him cold in his tracks. Someone was forcibly entering the house.

Men's voices growled commands as heavy footsteps trod into the front room.

Peter stepped backward into the bathroom and eased the door closed to a crack so he could peer into the living room. Men in black uniforms flashed by the living room—one, then another. Peter knew the soldiers weren't interested in the women. They wanted him and Jazmin, and would soon search the rest of the house.

Jazmin still stood on the balcony, frozen in panic. Peter opened the door and gestured her toward the closet. Their only hope of survival depended upon surprise.

He covered the small bathroom window with a towel to darken the room, then eased back to the door and listened.

A soldier asked questions of the women while another stepped down the hall, toward the bedroom, stopped, and then continued inside. He heard the closet door open, and braced for a quick burst out of the bathroom, but there were no sounds of a struggle.

Peter removed a wrought iron crucifix from the bathroom wall, praying the soldier would not kick the bathroom door in, exposing him before he could wallop him.

Footsteps came across the bedroom floor toward him, and he trembled as the door opened halfway. The dark barrel of an M40 carbine appeared first, but the soldier moved casually, as though not expecting to find anyone inside. When the man stuck his head through the darkened doorway, the black uniform sent shivers through Peter. He brought the cross crashing down on the soldier's head, and the man dropped to the floor, out cold.

Peter picked up the weapon, then peered through the door and down the hall. The other soldier still stood in the front room, watching over the women. He hadn't heard the commotion.

He dragged the unconscious soldier the rest of the way into the bathroom, crept out and closed the door, gritting his teeth at the small click of the door's hardware. Easing across the hall to the bedroom, he stepped onto the balcony, peered around the corner, and found Jazmin hugging the outside wall.

She exhaled with relief when she saw him. "I expected a soldier," she whispered.

He pointed to the house, indicating to her that another soldier was inside. She crept into the bedroom and began taking the sheets off the bed. Peter had no idea what she was doing.

She tied the corners of two sheets together and cautiously returned to the balcony. He stayed in the bedroom, watching for the other soldier. She tied one end of the sheets to the railing, knotted it tightly, then threw her handiwork over the railing. The sheets nearly reached the ground. He signed thumbs up, and signaled her to go first. She hitched up her borrowed nightgown and threw a leg over the railing, then worked her way to the courtyard floor, breathing hard.

Peter moved toward the balcony, glancing back into the room just when a heavy-set soldier burst in, a few feet separating the two men. Their eyes fell on one another, and for a brief moment, the soldier froze.

In that stolen moment, Peter kicked the rifle from the soldier's hand and slammed the butt of it into his head. The man reeled against the wall, but recovered quickly.

With terrific force, he shoved Peter across the room and onto the balcony, nearly hurtling him over the railing. Bent over the railing, they pushed against one another, their faces inches apart, eyes locked. Peter was losing the battle to maintain his position, his lower back arched over its edge of the railing. The soldier smiled unexpectedly, a grin filled with hatred. He wanted Peter to know he would enjoy killing him.

Then, in a fleeting moment, the soldier became a Maya warrior, with the same malevolent smile as in his vision at *Na-Bolom*. Rage replaced fear, and he threw the man off balance, kneeing him in the groin. But the soldier leaned hard into Peter in his struggle to recover, throwing him precariously off-balance atop the low railing. They sailed together from the balcony.

The soldier flipped over Peter, and they plummeted a dozen feet to the cobblestone courtyard. Peter cried out in pain as they hit the floor, but the soldier lay quiet and listless under him. The stout man had broken his fall and lay unconscious, but still breathing.

"Thanks for the ride," Peter gasped.

"Peter, are you all right?" Jazmin cried, running to his side.

"Yeah, I guess," he sputtered, trying to catch his breath.

Rosa appeared above them on the balcony.

"Thank God you were not hurt." She crossed herself, tears running down her cheeks. Several women followed her out, and when they looked down, their hands fluttered rapidly in the sign of the cross.

"Are there any more soldiers?" Peter asked in a hushed voice.

"No. There were only the two, but more are down the street."

"That's strange," he said. "They must not have known we were here."

"They are going from one house to another," Rosa confirmed.

Peter ran back upstairs and dragged the soldier from the bathroom down to the courtyard. He bound both soldiers' hands and feet, and shut them in a shed at the far corner of the courtyard.

Rosa and her friends gathered around.

"We have to make a phone call," he explained.

"*Sí, sí,*" Rosa agreed.

Rosa and Petra, her best friend, led them to a back gate and into a narrow, quiet lane leading away from the soldiers. They casually strolled toward the *zocalo*, the town square, and a hotel with a phone. Luz gave Peter a battered sombrero to shade his face, and a striped poncho to hide his handgun. He tried to slouch to disguise his height and hoped he wasn't drawing more attention to himself.

They neared the square and peered around the corner of the pink stucco hotel. Several military jeeps idled in the middle of the square, and a soldier sat inside one of the vehicles smoking a cigarette. Two guards stood at the hotel entrance, machine guns and canteens slung over their shoulders. No doubt more soldiers waited inside.

He turned to Rosa. "They're one step ahead of us. Someone must have informed them, or they figured we'd look for a phone. Are there any other phones in town?"

Rosa thought before answering. "Since the soldiers are here, they'll also be at the telephone office. But there is a wealthy old Mestizo five minutes away. He has a phone."

"We need to get to it before they do."

"*Sí*. We go," she said.

Rosa led the way, walking twenty to thirty paces ahead of Peter and Jazmin. A dozen brightly attired Tehuantepec women caught up to their small group and surrounded them.

"We're about as inconspicuous as a neon sign," Peter whispered to Jazmin.

A half-block away, several soldiers conducted a house-to-house search on a side street. Rosa paused until they barged into the home, then signaled the group across the street. The few local citizens who dared roam the streets spoke excitedly, their eyes filled with fear as their group encountered them.

"Look at these frightened people." Anger crept into Peter's voice. "They're scared half to death."

"So am I," Jazmin said. "These people were leading peaceful lives until we came. I feel terrible."

He extended his hands, palms up. "Me too. I had hoped this was over." They walked the distance of several city blocks, and neared the Mestizo's home, looking like a flock of colorful birds. The modest, single-story adobe house was rundown, contained by a low adobe wall with a wrought-iron gate in the center.

"I thought you said this fellow was wealthy," Peter said.

"*Sí*. Very wealthy," she responded, nodding her head.

A single strand of wire ran along the street from pole to pole and into the man's home.

"Anyone with a phone must be considered rich around here," he told Jazmin in English.

No troops were visible from their vantage point, but they were exposed. Peter directed his companions off the road and into a thicket of trees, where they could observe the house. They saw no activity after watching it for several minutes. He told Rosa he would slip to the front door and knock. He started out of the brush. Halfway across the road he looked behind, startled to see the entire entourage of women following him.

"No, no," he pleaded, waving them back. "Stay there."

They froze in the middle of the road, listening as the sound of a jeep made itself apparent as it came around a corner. Everyone scurried back into the cover of the trees. A green jeep sped around the corner, enveloping everyone in a choking cloud of dust.

"Mexican drivers," Peter mumbled.

Three men in black uniforms pulled up to the house and jumped from the jeep. Two of them carried rifles, the third a handgun in a hip holster. The soldier with the holster appeared to be the officer in charge. He looked oddly familiar to Peter. The officer and one of soldiers approached the house. They knocked loudly with the butts of their guns. The door opened a crack, then a few inches. The soldiers barged in, pushing the man peering through the doorway back into the house.

"Pleasant guys," Peter said.

Jazmin looked at him, alarmed. "What do we do now?"

"I don't know. We'll never make it to another town. They'll have all the roads covered."

"We'll have to think of something," she said. "Let's sit and try to clear our minds."

Peter and Jazmin sat cross-legged in the tall grass, shut their eyes and tried to relax.

The minutes passed quietly. Nothing happened. When Peter finally opened his eyes, all the women stared at them as if expecting some far-reaching revelation, or spirit appearance over their heads. He looked at Jazmin and shook his head. She returned his look of despair. The soldiers had not exited the house, and no one had come up with a plan.

"They must be waiting for us," he said.

After watching the house another quarter hour, Rosa stood abruptly, and spoke with exaggerated dignity. "I have an idea. I will go to the house, knock, and when the soldiers come out, I will say I have seen the gringo and the woman they are looking for. Then I will lead them across town, only to come up empty-handed. By then you will have made your phone call, and all will be well."

Peter and Jazmin exchanged glances and shrugged. The plan was feasible. A quick glance at his watch told him it was nearly eight. He turned back to Rosa. "These are violent men. What if they suspect a ruse? Are you sure you're up to it?"

She gave him a haughty look. "I shall have them eating out of my hand."

Without hesitation, Rosa walked with determined strides toward the house. By the time she reached the parked jeep, the front door of the house swung open. The officer brandished his handgun, a military-issued Beretta just like Peter's, demanding answers for his questions with exaggerated movements of his arms. He took Rosa by the arm, and escorted her to his jeep. The other soldiers piled in behind them.

The jeep jolted to a start, then stormed off in a cloud of dust in the direction they came from.

As the dust rolled over Peter, Jazmin, and the Tehuantepec women, Peter signaled everyone to stay put. He and Jazmin stood, then crossed the road to the house. He knocked softly but rapidly on the door. It opened slowly, creaking on its hinges, and a small Mestizo man peered out.

Peter barged in, much as the soldiers had, pushing the little fellow aside. "Sorry," he said, hoping he sounded apologetic. "But we're in a big hurry."

"*Sí, Señor. Mi casa es su casa.*" The frightened man looked at the floor and bowed politely.

"Where is your phone?" Peter skipped any polite introduction and glanced around the room. "This is an emergency. We need to call the American embassy in México City."

The homeowner pointed to the phone on the far side of the small but well-furnished room, and Peter rushed over to it as the man retreated into his kitchen. He lifted the antique phone to his ear, but heard no dial tone. Then he tapped on the lever that cradled the handset because he had seen it done in old-time movies, smiling in surprise when an operator answered.

"*Hola, Manuel,*" said a woman's voice in Spanish. "Do you wish to dial up Liliana?"

"No, no, *Señora,*" Peter stammered. "I'm a friend of Manuel's. I need to dial the United States consulate in México City. This is an emergency."

A pause. "*Sí, Señor.* I will try to reach the long-distance operator." Another long pause. Jazmin watched out the window. Drops of sweat ran down Peter's face as he waited for the operator to come back on the line. "Any millennia," he mumbled. What could take so long? Could it be a trap? Was she talking to the *Federales,* informing them of their location?

"Long distance. May I help you?" a voice finally asked.

"Please, I need to get in touch with the U.S. consulate in México City. Please hurry. This is an extreme emergency."

"One moment, please."

Seconds ran by. Jazmin turned toward him. "I hear a car," she said, her voice rising in urgency.

"It's ringing!" Peter exclaimed.

"This is the United States Embassy in *Ciudad México*. Currently all of our lines are busy..."

"Damn," he exploded. "We may have to run for it."

Peter noticed French doors open to a back patio and considered his options. They might be able to escape unnoticed, but not likely. He couldn't see much vegetation at the rear of the house. No place to hide. He took a deep breath to clear his mind, and glanced at a photo on the wall. José Aguilar, the president of México, sat in an ornate chair. *El Presidente's* steely eyes glared at him. Somehow, his suit and tie looked out of place. The Maya chief of his visions formed over the photo, sending a cold shiver through his body.

This was the man on the pyramid in *Na-Bolom*, the man who had savagely killed him.

He stalks me still.

"The soldiers!" Jazmin cried out. "One just came around the corner. We should go . . . Peter?"

A tremor of rage ran through Peter's body, and he glared back at the photo. Then something in the picture caught his eye. The chair *El Presidente* sat upon had a high decorative back. Carved into its design was the image of a raven, positioned as if perched on his shoulder. He had the distinct impression the raven held *El Presidente* down. Suddenly the phone line felt like an umbilical cord. It was their lifeline.

"We stay," he ordered, astonishing Jazmin.

"The jeep is pulling up to the house," she implored.

"U.S. Consulate," a voice answered. "How may I direct your call?"

"I need to talk someone in charge," he blurted. "This is an extreme emergency."

"One moment please. I'll see who I can reach."

Seconds ran by as he listened to the low hum of an engine and the squeal of dusty brakes outside as the Special Forces jeep pulled up to the house.

"This is Ambassador Richardson. May I help you?"

"You sure can," he said. "You can save our butts for starters. This is Peter Campbell. I'm a U.S. citizen. My girlfriend, Jazmin Rivera, and I are at a home in Tehuantepec surrounded by *Federales*. They've been chasing us all over the jungle, and they'll be bursting into this house any second."

"Dr. Campbell, we know about you. Your employer has been in contact with us. They're quite concerned about you and Ms. Rivera."

"The soldiers are coming up the walk," Jazmin reported, her face white with fear. She turned to see the Mestizo man quietly exit through a back door in the kitchen.

"Mr. Ambassador, I'll be blunt—in a few seconds Mexican troops are going to burst in here with automatic weapons, and I'm not sure we'll be able to finish this conversation."

"Mr. Campbell, are you absolutely sure those are Mexican troops chasing you?"

"Yes, for months—Special Forces."

"Special Forces? We've stayed in close contact with the Mexican government," he responded. "They said they knew nothing of your whereabouts."

"Oh, they know all right," he replied, glaring again at the *El Presidente's* photo. "And if you aren't on the phone with President Aguilar in the next thirty seconds to tell him to call off his dogs, there's a very small likelihood we'll ever have the opportunity to speak again. I hope I'm making myself perfectly clear."

"Peter!" Jazmin screamed as the front door of the house burst in.

Peter found himself suddenly staring down the cold blue barrel of a Colt M40 carbine. The officer entered, walked directly to Peter, grabbed the phone from his hand, and slammed it down on its flimsy cradle. The large barrel-chested man scrunched his heavily pockmarked face close to Peter's face as if memorizing his features.

"*Buenos días,* Dr. Campbell," he said. "So, we meet again."

Peter recognized the officer—"*El Capitán*"—from the checkpoint outside San Cristóbal. But this time the man's voice was casual and surly. This could get ugly fast.

"As always, the pleasure is all mine," Peter said.

"With whom were you speaking?" the captain demanded, his voice suddenly harsh.

"The U.S. Embassy."

"Nonsense. You have not had time to make such a call. It takes hours to get a call through from a flea-bitten town like this. You are a cunning man, Dr. Campbell, but we finally caught up to you before you could kill any more of my men."

"I didn't kill anyone," Peter blurted, surprised at the accusation.

"Your soldiers died in the marshlands when they fell into quicksand. There was nothing we could do to save them."

El Capitán slapped Peter across the face. His head jerked to one side from the impact, but he made no other move, aware of the gun barrels still pointing at him.

"Don't insult my intelligence. My men are professional soldiers. They do not drown in swamps. Tie them up, and put them in the jeep," he ordered. "Perhaps we can find a swamp for you to rest in as well."

The telephone rang. Everyone froze and stared at the antique device as it emitted a noise more a chirp than a ring. One of the soldiers reached for Peter.

"Aren't you going to answer it?" Peter asked *El Capitán*. "It's for you."

"Don't be insolent," *El Capitán* barked, as more soldiers entered the house. "How would you know who it is for?"

"Why don't you find out for yourself?"

The phone continued to ring, rooting everyone in the room as if its sound magically bound them in time and space. *El Capitán* looked hard at Peter, and then took a step toward the phone. He jerked the receiver from its cradle and spat into it in an accusing tone. "Who is this?"

The soldier listened, holding the receiver tight against his cheek. As if choked by an unseen entity, his face turned red and lost the surly look.

"*¿Señor Presidente?*" he stuttered. "*Sí, sí. Comprendo.*" Then, like a blow-up doll with air leaking out, the captain's face sagged. Without ceremony, he turned and shoved the phone in Peter's face. "*El Presidente* wishes to have a word with you."

"Oh." Peter smiled, trying to sound confident. "My mistake. I thought it was for you."

He raised his eyebrows at Jazmin, and put the phone to his ear. One of the soldiers gripped her arm tighter. All eyes fixed on Peter.

"This is Dr. Campbell."

"*Buenos días,* Dr. Campbell. Please allow me to introduce myself. I am *Presidente* José Aguilar. I'm delighted to hear my soldiers have finally found you. Your embassy informs me that you have been pursued through the jungle by people masquerading as my soldiers."

"They looked like your soldiers to me," Peter said bluntly. "And your *capitán* seems to be taking their accidental deaths quite personally. In fact, he already admitted that they were his soldiers."

Peter heard what sounded like *El Presidente* pounding his fist on his desk. "I assure you my soldiers are there only for your protection." Ambassador Richardson had been quick to act, and apparently had some fire of his own. A scandal of this magnitude would jeopardize President Aguilar's NAFTA deal, if not his presidency and his life.

"The spirits of the jungle led us to *Na-Bolom*. You remember *Na-Bolom*, don't you, *Señor Presidente*? I believe we've both been there before."

For a moment, there was only silence on the other end of the phone. "Dr. Campbell, I do not know of this *Na-Bolom*."

"Sure, you do. Even your old friend, the jaguar, was there."

El Presidente's voice turned menacing. "What is this nonsense?"

He raised his voice in return. "Your men tracked us through the eyes of the jaguar, didn't they? There is no other explanation. They could not have followed us through the rain and swamps otherwise."

Another long silence gripped at Peter's throat. Exposing the most powerful man in México was risky. *El Presidente's* involvement was impossible to prove, but threatening the man might loosen his hold on them as well as on the tribe.

"Perhaps you were in the jungle too long, Dr. Campbell. I assure you neither I, nor my soldiers, mean you any harm."

"Then, as a token of your sincerity, tell your *capitán* to leave Tehuantepec and take his soldiers with him. They're stinking up the place, and frightening the beautiful women here."

"As you wish," *El Presidente* replied in a tight, controlled voice. "Apparently, they cannot be of any more service to you."

Peter breathed a sigh of relief. "Before I give the phone back to your *capitán*, I have one other thing to say to you. If your soldiers kill even a single Lacandón man, woman, or child, I'll hold you personally responsible. And I'll make sure every newspaper in the America knows about it."

The long silence made Peter think the connection had been lost until Aguilar cleared his throat with a low growl.

"I assure you, I will do everything in my power to protect your tribe," Aguilar replied stiffly.

"Don't you mean *your* tribe, *Señor Presidente*?"

He handed the phone back to *El Capitán*, raised an eyebrow at Jazmin, and smiled.

El Capitán sputtered and turned red as he listened to his instructions.

"*Sí, sí, sí,*" he kept saying, then slammed the phone receiver down. Ignoring Peter, he turned toward his soldiers.

"*Andalé pronto,*" he shouted in frustration, herding the soldiers out of the house.

The soldier gripping Jazmin's arm reluctantly let go. With tears of relief running down her face, she ran to Peter, wrapping him in a tight embrace.

"It's over, sweetheart," he whispered, kissing her wet face. "It's over." They continued to hold each other, letting their tension dissolve as the soldiers pulled away in their jeeps.

Jazmin gathered herself together, and looked up at him. "What happened?"

He turned and pointed to the photograph. "The Raven. I ignored a sitting raven once, but not a second time."

"You sound more like Chan all the time."

"I guess I do."

The Mestizo homeowner slipped back from the kitchen to the living room. He stood before Peter and Jazmin with a quizzical expression. They apologized profusely for intruding into his home and exchanged introductions before making their way to the front door. He smiled graciously, holding the door wide for them. To their surprise, several hundred Tehuantepec citizens lined the street and filled the yard, cheering as they stepped outside.

"It looks like all of Tehuantepec is here," Jazmin exclaimed, her face lighting up.

Rosa rushed out of the crowd to embrace Jazmin, passionately kissing her, sobbing with relief. The people gathered around, cheering and tossing flowers around Peter and Jazmin.

"They've brought flowers," Jazmin yelled over the noise of the crowd. The fragrant beauty of the flowers and the people's affection intoxicated Peter. He picked up blossoms and tossed them back, to the crowd's delight.

"Maybe they thought they were coming to our funeral."

"Peter, don't say that!"

"We had faith you would defeat those horrible soldiers. We prayed you would come out alive," Rosa said. "We knew when you came out of this house, it would be your rebirth."

"Told you so." Peter smiled.

"You have survived the Forbidden Jungle and those evil demons. My people say you are saints."

"Oh boy," Peter said. "Here we go."

"Maybe we are saints." Jazmin beamed. "We survived earthquakes, jaguars, assassins."

"No, don't tell them about the jaguar."

He wondered how his tribulations in the jungle might have changed things, but could only guess as he stood among the people of Tehuantepec, thankful for the moment. The women continued to throw flowers, bathing them in their fragrance. The flowers' fragrant beauty and the people's affection intoxicated them as they continued walking back through the city.

Then Peter's vision changed as it had with *El Presidente's* picture, and in *Na-Bolom*. The cheering crowd of women turned into an ornate army of warriors in battle dress. Instead of flowers, they tossed golden coins and exotic gifts. The Maya army of *Na-Bolom,* clothed in leopard skins and equipped with obsidian-tipped spears, faded back to the citizens of Tehuantepec. The image passed quickly, but the distinct feeling that the women of Tehuantepec were the warriors in his vision lingered as flowers continued raining down around them.

Peter wondered if humanity had reached an evolutionary peak only to face darkness and despair, or if mankind had raised its vibration enough to turn the tide of extinction.

It seemed that the dark, ancient city of *Na-Bolom* had dissolved into the City of Flowers. It was a good sign, a very good sign, and Peter decided to go with it.

CHAPTER 29

The tree stood about twenty feet tall, its saucer-sized flowers blossoming in fabulous clusters throughout its branches. Peter recognized the blossoms as one of many local flowers tossed about in celebration when he and Jazmin had foiled the plans of *El Presidente* and his Special Forces.

"What's the name of the tree that has the tissue-white flowers with red throats?" Peter pointed beyond Rosa's patio, asking no one in particular.

"It is the *cazahautl* tree, one of my favorites," Rosa said.

"*Ipomoea aborescens*," Jazmin added. "The morning glory tree grows all over southern México and Guatemala."

The momentary diversion turned from the tree back to their plans. "Why must you go back into the jungle, *Señor* Peter?" Rosa asked again with sorrowful eyes. "You both still recover from your cuts and bruises. It is dangerous. If the soldiers do not kill you, the jungle will. You have risked your lives enough. *Por favor*, stay here with us. You will live long lives surrounded by those who love you."

"*Sí, sí,*" the ladies said, crowding around, pleading, and nodding their heads in unison.

"I don't like the idea any more than you do," he said. "Believe me." Jazmin reached out for Rosa's hand. "We realize it's risky, Rosa. But we know in our hearts that we must find Chan and his people. They need our help in ways we cannot explain. Spirit sends us back." Peter looked from Jazmin to the tree-lined horizon. The rains had subsided, and they could skirt the Forbidden Jungle, making their journey infinitely easier. Besides that, in his heart of hearts, a part of him missed the Lacandón forest and the tribe. Then there was the jaguar, who continued to call to him in his dreams. He knew his deepest fears would not dissolve until he confronted President Aguilar directly. A driving force would not allow him to turn his back on the Lacandón.

"When we know with certainty that Chan and his people are thriving," Jazmin continued, "then we will do what we must to ensure the tribe is free to live on their land without fear from the government. Rosa, we are the only ones who can find the tribe in that jungle."

Rosa conceded, her eyes filling with tears. "We know what it is like to live for the land. *Vaya con Dios.*"

Peter talked at length with Ambassador Richardson, and to John Bishop, his boss in Denver, documenting their ordeal. John, like the people of Tehuantepec, had tried to dissuade him from returning to what he considered certain death. "Come back for a few weeks and then make your decision," he argued.

"We've notified the press back in the States," Peter explained, "asking them to hold the story, but if the embassy hasn't heard anything from us inside a month, the article will appear in every paper in North America the next day. To publish it now risks playing our hand too early. If *El Presidente's* treachery is exposed now, he may kill the tribe simply out of revenge. I don't like the idea of going back into the jungle either, especially with the possibility of running into Aguilar's troops. But I have to."

After waiting two weeks to rest, heal, and gather new supplies for their journey, Peter and Jazmin quietly left town during the night.

They traveled for a day in a hay-laden cart pulled by horses, manned by a Tehuantepec youth through the narrow back roads of southern Oaxaca, taking every precaution to avoid *El Presidente's* soldiers. They encountered only friendly natives who waved and shouted *"Buenos días,"* and *"Buenas tardes"* as they passed through dozens of small villages that lined the bumpy road into the mountains toward Chiapas.

When the road deteriorated into a rocky trail, they bid their young friend farewell and started out in a fresh set of clothes and new huaraches, the woven leather and tire tread sandals worn by Mexican peasants throughout the country. Adjusting their packs, they continued on foot along the trail.

Dropping away below them were hundreds of square miles of green valleys and mountains whose summits mingled with cloud veils of virgin white. Blue skies filled with billowing white cumulus clouds, and a warm sun called forth a day of promise, lifting their heavy and uncertain hearts. Descending the eastern face of the Sierras, they found themselves in a land of immense fields scattered with the flowers of yellow salvia, and watered by shallow rivers and creeks so clear the sandy bottoms shone golden in the sunlight. Cattle and oxen filled their bellies on the abundant flowers, and friendly farmers waved in greeting. Peter looked at Jazmin, and each knew the other wanted to linger there, a tropical Shangri-la. But their mission drove them forward and the pasture land soon merged with the jungle that loomed before them.

Days into their hike, they entered the tangled, remote valley the Lacandón called home. Standing on a high plateau, they gazed across a pristine valley now flooded only with memories. They carefully made their way through the forest's deep recesses, guided by intuition. The jungle seemed to regard them with a measure of tolerance, even gentleness, as though it knew they belonged to the land.

The air was heavy and motionless, with many familiar and unfamiliar fragrances mingling in a sweet, heavy musk. Exotic bird calls floated through the canopy, whetting their curiosity and imagination, as sun and shadows played on the forest floor, flirting with their senses. Once again, the wilderness honed their attention, and they found themselves moving in step with its rhythms. The jungle was a great teacher, and they took pleasure in knowing they had learned how to survive its lessons.

One week into the journey brought them to the shores of the Rio Jataté, where Chan and his people had made their escape. The wide river flowed quietly, and they bathed with caution on its shore, watchful for crocodiles and soldiers. But they saw no sign of either, nor were they given any clues to the tribe's whereabouts from the spirits of the forest. After two days hike along the river bank, they turned up one of its tributaries. Fruit was plentiful after the long monsoon, and they easily lived off the land. Now that the driving rains had abated to gentle afternoon showers, they easily traversed the land.

Jazmin gestured "time to stop" beside a creek, attracted to its gentle sound. They pondered their next move, unsure of their direction in a jungle encompassing hundreds of square miles.

"We could wander in this forest forever, map or no map," she said. "We're falling into our old pattern of forgetting to ask the jungle for help. Let's stay here until the spirits offer us a message."

"Okay," Peter said, his voice tinged with frustration. "But they've had plenty of time to speak. I'm beginning to think the jungle spirits have deserted us."

She sighed and looked at him wearily. "The trees have been quiet, but they seem at peace with us, *amor*. At least we're not fighting our way into this jungle as we did before."

"You have good instincts about these things," he conceded, accepting her counsel. They lay down on the bank and let the delicate sound and refreshing scent of the water soothe their minds. He gradually allowed his thoughts to drift away with the current. The creek slowly drew him out of himself, absorbing his tension. Finally, he set his mind to rest. As time slipped by, everything around them became unnaturally quiet. He heard no birds or insects buzzing, no leaves rustling in the wind— nothing but the gentle trickling of water. It was as if the stream wanted to tell him something. He stayed with the moment, absorbed by the sound, the voice, and rhythm of the ripples.

"I'm not getting anything," Jazmin said, shattering the serenity of the moment.

He held out a hand, appealing for silence, but it was too late. Her voice had already ushered the cacophony of the jungle back into his awareness.

"What is it?" she whispered.

"I don't know exactly. You interrupted."

"Ah! I'm sorry, Peter . . . What was it?"

He took a deep breath, not wanting to engage her in dialogue. Then chided himself—the moment had passed. "I was listening to the water."

Jazmin ran her hand in lazy circles in the cool creek. "The water? You were just listening to the water?"

"You interrupted me," he said again. "I was just getting into it." They stared at one another for a moment, then tried to return to a meditative state, but nothing was the same as it had been a moment ago.

"I don't know if I was on the verge of getting something, or not."

Jazmin nodded, and skipped a stone across the shallow creek. Peter stood, then noticed something drifting toward him, ten or twelve inches long, and black. There had been a steady stream of unremarkable leaves and debris, but this particular object caught his attention. He gripped it with his eyes as it surged closer, then plucked it from the water as it floated past. He held the dripping object out to Jazmin.

"A feather," he muttered, as though talking to himself.

Jazmin glanced over her shoulder, smiled weakly, and turned away.

"A feather," he said again, louder this time.

The long, black feather gave off a blue sheen in the direct sunlight. He stroked it absentmindedly, running his fingers along the soft edges, admiring it, recognizing its qualities without considering its implications.

Then the realization hit.

"My God, Jazmin! Look," he said, showing her the feather again. She turned and squinted at it this time, taking a closer look.

"A raven's feather?"

"Yes!"

"What does it mean, Peter?" she asked, suddenly excited. "What does it mean?"

He cocked his head and appraised the feather. "I'm not sure. What do you think it means?"

She stood impatiently, and took the feather from his hand. "Didn't you say the creek was trying to say something to you?"

"Yes. And then I saw the feather bobbing down the creek. We've been asking for direction, so the spirit of the creek brought us a feather. Not just any feather—the feather of a bird that doesn't live in the jungle—a raven's feather."

"Well, Sitting Raven, what is the message?" She baited him, eyebrows raised.

He pointed downstream. "We need to follow the water."

"Chan will make a good shaman of you yet," she said, lifting her pack. He smiled, and helped her adjust the pack on her shoulders. They followed the creek, alert for more signs as they hiked. For several miles, they saw nothing unusual, and agreed to camp for the evening as the late afternoon sun faded into dim pools on the forest floor.

Peter yawned and started to pull his backpack off, when something caught his eye in a thick grove of trees a few hundred feet away. A movement. Someone was coming. He signaled Jazmin to take cover, and drew his gun. Moving quietly toward them were several men . . . in white tunics.

Peter exhaled in relief and looked to Jazmin as K'in emerged from the trees and signaled to them. His sharp eyes had already seen them. Jazmin tore off her pack, and ran to greet them. The young men of the tribe responded with wide grins, excited gestures, and smiles. Everyone embraced, speaking rapidly with tender words, few of which Peter understood.

Jazmin unleashed months of worry and uncertainty into radiant joy. Tears wet her face as an explosion of emotion poured from her. The terror of that last frightful night in the village was rekindled, and then discarded in a joyous reunion that dispelled past uncertainties.

The group looked for a comfortable place to rest, and sat in the shade of a grass-covered dell to discuss the details of the past few weeks. Peter nestled into a comfortable sitting position against a shade tree.

"Is everyone well?" he asked, gazing at K'in, enjoying his warm, mannerly disposition.

"*Sí.*" K'in nodded vigorously.

"Where is the village?"

Upon hearing this question, K'in stood abruptly. "Come! I take you."

"We don't have to go right now, K'in . . ."

But before Peter finished speaking, K'in and the other men had already hefted his and Jazmin's packs on their shoulders, along with their own gear, and started down the trail. He grinned at Jazmin, they shrugged in unison, then hastened down the obscure path after the scouts.

The trek continued until sunset, and they easily kept up with the scouts without the burden of their packs. Within an hour, they were within sight of the village. When the people of the village caught sight of Peter and Jazmin, the children ran to them, screeching with laughter. A dozen pairs of bouncing arms and legs soon surrounded them. The women soon caught up to the children and sorted their way through the mass of little bodies toward Jazmin. Peter knew he had seen the last of her for a while. They cried, and hugged in unconditional love and affection. The trauma in their lives had brought them closer.

Peter embraced women and children, then followed the scouting party into the village. As before, the structure of the makeshift village was barely visible under the tall canopy, yet somehow it looked like home. The venerable Chan lay in his hammock as they entered. An unexpected emotion gripped Peter, and he paused to regain his composure. Chan rose quietly and stretched out his arms. Peter stepped quickly to him, and they embraced while the others gathered round.

Chan pulled back, studying him. "What took you so long?"

Peter grinned at Chan's thoughtful stare. "It's a big jungle out there." He shrugged. "I guess I'm not as clever a student as you thought."

A faint smile illuminated Chan's face, as he sat back down in his hammock. Peter joined him in a hammock next to his and lay back, thankful to be off his feet.

"No, no," Chan responded. "The Lacandón forest is very big, even for the eyes of the raven."

CHAPTER 30

As usual, Chan had somehow known to expect Peter and Jazmin, and the tribe had prepared a feast in anticipation of their arrival. Everyone gathered to eat and share their stories near the *ramada*, an open-air arbor built from sturdy saplings with a thatched roof.

Chan sat on Peter's right, Jazmin on his left, with a throng of women and children around them, and the men lining the perimeter. Wild banana trunk hearts, steamed in *maxan* leaves and covered with toasted squash seeds, was the main course. Side dishes of fruit and vegetables prepared in many ways were arranged on straw mats upon the ground.

Everyone chattered about their escape into the forest. From what Peter could discern, the tribe had traveled but a few miles downriver before abandoning the canoes. The canoes put some easy distance between them and the soldiers in the early morning hours before sunrise, but Chan knew they would be easily spotted from the air once daylight came. He sent the canoes further downstream. This way, the soldiers would not be able to track them. The scouts took the canoes thirty kilometers downstream to a safe hiding place, then made their way back on foot. The soldiers were led far down the river, away from the tribe. Peter marveled at the old shaman's cunning, but felt a renewed concern about what the future might bring to these people. "How long do you think you can hide before the soldiers find you again, Chan?" he asked. "I'm certain that my conversation with *El Presidente* in Tehuantepec angered him."

Chan's answer came casually, and without hesitation. "One day."

An old shiver shot through Peter's back, and he sat up straight. It seemed Chan had anticipated his question, but the response was so incongruous, Peter decided he must have heard the question incorrectly. "I mean how long do you think we can stay *here* before the soldiers find us?"

Chan looked up at him for a long time as if searching for the right words. "One day," he repeated.

Peter looked at Chan with disbelief and turned to Jazmin. Her face fell in confusion.

"The soldiers will come tomorrow?" she asked.

"*Sí*. We go with the morning sun," Chan answered in a relaxed tone.

"Go where?" Her face flushed. "Do you have a plan?"

"South. We go deep into the forest. This is what I am told." Chan seemed content with his statement, and offered nothing more. Hearing this, the tribe became animated, but when all had shared the information, they settled into quiet contemplation.

The tribe stayed up late into the night. Peter fidgeted with his gun as the uneasy villagers chatted among themselves, occasionally casting furtive glances into the darkness. Several of the children hung on Jazmin's shoulders and lay in her arms, while the women combed her hair and fussed around her. No one wanted the night to end, and it was not until the wee hours of the morning before anyone fell asleep.

Peter lay tossing and turning on his mat, straining at every noise in the jungle. At first light, Chan had everyone up, and with the efficiency of a military operation, they broke camp and started out. The clouds had dispersed in the night, and the morning air was brisk. Parrots greeted the morning sun with raucous calls as the tribe started down an unseen trail.

Despite the fine day, a growing anxiety chewed at Peter's stomach.

He remembered the words of a great Native American chief: "It is a good day to die." He couldn't help but wonder if this was his day. Chan looked occupied with his own inner world, perhaps reluctant to speak.

Silent and watchful, the tribe hiked until the sun shone overhead through a magical land of giant trees and waterfalls. The long trek brought them to the head of a canyon inside the untouched world. Remote and difficult to approach, the canyon was a perfect place to hide, but its apparent lack of escape routes bothered Peter.

Huge broadleaf trees surrounded them, radiating a peaceful presence as the tribe relaxed in the midday sun. Then a sudden realization struck Peter. They were back in the same forest Chan had brought them to months ago. This was the outskirts of Chan's sacred forest, the land of the giants. It seemed comforting to the tribe, but even in the midst of this forest, Peter was uneasy. His hands began to sweat and a sense of pending entrapment enveloped him. Jazmin anxiously studied his face as a dark cloud of fear pressed in on him, crawling along his flesh like a serpent. Suddenly jumpy and irritable, he felt someone was watching them. He wanted to run.

The tribe was eating a mid-day meal of cold tortillas and vegetables when one of the scouts spotted a movement beyond the trail. He motioned everyone to hide with a sweep of his hand, but the sharp eyes of the tribe had already seen the movement and everyone had turned dead silent.

The stalkers moved silently along the far side of a meadow, blending in with the jungle's undergrowth. Peter's heart thumped. Hoping not to give away their position, he moved his head slowly toward Jazmin and the others. The tribe was silent and motionless, especially Chan, who sat with legs crossed and eyes closed, radiating a sense of calm. Was he unaware of the danger?

Peter whispered into Jazmin's ear. "Soldiers."

She nodded almost imperceptibly, sweat beading across her forehead.

Somehow, the soldiers had moved past the scouts. Peter gazed around at the tribe, searching for clues. How could the soldiers have gone undetected? What treachery had brought them here? The young tribesmen were some of the best scouts in the world. The image of the jaguar flashed through his mind, and his stomach clenched with the old pain. He took deep breaths into his solar plexus, but the fear remained.

There's no getting away from these murderers. Chan knows that.

Some of the men glanced wide-eyed at Peter. Several women and children crept behind a fallen tree, some five feet in diameter, which offered good protection against rifle fire. But Chan continued sitting in the relative open, apparently unaware.

"Where are the scouts?" Peter whispered to Jazmin. "Why didn't we get a warning?"

Jazmin glanced around at the tribe, then back to Peter. "My God." She exhaled. "They're all here with us. Chan didn't send any of them out. Why did he do that, Peter? Why?"

"I don't know! He never said anything to me." Peter shrugged with a nervous tic. "Hell, I never know what he's up to anyway."

Anger and frustration welled up inside him. He motioned at the men to fall back. Rather than retreating, they looked at Chan, who continued to sit in a meditative pose.

"There is no more retreating," Chan said unexpectedly, his eyes still closed.

Peter wanted to scream. "Why, Chan? Why did you call the scouts in? We're trapped now."

"It is time to face your death, old friend."

A nauseating fear sent a tremor through Peter's body. He looked around, saw more movement to the opposite direction. Soldiers moved stealthily through the trees and high brush. Less than fifty yards away, the soldiers stopped and took up positions.

"How did they know we were here?" Peter asked, even though he knew the answer. "They don't seem to see us yet."

"The eyes of the jaguar are on us," Chan answered. "Do you not feel them?"

That explained his sweaty palms.

Peter whispered to Jazmin. "They're on two sides of us now. We'll get caught in their crossfire, with only my gun and a few bows and arrows to defend ourselves."

"Surrender to the day, old friend," Chan said.

Peter's astonishment turned to anger as he spoke. "You hand us over to those murderers? Why, Chan? You know them. They've killed me before, for God's sake."

"No, not for God's sake," Chan said softly. After a silence, he added, "You, old friend, must face them without fear."

Peter froze, unable to breathe. More than the words, the hint of sadness in Chan's voice startled him.

"It is time to say goodbye . . . again."

Peter's heart pounded in a tattoo of drumbeats. He couldn't fathom dying at the hands of these cruel men.

Jazmin embraced him, and began to sob. Peter took several deep breaths and focused on the ancient giants around him. The trees began to calm him, to give him strength. He regained some composure, then pulled away from Jazmin to face Chan.

"You're suggesting I give myself up to those men?"

"No, you must give up your . . . *self*," Chan said deliberately, eyes still closed. "There is no other way."

Automatic gunfire shattered tree branches over their heads.

Everyone dove to the ground as branches and chunks of bark burst into fragments and plummeted down around them. Children screamed in fear, and the low murmur of their mothers' reassurances wafted through the group like a prayer. The gunfire cut down branches, leaves and debris like an indiscriminate chainsaw on a rampage, raising dust and sending forest creatures scurrying for the underbrush.

Jazmin and Peter crouched low behind the fallen log. More bullets tore through the air. Everyone in the tribe hugged the ground, paralyzed by the raging bursts. Peter glanced in Chan's direction. He had not moved a muscle. Neither had the old shaman even opened his eyes.

As abruptly as the assault had started, the gunfire ceased. The jungle turned eerily quiet.

"Dr. Campbell!" The familiar voice sent shivers down Peter's spine. It was the same harsh voice from his encounter in Tehuantepec just weeks ago.

"Dr. Campbell, you cannot escape. You are surrounded. Give yourself up, and we will spare the others. You killed three of my soldiers. Now you must pay."

Peter's mind raced. Why did everyone in this damn jungle want him dead?

"Don't go out there, Peter," Jazmin begged. "He's lying. You know they will kill all of us. They have to. They want this land, and we stand in their way."

She was right. The soldiers would never let her or the tribe walk free. They could execute the tribe, and no one would be left to tell their story.

"Dr. Campbell, please do not risk the lives of others simply to prolong your own pitiful life. You are a coward, hiding behind a woman's skirt. Leave this world like the proud jaguar!"

Proud jaguar. Odd to hear the soldier call him that. Words from another lifetime.

Everyone seemed to designate him as the sacrificial pig. Even Chan. Perhaps the soldiers would be satisfied with him. Maybe the tribe could escape and Jazmin could leave the country while they were busy with him. Sacrificing himself seemed the only way to save her and the tribe.

"I'm coming out!" Peter yelled so abruptly, he wasn't sure he or someone else had uttered the words.

He raised his head, pushed himself up cautiously from all fours, and held out his Beretta to Jazmin. With tears in her eyes, she reached up for the weapon, dangling it from her fingers like a dead animal. He knew she would never use it. She didn't have it in her to kill another living thing, not even one who threatened her life. He knelt again, and held her face close to his.

"I love you so much, Jazmin. It's been a hell of a ride—the jungle, Chan, the tribe. I wouldn't trade it for anything. It's been the most wonderful part of my life."

"*Mi amor*," she cried, holding him close. "I don't want to live without you."

"The jungle will take care of you," he said, lifting her chin to look into her eyes one last time. "I love you so much. I'll love you the next time around, too—forever."

She covered her face in her hands, not wanting to face the nightmare ahead, her lean body racked with heaving sobs as he turned away.

Peter glanced back at Chan one last time. He had not moved, and looked as calm as the day they had meditated in this part of the forest months ago, rooted to the ground, an inextricable part of the forest.

"Goodbye, old friend," Peter whispered.

His negative thoughts of betrayal drained strength from his body. He turned with heavy heart and began to walk toward the soldiers. But he acknowledged the only chance the tribe had was his surrender. He could only hope the soldiers would give the tribe time to flee.

The sunlight striking Peter's face made him feel more vulnerable as he moved into the open. Raising trembling arms above his head, he stepped around a fallen tree, his heart racing and his breath coming in sharp gulps. He made his way across the meadow, separating himself from the tribe, each step forward requiring extra effort as he moved farther away from those he loved. The rifles pointing at him seemed eager to cut him down as he approached the tree line where the soldiers waited. He wondered when *El Capitán* would give the order to shoot.

Dark and menacing in their soiled black uniforms and blackened faces, the soldiers swaggered and sneered as he approached. Stopping before their ranks, Peter counted some twenty men, all wearing Special Forces' uniforms with a black panther emblem on their shoulders.

"So we meet again," one of them barked.

Peter squinted into the bright sunlight and recognized the captain, his fat face grinning with malice. "Still killing innocent people for a living, *Capitán?*" he said, hoping for the final word.

El Capitán raised his revolver, pointed it directly into Peter's face, and started to bear down on the trigger.

Someone shouted from behind the line of soldiers. "*¡Alto!*"

Peter searched the shadows, unsure where the voice had come from. A large, powerful-looking soldier stepped from the trees. As though consumed by the jungle's dark shadows, the man seemed to come from nowhere, his cruel face emerging in fragments. A fierce jaguar adorned the man's black beret, triggering Peter's memories of past lives. His body trembled with recognition of the man before his mind could recall the features from his visions or from photographs. The uniform could not hide the soldier's identity. He had seen the face in many different guises. There was no mistaking his long-time nemesis, José Aguilar, *El Presidente de México.*

The large man looked surprisingly fit for a desk-ridden politician. His smooth, cat-like movements made him all the more menacing as he approached.

Peter took an involuntary step back, his guts knotting up as *El Presidente's* thin lips bent into an angry grin. Aguilar stepped directly in front of him, inches away, locking his steely gaze on Peter's eyes.

Aguilar's arm shot out. Peter buckled to his knees, holding his abdomen and gasping for breath.

"So, you still know your place when confronted by superiors,"

Aguilar sneered. *"Bueno.* I like that quality in a man. But it is too late for a show of respect. Too late for you, *mi amigo."*

"I'm . . . not . . . your . . . friend," Peter gasped between words.

A sudden sharp blow to the ribs sent Peter rolling along the ground. He winced in pain. Tears flushed from his eyes and disappeared into the dark soil. He grieved for Jazmin and the tribe, wondering why Chan had deserted him. Another blow to the midsection knocked him from his thoughts. The soldiers gathered around to have fun with him, snarling obscenities and flicking their cigarette butts at him.

"We could hang him upside down, and whip him bloody," he heard a soldier say.

"Sí, and tonight we could watch insects and vampire bats eat the flesh off his bones," said another.

Unfazed, Peter paid little attention to the soldiers' antics. He instinctively tried to clear his mind, knowing he had little chance of survival if he operated from fear.

Peter began praying to the spirits of the jungle, asking for guidance and forgiveness. But he had failed them, so how could they save him now?

As he prayed, another voice interrupted his inner dialogue. There was something odd—the voice came from inside his head, but it was not his own! He strained to make out the words. The tone of the voice soothed, comforted, yet was difficult to hear over the soldier's jeers.

You are not alone.

We are with you, several voices chimed in.

Peter took a deep breath and tried to focus on the voices. His hands stopped shaking, and his heartbeat slowed. At least he would die with dignity. It seemed as if the ancient trees had gathered around him, trying to protect him. But the soldiers were gathering closer too, laughing uproariously at their own hostile remarks, shoving and kicking him. A sudden blow to the head blinded him, and he dug his fingers into the damp earth.

276

As Peter struggled to regain his vision, a light caught his attention. He turned his head to get a better look, but the soldiers obscured his view. He glanced up at *El Presidente*, who loomed over him, then gazed again in the direction of the light. Why weren't the soldiers reacting to it? They seemed not to notice.

The light behind the soldiers suddenly brightened, emanating from all directions. Peter looked around, searching for the source. Its brilliance engulfed everything, but the soldiers still did not acknowledge the strange phenomenon. How could they not see it? It surrounded them now, illuminating the forest.

Peter began pulling himself to his knees when another blow slammed into his gut. He crumpled back to the ground, struggling to breathe as the soldiers laughed and resumed their taunting. Distracted by the light, he ignored *El Presidente* and his soldiers even as they continued their abuse. The trees' illumination increased in brilliance as another blow from the butt of a rifle flattened him. He cringed in pain, hugging the earth.

"We are here with you," the strange voice whispered again. Peter wiped tears from his face. Would the spirits of the forest deliver him from the Earth plane? He sat up and looked toward the light again.

"What are you looking at, white trash?" A round-faced soldier yelled into Peter's ear, striking him in the side with his weapon, sending him sprawling on the ground. He cried out in pain, sucking in air that had been forced from his lungs.

The soldiers appeared to be working themselves into a killing frenzy. How much more could he take?

The soothing inner voice returned, speaking in long phrases. This time it sounded like his own voice. Or was it Spirit? It began a narrative, explaining the circumstances of his situation. Peter's many lives through countless millennia unfolded before him. His problems had not started in the jungle with *El Presidente* and his soldiers, nor had these begun when he was born into this life. This drama began millions of years ago, when he'd had his first fearful thought.

El Presidente pulled him up roughly by the shoulders, and stared into his face. His thin smile filled with hatred as he drilled Peter with steely eyes blacker than he'd ever seen, eyes that evoked an irrefutable power.

Aguilar grasped him firmly by the hair. Peter felt sick to his stomach again, but from the corner of his eye, he could see the strange light growing, first to his left, then to his right. So comforting was its magnetic presence that he relaxed, seeking the calm within it.

Struggling free of Aguilar's hand, Peter found the strength to turn his head. *El Presidente* laughed and taunted him, but he paid little attention, for the remarkable illumination was more alluring.

Aguilar pulled Peter's head around to glare into his eyes. As *El Presidente* stood gloating, enjoying his victory, Peter's emotions shifted from the dark fear of death to an unexplainable exaltation. Somehow, the outcome of this drama no longer mattered.

An exquisite calm filled his body, growing with every breath. The soldiers could not see the magnificent light, but how could they not feel it? Such warmth and calm, such love. Did it not affect them? Peter searched their eyes for clues. He gazed at the soldiers, then beyond to the heavenly light streaming through the trees.

El Presidente continued to mock Peter, imagining he feared his impending death. "You are a fool," he gloated. "Did you really think you could come into my country, kill my soldiers, and live to tell about it? Did you really think you could defeat me? Escape the House of the Jaguar?" His voice quivered with anger as he worked himself into a rage.

Peter held his bruised ribs and leaned forward to whisper into his adversary's ear. "You, my enemy, do not comprehend the power that stands before you."

Peter was not sure where he had found those words, or even if he had delivered them.

"You stupid swine!" *El Presidente* growled, slapping him across the face. "You are a bigger fool than I thought."

He lurched from the blow but the big man held him up. José Aguilar directed Peter's gaze to his eyes again. Deep and oppressive, they evoked great power and disturbing memories. This time he returned *El Presidente's* gaze without blinking, though a familiar, bleak emotion threatened to fill him. Deeper and deeper he went into the hell of those eyes, until only darkness remained. There, a subtle movement caught his attention . . . a jaguar, stealthy and black as the shadows whence it arose. As the image solidified, Peter observed its agitated pacing, the same restless movements as in his nightmares.

The jaguar stopped in its tracks, and turned its fierce yellow eyes on him. The eyes were full of malice, but now Peter felt only a sense of sorrow and compassion for the creature. Something within him had shifted. How or when, he could not tell. But some indefinable part of himself looked on the spirit of the jaguar, and found it no longer claimed a hold on him. At this realization, the image of the jaguar disappeared into darkness, jolting him from his trance and back to the riveting eyes of José Aguilar.

Aguilar's face filled his field of vision, but now he evoked a different emotion. Peter saw only emptiness before him. *El Presidente's* power had vanished with the jaguar.

Aguilar angrily pushed him away. "How did you do that?" he demanded in a hoarse whisper.

Peter stumbled and caught himself. "The House of the Jaguar no longer rules me, or this land. A greater wisdom rules this forest now. Do you not see the light?" He swept the horizon with his hand.

"Nonsense!" Aguilar screamed, shaking a finger in his face. He looked to his soldiers. "Kill him!"

Peter turned to face them, ready for the sudden rush of bullets to pierce his body. But the soldiers seemed confused and disoriented, glancing about with flinching, twitching movements. He hadn't noticed their distress until now. He looked up to see thousands of white lights streaking from the trees, intersecting in a brilliant web among the circle of men. The soldiers sensed the light piercing their bodies and looked around wildly, searching for the source.

Some raised their firearms in response to Aguilar's orders, but their faces filled with uncertainly as their muzzles turned on Peter.

Losing patience, *El Capitán* stepped forward and thrust his handgun in Peter's face.

Peter studied the cool, shiny steel of the long-barreled revolver, sweat running into his eyes.

El Capitán's forefinger closed over the trigger.

Peter sucked in a breath and closed his eyes, awaiting the explosion. Instead of the ear-piercing muzzle blast, he heard only silence.

El Capitán's gaze moved from Peter's face to the gun. His finger would not move to squeeze the trigger and his hand began to shake. The officer's face tensed in concentration as he willed his index finger to pull back the trigger, but it would not move. He turned red with fear and anger, glancing at his men, then at Peter, and finally at the revolver again. His arm trembled with the exertion of his attempt to fire the weapon. Confusion and humiliation mixed with fear as his body trembled out of control. His soldiers could only watch as their captain's knees buckled, sending him crumpling to the ground in violent convulsions.

The soldiers took a step back, staring open-mouthed at their commander. Some threw down their weapons, clutching their chests or throats as if in great pain. Others simply trembled. One young man dropped his gun and ran, screaming incoherent warnings to his comrades, while others dropped to the forest floor with loud moans, casting their guns aside. Some dropped to their knees, crossed themselves, and began to pray.

"Cowards!" Aguilar shouted in despair. "What is the matter with you? You are all cowards." He lunged for *El Capitán's* revolver and grabbed it, still cocked, from his trembling hand, and pointed it in Peter's face. "This is the last of your trickery, you coward!"

Absorbed and exhausted by the confusion, it had not occurred to Peter to take action until it was too late. He froze as Aguilar aimed the gun between his eyes. In some way, this man had been in control over his life for eons, and now he could only accept his fate. Sweat ran into his eyes as *El Presidente* curled his swarthy forefinger over the trigger. Peter froze, awaiting a second time the explosion that would end his life. Flinching when the hammer slammed against the firing pin, he heard only a click instead of an ear-piercing ignition.

A misfire!

Aguilar moved to fire again, but Peter lunged forward, grabbed the revolver, and caught it by the barrel just as Aguilar fired again. The bullet erupted near Peter's shoulder, but zinged harmlessly off into the forest as they struggled.

A knee to his stomach buckled Peter to the ground. He clung desperately to the revolver, bringing Aguilar down with him. They tumbled through the clearing, rolling and kicking. Dirt, elbows, and fists flew, every muscle pushed to its limit as they grappled for possession of the revolver.

He fell under the large man, struggling for air. Peter thought he had a firm hold on the gun, but Aguilar had the better grip. The barrel inched closer and closer to his face. He shuddered as a deafening blast exploded near his ear.

The streaking piece of lead blew a hole in the ground, sending dirt into Aguilar's face. In that instant, Peter threw his weight to one side, casting *El Presidente* off. But he also lost his grip on the gun.

Rolling on the ground, Aguilar recovered quickly, bringing the revolver to bear on him again. Peter met Aguilar's move, kicking it out of his hand. They scrambled for the weapon again. *El Presidente* reached it first. Peter aimed a ferocious kick to Aguilar's side, buckling him over. He grabbed the revolver and pointed it in his adversary's face, hands shaking with tension and anger. "Don't move," Peter growled.

Aguilar climbed to his knees. "Kill me," he screamed. "Kill me, so I can return to hunt you down like a dog!"

His finger caressed the trigger as *El Presidente* kneeled before him, now a crumpled heap on the forest floor. No longer threatening, no longer a symbol of power. The light brightened then. Peter's feelings sickened him as he looked down at the defeated man. His fear and hatred evaporated, replaced with feelings of shame and disgust. The dark cloud of fear that had hung over him for months lifted. He breathed in deeply and lowered the gun, grateful the man before him could no longer haunt his dreams.

"Kill me!" Aguilar pleaded.

"No."

"Kill me!"

"That's what you would have me do?" Peter shook his head. "No, I won't shoot you."

José Aguilar began to weep in frustration at Peter's refusal to play by his rules. And even as the broken man raged, the rays of light penetrated his body.

"Can you not see it? It's all around us. Look!" Peter motioned to the light.

Aguilar glanced up, bewildered by the luminosity of the forest, uncomprehending. "This is just another one of your tricks." His voice cracked, reflecting his near-hysteria.

"No, *Señor*, oh no. My bag of tricks is empty now. The spirit of the jaguar is free to roam the jungle. I cannot hold onto my anger any longer, or use lesser beasts to further my hatred. I cannot kill you, for I would live to see your ugly face again another time. And believe me when I say I've seen enough of you."

Aguilar whimpered, a small animal sound.

"No, to kill you now would just prolong the fear between us. Maybe you love this game, *Señor*, but I'm sick of it! So, I'm going to stop this violence here, today, with the hope that my people will live in peace in their jungle."

"Tricks!" Aguilar cried in anguish, beating his fist on the ground. Nearby, soldiers lay tucked in fetal positions, whimpering or shouting aloud. Several had run off, and some had discarded their firearms, which lay strewn around them. *El Capitán* was nowhere in sight.

Peter turned to see Jazmin running across the clearing toward him. Nearly out of breath when she reached him, she fell into his arms.

"Oh, Peter. We heard the gunfire," she sobbed. "I thought you were dead."

Peter embraced her with what little strength he had left. "I thought so, too. But I'm fine . . . I'm just fine now."

"Fine?" Jazmin said, wiping away tears. "Look at you! You have blood and cuts and bruises all over! You can hardly stand up straight. What did they do to you?" She loosened her grip on him, and pointed toward Aguilar and his soldiers. "And what did you do to them?"

"I didn't do anything. The trees did. I could hear their voices. Don't you see their light?"

"*Sí.*" She glanced about, beaming. "It is so beautiful—the whole forest is alight."

"What did you do back there while I faced the soldiers?"

"Pray."

"You prayed?"

"That's what Chan asked us to do," Jazmin said. "He said there was no more running, and that we had to help you by praying to the trees."

"Chan must have led the soldiers here knowing the trees would help us," Peter said. "He knew what he was doing all along."

"He knew the trees would give us strength."

"And take *their* strength," he added, pointing to the soldiers on the ground. "The darkness in their hearts could not coexist within the trees' light."

"That's true. But I was so frightened," she said. "I don't think I was much help."

"If it wasn't for you, I wouldn't be here. Your love for these people and their land made this happen. You've done more than you can possibly know, Jazmin. You, Chan, and everyone else." He gazed around at the soldiers, then at the pistol that still hung in his hand. "Even this gun helped me. It misfired when *El Capitán* tried to shoot me the first time."

They watched as K'in cautiously led the men of the tribe to the clearing, while the women, children, and elders gathered nearby, staring at the broken men lying unconscious on the ground.

Jazmin pointed to the soldiers. "What happened to these men?"

"Hummingbird energy," K'in replied, stone-faced.

Jazmin's eyes widened. "Chan said Earth's energy is moving fast now, that life is changing quickly. If we don't adjust our vibration to this higher frequency, we will be swallowed up by it."

"Apparently so." Peter glanced around. Nature assists those whose intentions are good."

"Where's Chan?" Jazmin turned to K'in, who simply pointed back into the woods. They supported Peter as he hobbled across the clearing.

Chan sat among the trees where they had last seen him, his eyes closed in deep meditation. "He never moved through all this . . ." Jazmin whispered, sharing a look of amazement with Peter.

A shiny object in Chan's lap reflected a glimmer of light. Peter blinked in disbelief as Jazmin bent down and gently picked up an unfired .38 caliber bullet, holding it up between her dainty thumb and forefinger.

Peter dropped *El Capitán's* pistol to the ground, kneeled before the shaman, and wept.

A breeze set the forest canopy swaying and rustling overhead. Chan stirred from his meditation, inhaling strongly through his nose. His deep-set eyes opened and sparkled with joy.

Chan placed a hand over Peter's heart. "I told you the trees would not forget you . . . welcome home, old friend. Welcome home."

ABOUT THE AUTHOR

A stranger and occasional customer handed me a library book one day in 1983 while I was selling burritos in the streets of Juneau, Alaska. He said I could read *Quest for the Lost City* (1951), a narrative written by a couple from California who had searched for a lost Maya city in the jungles of México in the 1940s. (Dana and Ginger Lamb eventually spent time with the Lacandón Maya in Chiapas and found the lost city).

Alaska Airlines offered a round-trip fare from Juneau to México City for $100 later that same year, a bargain too good to pass up. So, my girlfriend and I took off for México. Someone told us about the artist town of San Cristóbal de las Casas, high in the mountains of southern México. When we tired of the beach scene, we flew into Chiapas and shared a taxi for the thirty-mile trip through the jungle-covered hills to San Cristóbal. One of the other passengers, a museum curator from New Mexico, told us of a place to stay called *Na-Bolom* that was nice, cheap, and safe, a compound surrounded by a ten-foot adobe wall. When we entered the hotel through a large, hand-carved door, I immediately noticed pictures lining the walls of the Lacandón Maya in *xikul*, their customary white cotton tunic. Unbeknownst to me, I had been delivered to their front door.

My own experiences in the area, bolstered by the Lambs' adventures, started rattling around in my head, inspiring a short story. One evening in

1988, I sat down and started writing the rough draft that is now Chapter 3 of *Na Bolom*. From then on, I was hooked. I didn't begin with the idea of writing a novel. Just a three- or four-page story, then another, and another. In time, it became apparent that these short stories were part of a larger tale, and I began tying them together. I never developed a storyline or outline. *Na Bolom* just sort of wrote itself. There was something compelling about the story coming through me and I became passionate about recording it.

It was my passion for this story that drove me. Sometimes I would write for eight, ten hours day and often past midnight. At one point I was unemployed and wrote seven days a week for a year. You might say I was obsessed, or possessed. So, the reason I'm a writer is because of this story—I had to get the damn thing out of my head!

Born and raised in the Southwest, I currently reside in Prescott, Arizona.

Forrest Hayes
✸ 2016

Hidden Jungle Press
PRESCOTT ✣ ARIZONA